A *WHIFF* of *SCANDAL*

A Spirited Spinters Sweet Regency Romance

ROBYN CHALMERS

Join my Readers Group
https://www.robynchalmers.com/newsletter

Find me on Facebook
https://www.facebook.com/authorrobynchalmers/

To Mum & Dad,
For all the nights at the library, for all the holidays spent reading.
School might have taught me my letters, but you taught me to love
books. I wish you were here.

CHAPTER 1

IN WHICH MISS DAVENPORT IS MOST IMPROPERLY PURSUED. READING, BERKSHIRE, 1810

Daphne Davenport stepped into Henderson's Perfume Emporium and quietly closed the door behind her. The pale morning sunlight streamed through the stained-glass window above the door, leaving a watery mosaic on the hardwood floor like a benediction.

If ever she needed one, it was today.

The shop was narrow and deep with a wooden bench running down the left hand side. Behind the bench, shelves to the ceiling were filled with vials and bottles of perfume and oils. Cakes of soap were stacked on porcelain platters like the finest macarons. Layers of musk, civet, and orange blossom filled the air, but they barely teased her nose as they drifted through her heavy veil. It was difficult to see through it, but it did have its benefits—nobody would know the Davenports had been reduced to *selling*. Finding a noble suitor for her beautiful sister would never happen if anyone discovered *that* little secret.

Father had been born a gentleman and was the grandson of a viscount. What he'd done after that should be irrelevant.

She inhaled deeply, using the fragrance to embolden her. She only came to Reading once a month on market day, when she could ride with Mr. Mulloway in his cart. Today's trip held more urgency than usual though, as the quarterly rent was due. If she didn't sell her whole basket, their situation would be dire indeed. The thought came with a frisson of alarm.

Daphne waited for the proprietress to notice her, but she was at the back of the emporium, immersed in arranging her dark glass bottles into neat rows. Daphne softly cleared her throat.

Mrs. Henderson let out a girlish shriek and spun, one hand clasped to her breast. "My, you give a body a fright, especially garbed in all that grim black."

Not a wonderful start. Daphne forced a smile, though it was unlikely Mrs Henderson would notice given the veil's thickness. "What is Lady Spellwater without some mystery?"

Daphne lifted her basket onto the counter and then adjusted her bonnet, keeping her veil firmly in place. "In any case, you will forgive me when you smell my newest creation. This puts By a Lady in the shade." Though she personally still loved her first perfume, as she had composed it especially for Celeste.

"Do show me, my dear."

Though Mrs Henderson walked across to the counter in a friendly enough manner, Daphne couldn't help but notice that she seemed ill at ease. She pulled the linen from over the basket to reveal rows of small round snuff tins.

"Snuff?" Mrs. Henderson raised a brow, her expression filled with doubt.

"No," Daphne replied. "A solid perfume set in a tin. The fragrance is so exotic, it had to be imprisoned in beeswax to preserve its beauty. I call it Scandal. I have been working on it for months." She had the notebooks full of failed versions to prove it. The current blend of rose, neroli, basil, and patchouli was number seventy-five.

Though her expression was still doubtful, Mrs. Henderson leaned forward to peer into the basket. "A solid, you say?"

Daphne nodded, trying to stop her shoulders sagging with

relief. Perhaps her luck would hold, and she'd sell another basket full. "It's unbreakable. Ladies can take it anywhere without fear of spillage."

It was hard to keep the excitement from her voice and maintain the aloofness Mrs. Henderson expected from someone of the gentry. Nothing about this perfume made Daphne feel aloof. It was the most exciting perfume she'd ever created. To think she'd found the rare ingredient stored in the barn with all of Father's mundane spices. It still made her shake her head in disbelief.

She picked out a tin and offered it to the older woman. If Mrs. Henderson purchased every tin, maybe she could afford to do more than pay the rent or buy food for the table. A trip to London, perhaps. An image of her sister dancing at a ball in a new gown had a smile tugging at her lips.

Mrs. Henderson sighed regretfully and pressed the tin back into Daphne's hand. "It's lovely, but I'm afraid I can no longer sell your goods."

Daphne wrapped her fingers around the tin, gripping it tightly. "Cannot sell them? Why ever not? Don't your customers see how superior, how complex, my fragrances are?"

Mrs. Henderson's eyes darted over Daphne's shoulder toward Broad Street. Then she wrung her hands and strode over to close the shade. "No, no, they still like it. That's not the problem. It is the gentleman who paid me a visit."

Her ominous tone made the hairs on Daphne's arms prickle. "Surely many gentlemen pay you a visit. After all, it endears them to their wives." *Laugh, Mrs. Henderson. Please. Tell me this is all nothing but a bad jest.*

Mrs. Henderson folded her arms over her ample bosom. "I'm sorry, Lady Spellwater," she said, using Daphne's business persona. "The gentleman who called was looking for you, and he was not the sort of man to whom one said no."

Fear bloomed in Daphne's stomach, and she gripped the basket handle to stop a shudder. "Did he say why he sought me?

Perhaps he meant to pass on his compliments. Gentlemen do strange things when a scent catches their imagination."

"I think not, madam. He asked me ever so nicely if I would cease stocking your products. The words 'criminal' and 'fraudulent' were bandied about. He said the ingredients you used were new and uniquely imported by his family's enterprise."

Alarm jolted through Daphne, right down to her toes. "I have never—and would never—steal my essences, Mrs Henderson." She paused. "Did he say which ingredient he was referring to?"

The shopkeeper frowned. "It started with P..."

"Persian Essence," Daphne murmured, feeling sick.

"Precisely!" Mrs. Henderson looked at Daphne through narrowed eyes. "He said their entire stock had been stolen before they could even distribute them."

Dear Lord. She'd been using the various oils Father stored in their barn for almost two years now, and had only recently found the Persian Essence buried deep in a mountain of boxes. Though it was rare, she'd presumed it was simply old stock, just like all the other oils. It had seemed like a waste not to make it into perfume.

Of course, had Father been around, she would have simply asked him about it. But he had not visited them for months. He was too busy flitting between London and India, trying to find investors to fund a new cargo shipment, and had all but forgotten his daughters. The short letters they received with a small amount of money enclosed was barely enough to pay the rent.

It had been that way ever since his release from debtor's prison. No matter how desperately he tried to regain the business he had lost, every attempt failed. And with each setback, the length between visits was longer. She loved him and wanted him home, but she now also couldn't help wondering if, perhaps, in his desperation to avoid further time in debtor's prison, he'd done the unthinkable.

"I've done nothing criminal," Daphne said calmly, yanking the linen back over the top of the basket. "This gentleman cannot be the only supplier of Persian Essence."

"Of course, my lady," Mrs. Henderson said formally, clearly not believing a word. Daphne could explain that her father had been a spice and fragrance merchant too—but then Mrs. Henderson might tell the gentleman and lead him straight to her door. There weren't that many spice merchants in England.

The store suddenly seemed very small, and the mixture of musk, civet, and orange blossom that had been so alluring when she arrived now made her stomach turn.

Someone sought to uncover her secret. Or worse still, lay the blame for her father's supposed crimes at her door.

She unfurled her vice-like grip on the basket handles.

No.

"What did you tell him, Mrs. Henderson?" *Why did she keep staring at the door?*

"Nothing, although what do I have to say?" She sounded thoughtful. "You've been careful not to disclose your true identity or direction. After almost two years, it's slightly suspect, isn't it?"

Daphne briefly closed her eyes. This was the beginning of the end. A man tracking her, and her best customer looking at her like she was the worst kind of scoundrel. She swung her basket around and made for the door. She had to escape this cloying little shop.

"No, it is not suspect," Daphne said, lifting her chin. "It is merely the protection of my family's reputation."

Mrs. Henderson sighed. "Whatever your reasons, perhaps you should use the back exit. I have a bad feeling about the front door, and that's all I can say to help you."

Cold dread overcame her. Daphne rushed to the shop window and peeked through the shade. As she did, a coach stopped across the road, its black door swinging open. A tall gentleman leaped to the ground without waiting for the steps to lower. He turned, his face darkly handsome. Daphne inhaled sharply.

Hugh Mandeville?

The memories that came flooding back at the sight of him were from a very different time and place. Memories of the Maharajah's garden and sweltering monsoon days. Of Hugh smiling at her as he handed her mango from a platter, or lying under a banyan tree together, looking up at the glossy green canopy. Her almost psychic ability of knowing the moment he entered the room. Even a crowded ballroom. Her heart still ached from the intensity of how she'd loved him, surrounded by the kaleidoscope of scent and color that was her beloved India.

Her mind whirled. Did Hugh think she was stealing his product?

One thing was certain: the son of her father's ex-business partner would not stop until he found her and ruined her family all over again. That was just what a Mandeville did, no matter how desperately one fell in love with them. And if the theft from the Mandevilles was on such a large scale that Hugh himself was involved, someone was going to pay dearly, but dashed if it would be her.

She snapped the shade shut and turned to Mrs. Henderson. "The back suddenly looks vastly appealing." She almost laughed at the level of understatement as she swept past the counter and out the back door, slamming it so hard the locks rattled.

Damnation. Ladies did not slam doors. Daphne sighed. They also did not say *damnation* or scurry around selling their wares. And most assuredly, ladies did not have gentlemen making polite enquiries about them for thievery and fraud. But then, the longer she had to labor for her family's survival, the more her gentility felt like a facade. A lady is as a lady does, after all.

HUGH, Lord Mandeville, threw open the front door of the shop, only to hear the back door slam.

"My thanks for the signal, Mrs. Henderson," he said to the shopkeeper who had closed the blind as they agreed she would if Lady Spellwater arrived. He took chase, reaching the alley only to see a swirl of black already halfway down.

"Going so soon?" he said under his breath. "What a surprise."

The faint hope she was innocent of using stolen goods faded. But at least he had done what Bow Street failed to do—find Lady Spellwater. Now he just had to *catch* her, and, by Jove, she was fast.

He ran, battling to keep his balance on the slippery, uneven flagstones. Blood pounded in his ears, silencing the sounds of the nearby marketplace. He paused briefly at the busy crossroad, looking right and left before catching sight of her walking swiftly toward the market. "Lose me among the potatoes, will you? I think not."

He ran on. She must have heard him behind her, for her pace picked up. But he was gaining on her. Ten steps, five, then one. He reached out to grab her, then stopped mid-stretch, not wanting her to scream. Instead, he fell into step with her, each of his long strides measuring two of hers.

"Madam, if I could…"

She only came up to his chin but somehow increased her speed to outstrip him. In her wake, the basket she carried left the sweetest smell the decrepit alley had ever held. He slowed involuntarily, hoping to keep himself in the ribbon of beauty she trailed behind her.

"Madam," he repeated, a little more firmly. "Lady Spellwater." He felt like a fool uttering her self-proclaimed title.

She kept walking, lifting her basket high like a wicker shield. "I am not acquainted with you, sir. Please stop accosting me."

Her voice was honey, pure, rich, and smooth. It pulled at his memory, but he couldn't place who she was. The breathless quality of it might have been naturally hers or due to running. But it was unmistakably the voice of a lady, and unintentionally answered his first question about her identity. How he wished he could draw back her heavy veil and have all his answers.

"Come now, I mean you no harm. Just to ask a few simple questions."

She stopped abruptly. "You mean me no harm?" She turned to look at him. Two long awkward moments passed in which she seemed to search his face through her veil, then shook her head, as if to clear it. "You have already harmed me. Mrs. Henderson was my best customer."

They were spirited words, but they wavered, showing her fright. He took a deep breath, trying to look less intimidating. He knew the effect his stern features had on females—fear, trepidation, flight. All the things normally reserved for a monster rather than an expensively dressed earl.

"I could repair the damage if you answer my questions." He offered her his arm to continue the walk down the alley. "In fact, I'll buy your whole basket for the answer to just one."

She stopped short again, ignoring the proffered arm. "All of it?"

He smiled reassuringly, although he had no idea how much she could see through that veil. It was worth the wad of bills he had in his pocket to get this answer. "One question, and not only will you sell all your perfume, but our paths need never cross again." It caused a slight pang to know he would never see what was beneath the veil, the face to match the voice.

She seemed to consider it and tilted her head to one side. He got a fleeting glimpse of an elfin chin under the black netting. "Very well. Ask your question." She loosened her grip on the basket, letting it sway at her knees. He'd won. Elation stabbed through him.

"Where did you source the Persian Essence?" He steadied his voice, to sound more calm and rational than he actually was.

8

Crossing swords with the woman he'd searched months for was a heady thing.

She sighed, but it was shaky. They were so close he felt the air stir with her breath. "I did not buy it. It has been in my family for years. May I have my payment? Mrs. Henderson pays ten shillings."

He ignored her request. "Then I think you have received stolen goods." He picked a tin out of her basket, turning it over in his hand. He opened it, lifted it to his nose and with one inhale, knew her to be a master perfumer.

It was fruity and rich, like a hothouse garden, but the image it raised was not of flowers, but of the bedroom on a sultry summer afternoon. Of silk sheets warmed on a woman's skin. Of a lazy smile and lazier love, languorous waves of pleasure...or something equally ridiculous. He rolled his eyes at his own folly.

Her knuckles had turned white from clenching the basket, and he could hear her breath coming in tiny, angry bursts. "As I said, the oils are old and belong to us. Not to you."

He put the tin back in its neat hole beside the others. "So you say, but there is no way you could have had this perfume in your family for years. The process by which the jasmine is extracted has only recently been perfected."

She pulled a piece of material over the tins with impatience. "Piffle. The Indians and Chinese have been doing this for centuries."

"Not like this, they haven't. This is India's answer to France's Jasmine de Grasse. A new variety, bigger, fruitier and picked only from midnight to dawn. I met the developer. He extracts the aroma using chemicals. It's revolutionary. We are the first to import it."

"'We' being who, sir?" She tapped her foot on the cobblestones, and he imagined her eyebrow rose in disdain. "You are not the only importer of oils in England."

She clearly believed what she was saying, but that didn't mean she was right. "Can I see your stock, then? If you have nothing to hide, it shouldn't be a problem." He shrugged.

"But I do have something to hide. My identity. We both know ladies cannot be in trade, and I most certainly am. I will not embarrass my family."

So, she had siblings she felt responsible for. Young enough not to have her own children, then.

She backed away from him so he tried to hold on to her arm. "Listen—"

She jerked away, but he held on. Her arm was so slight his hand encompassed it. Too thin.

He heard a small ladylike gulp, and her whole body shuddered in fright. "I can tell you no more and beg you not to ask."

What had this situation turned him into? He loosened his grip. "I'm not trying to hurt you or expose you. Just to warn you."

It was impossible to see her expression or gauge what she was thinking, so he pushed on. "You are at risk in the worst possible way. If society would be severe on a genteel lady dabbling in trade, how do you think a lady with criminal connections would fare?"

"You would say that about me?" Her voice wavered with what might have been either anger or fear.

He shook his head. "Of course not. I've already promised not to expose you. But I will expose this thief and have justice done. You could easily be caught up in it."

It was hard to say what convinced him she had nothing to do with the actual thefts. Probably the last remnant of hope that beneath all her deception she was an honest woman, and he didn't have to continue stalking her. And her voice. Outrage like that was difficult to feign.

"I'm aware of the risks," she said primly.

"I don't think you are. What would happen to your family if you're taken into custody by the Magistrate? It's not worth ten shillings. Lay low for a while."

She scoffed. "And what would you have me do? Rely on the charity of others? All the things I've been taught to do are useless in providing for my family. All except this." She motioned to her basket.

"Would finding a husband be intolerable?" he said softly, to see what she would say.

"The worst possible outcome," she bit off.

"How so?" He must have looked astonished because she chuckled.

"You assume I dislike plying my trade like this, but I love making perfume. I love smelling it on the wind as I walk in the park. Nothing could make me give this up."

"Not even true love?" An innocent question, but it would tell him if she were married and had a partner in her industry.

She drew her shoulders back, but a hunch told him it was more pride than actual defiance. "This is my true love."

The passion in her voice moved him. How lucky she was to have that love and be free to follow it. His days before the thefts seemed to consist of the same things. Club, dinner, ball, Club, dinner, ball. And the future would be more of the same.

His maternal grandfather had been a trade mogul, building up Oriental Spice and Fragrance to the heights of him buying his daughter into the Ton. But now, he was supposed to give all that up when it ran in his veins like liquid fire. But if he had to give it up, so did she.

Although she might be brave, he didn't think she was stupid. "Can I convince you to stop making perfumes, even for a few weeks while I find my thief?"

She shook her head. Apparently, she was also reckless.

"No. I will continue. There are no stolen goods in my perfumes. I have nothing to fear." She broke away from him. "You promised to let me go if I answered your question. I have answered far more than one."

That voice. So deep and alluring. If he met Lady Spellwater on the dance floor, he'd know just by the strange spark that flashed between them. It was enough to make him look forward to going to balls again.

"So I did." She was a lady and had his word as a gentleman. If that point of honor didn't mean anything, then he was more lost than he thought.

He stepped back and swung his arm to motion her down the alley. "But I also promised to buy your stock." He fished into his pocket and pulled out a handful of coins. "For your basket."

She gave a throaty chuckle. "Oh, no, sir. Ten shillings buys you one tin, not the entire basket." She did the calculation in her head. "Simple. Twenty tins by ten shillings. That will be ten pounds." She held out her hand.

He laughed, the sound reverberating off the surrounding buildings. It sounded harsh and foreign, but maybe that was because he hadn't done it in so long. The three years since Father's death had been one long trial.

He pushed the coins into her outstretched hand. "I think not, Madam. You see, I have a strong feeling these belong to me, anyway. You'd best take what you can."

He curled her gloved fingers over the coins, enclosing her small fist in his much bigger one. She drew in a ragged breath and pulled her hand away, dropping the coins into the basket and pulling out a tin.

"One tin is all you get," she said defiantly. "Owning the ingredients doesn't mean you can make them into perfume." Without a curtsey, she took off like someone had lit a cracker beneath her skirts.

"Where can I find you?" he shouted after her. He could follow her, but did not want to cause her any more anguish than he already had.

"Glittering balls in London," she replied airily.

He bowed. "Until next time, my lady," he whispered, the tin like a hot coal in his hand.

She turned, lifting her hand in farewell, and he swore he saw the flash of a smile beneath the veil. Then she continued her glide down the alley, black cloak billowing out behind her.

It was funny, but by the end, he could swear she wasn't afraid of him at all.

CHAPTER 2

IN WHICH A DOG ENJOYS THE TRAPPINGS OF
A LADY

Daphne returned to their cottage on the outskirts of Reading. It was set back from the noise of the Bath Road and had once been part of a large farm, but the owner had built a new farmhouse nearby. The roof may have the sway back of an old horse, and the stonewalled interior might be icy in winter, but it was set in the midst of a large wild garden that more than made up for it.

She trudged up to her attic bedroom, changed out of her disguise, then went in search of Celeste. She found her in her usual spot by the window, surrounded by a mountain of sewing. It was a cozy scene, her sister's head bent in concentration, the sunlight streaming through the window turning her hair into a golden halo.

Celeste's future was the reason Daphne worked. She looked every bit a nobleman's great granddaughter, and she deserved the future Father had denied her by moving into trade.

Sir Barkley, their yellow-haired retriever, lay curled in a comfortable circle by the fire, but let out a small woof of greeting when Daphne entered the room. Celeste looked up, but her welcoming smile quickly faded as she searched Daphne's face.

"Oh dear," Celeste said. "Did it go badly?"

Sometimes it would be nice if Celeste couldn't read her expression so well. "The worst you can imagine. I'm not looking forward to telling Ayah."

The only blessing of returning to England had been that their childhood nurse and her family had returned with them. They lived in a cottage a short walk away.

Celeste lowered her stitching and clasped her hands in her lap so tightly her knuckles turned white. "You sold none? Dear Lord, what are we to do?"

This was where it got hard. Daphne drew her shawl closer. "Evade Mr. Slough until I sell more."

A difficult thing to do when collecting the rent was their landlord's favorite pastime.

"Did you sell any?"

"One. But guess to whom?"

Celeste pulled a face. "Just tell me. You know I hate guessing games."

"Hugh Mandeville." Saying his name out loud did not make the situation any less surreal.

Celeste drew in a shocked breath. "How very typical of a Mandeville to spoil your sale. They live just to ruin us."

Daphne nodded. "Apparently so."

The tragedy was compounded by her wickedly thick veil stopping her from fully drinking in the sight of Hugh.

But that voice.

She would have known it anywhere, even though the passing years had changed its timbre. It was darker, deeper, richer, but still did strange things to her nerves. Or perhaps that was the terror of being cornered. Beautiful and dangerous, Hugh Mandeville. Asking her about true love. As if she could ever hope for true love when she'd all but ruined herself. The perfume truly was all she had.

And how ironic that the one person who had always encouraged her to be reckless when she was a girl should be the one to stop her making perfume. Because the more she thought about it, the more she realized she *must* stop. He was right, the risk of being caught was too high while he looked for his thief.

Instead, it was time she tracked Father down to own his responsibilities. No more letters where he told diverting stories of news he'd gathered at the coffeehouse and implored her to keep faith with him. No more waiting for their fortunes to reverse. If he wanted her to trust in him, he would have to be more forthcoming.

"Devil it," Celeste said, with a frown. "Every time we make headway, something bad happens. What did he want?"

There was genuine fear behind that question—a fear they both knew but rarely voiced. The fear that they'd never escape this situation. That Father's business would never take off, and they'd be poor forever.

"He's looking for Lady Spellwater because he thinks she's using stolen ingredients in her perfumes, including Persian Essence."

Celeste's eyes widened. "I *told* you not to use it! I knew there was something wrong about that box."

Daphne closed her eyes briefly. "I know, I know. But we have no proof that it was stolen, either then or now."

"Do you remember when it arrived?"

"I think it was with Father's last visit, when he brought the wagon load. I'd never seen it before then. But Celeste, if he is importing, he would have things like Persian Essence."

"We're sunk." She closed her eyes and leaned back into the chair, shoulders slumped.

"Maybe, but I intend to find Father and make him explain." No need to admit how very scared she was.

The silence that fell between them had nothing comfortable about it. The worst part was suspecting that maybe Hugh was right. She loved Father, but he greatly enjoyed a bargain. He might have purchased stolen goods. It was a horrible thing to think, but not outside the realm of possibility.

Celeste's thoughts were obviously taking the same path. "Do you think they are one of Papa's bargains? That last letter said he thought things were looking up. Maybe..."

"That's what I intend to find out." Father could overlook all manner of things if the price was right. It was the reason he and the rest of the noble Davenport clan were not on speaking terms.

Daphne collapsed onto the sofa and pulled her rug onto her lap. The fire might be burning but the small room was draughty and far from warm. "We must find him and bring him to heel. But not right this minute. I need to recover my nerves."

It was best to let the proverbial dust settle before she decided her next move. She lifted her wrist to her nose to see how her latest experiment fared after a few hours. The lime top-note was perfect, uplifting and energizing. Just what she needed. That, and a change in conversation topic.

"What are you working on today? Looks like yet another re-trimming of Mrs. Allen's bonnet."

Celeste gave a small nod, lifted the bonnet, and shook out the ribbons. "She's had this bonnet for six years. I can still see where I sewed the cherries on it. Heaven forbid she buys a new one with all that pin money."

"Maybe she can't find another that becomes her so well." It was hard to find a good bonnet in the village, no matter how much pin money one had. "As long as she pays you this time, I can forgive her."

"I vow, if she doesn't pay I'm giving this bonnet to the dog." Celeste glanced over to the fire and smiled mischievously. "Sir Barkley, come."

"He's resting. Leave him be."

The dog unfurled and stood, slowly stretched out his back legs, then padded over to her, tail wagging. He sniffed the bonnet, then sat obediently, lifting a paw onto Celeste's knee.

"The cleverest dog in England," Daphne said, smiling despite herself.

Celeste settled the bonnet gently on his shaggy head and snugly tied the pink ribbons. Barkley's soft floppy ears poked out from under the woven straw.

Laughter bubbled up, making the day seem brighter. "Pretty, Sir Barkley," she said. The dog thumped the floor with his tail, causing slight puffs of dust to rise from the rug.

"At least we have found someone the bonnet truly becomes," Celeste said, scratching him under the muzzle. "When I am rich, I will have a portrait of him done wearing his bonnet."

"And we could put it in the family gallery. He wouldn't look out of place with those blond locks." Sometimes it seemed God had saved everything fair and sweet for Celeste and Barkley, while tossing Daphne the dark unruly looks that were never in fashion. The years that separated them sometimes felt like centuries. At eighteen, Celeste was blooming into womanhood, and at twenty-six, Daphne felt as though she'd entirely missed her spring.

They both sat staring at the dog in mute admiration. It was a common pastime. But the crunching of wheels on gravel brought women and dog alike to attention.

With an odd sense of doom, Daphne jumped from her chair and ran to the window. The same well-sprung coach with golden lamps and glossy black paint came to a halt in front of the house. Two tigers in tricorn hats jumped off the back, the silver buckles on their shoes glinting in the sunlight. The carriage was fine enough for a king, and if it had splashes of mud up its side, they did nothing to detract from the aura of excessive wealth.

"Mandeville?" Celeste whispered.

Daphne couldn't answer because her stomach had dropped somewhere around her ankles. He'd found her. Had he followed? No, she would have seen him from the back of Mr. Mulloway's cart.

She closed her eyes, praying it wasn't him so he wouldn't see their faded sofa and smell the sourness of their tallow candles. Melting the last box of beeswax candles for the new perfume now seemed a little rash.

There was no veil to hide behind.

Thank heaven, she didn't make the perfumes here. The smell would give them away instantly. Once again, her caution paid dividends. She pulled her sleeve down, to cover the scent on her wrist.

Celeste sprang out of the chair and pushed her way to a good vantage point. "What beautiful equipage he has. Do you think he's still looking for Lady Spellwater?"

Daphne put a hand on her arm, hoping Celeste wouldn't notice how badly her own hand shook. "No. I'll lay you odds he's looking for Father. He didn't recognize me, but he heard me speak, so if you can help me with the conversation, I would appreciate it."

Celeste paused, then straightened her shoulders and took another peek out the window. She threw Daphne a wicked smile. "I'll distract him."

Considering she had been distracting every young buck in the neighborhood since she turned sixteen, Daphne could well believe it.

When a liveried servant pulled the door of his carriage open, Daphne let the drape close and peered through a tiny crack. It was him, and everything she missed through her veil came into sharp focus.

Manhood had seen him grow tall and muscular in a way that spoke of vigorous exercise. It was easy to imagine him boxing or fencing, or shooting pistols at Manton's as she read about in the circulars their neighbors loaned them. His hair was inky and sat in poetic waves almost to his shoulders. The strong jaw she had been transfixed by as a girl held a hint of shadow and brooked no nonsense.

She closed the drape completely because his keen eye would never miss her standing in the window.

"I can't see," Celeste said.

Daphne slapped her hand away. "Sit. Unless you want him to spot you gawking." She led the way, rushing back to her armchair, grabbing a book off the pile on the floor.

The rap at their front door was so loud it sounded as if he was pummeling it with his cane.

"And remember, no talk of perfumes. Calm, controlled, lady-like," Daphne said.

"Amazed, scared, and excited," Celeste countered, her eyes flashing up to the door as Mrs. Pike entered the room. "Don't worry. He can't know we make perfumes because everything is at Ayah's house."

The cottage their old nurse lived in was far enough away not to raise any suspicions.

The housekeeper entered the room, ran her hands down her apron, and then held out a heavy rectangular card. Daphne tried to take it from her, but the job was made more difficult by Mrs. Pike's shaking hand. The card was thick and finely crafted, the black print of his name bold and strong.

Lord Mandeville. He was not Lord Hugh anymore, since his father died some years back. Not that any Davenport attended his funeral. Dancing on graves was definitely bad manners.

"He's ever so fine. Ever so tall." Mrs. Pike's cheeks were pink. "Wanting your father, he is. I told him he was out of luck, what with Mr. Davenport being in London and all. Shall I organize a tea tray? Mr. Pike offered to help take care of his horses before he makes the journey back."

"Tea would be lovely, Mrs. Pike." There went the last inch of tea she was saving for Celeste's birthday. "Please send him in directly."

Mrs. Pike bobbed and left the room.

The sound of twittering small talk echoed down the hall as

Mrs. Pike led their guest toward the sitting room. Daphne looked down at her oldest morning dress, re-cut from an even older dress of her mother's. The fabric was woefully thin, and the pattern shrieked of the last century. She pinched her cheeks to get some color into her face.

Sir Barkley, who had settled by the hearth again in his bonnet, pricked his ears and growled at the foreign male voice.

"Hush, Barkley." She looked down at him. *Dear Lord.* He was still wearing the bonnet, now at a very jaunty angle and with drool on the ribbons. The footsteps drew closer. Daphne raced to the hearth but didn't make it in time before Mrs. Pike entered the room, Lord Mandeville towering behind her.

As she announced him, Daphne turned her back to the fire, shielding Barkley in her skirts.

There was a moment of frozen silence after Daphne and Celeste made their most elegant curtsies and Mrs. Pike departed to fetch the tea.

Their little sitting room, with its golden drapes and well-mended sofas, had never seen anything like him. He somehow filled the room and looked ridiculously out of place.

Athletic and potently male, his skin held a hint of bronze that suggested he still travelled to faraway places. It made his eyes look very blue. Eyes that looked at her searchingly. He was probably trying to match the Daphne he remembered in India with the one that stood before him. There was precious little to match. England had wrung the color out of her. Every cold dark winter, she lost a little more of herself, until now she could only find hints of it inside a perfume bottle.

He smiled at her, and she shook her head to clear the sudden fog. She felt herself smiling back, unable to resist. Daphne, come to your senses. He's the enemy.

He strode forward and took both her hands in his. "Miss Davenport," he said warmly. Too warmly. "How do you do? Lovely to see you after all these years."

So much for having Celeste lead the conversation. Lord Mandeville seemed to only have eyes for her. She took a deep breath and schooled her voice to something lighter than the one she'd used for Lady Spellwater.

"And you. I think I was sixteen and hanging from a tree last time I saw you." She giggled nervously. *Keep that voice high and light. He'll never recognize you.*

"If memory serves, it was a woven vine of jasmine that promptly broke, landing you on your backside."

He smiled at the memory and she smiled along with him. Was that how he remembered her? A hoyden hanging from a vine? Considering she only climbed things to get a better look at him, it was quite ironic.

She glanced at Celeste. *Say something.*

"Daphne still likes to climb trees," Celeste finally gushed, then lowered herself onto the sofa with an audible sigh.

Brilliant.

Daphne grimaced. "I'm sure you will also remember my sister, Celeste."

He inclined his head. "I am as enchanted by the lady she is now as I was the precocious child back then."

Daphne snorted and Celeste beamed.

"How on earth did you find us?" Daphne asked.

"Your father left this address at the post office near your old house in Half Moon Street for any mail. They gave it to me quite readily."

"I suppose having a title does that for one." Some people were just born lucky. "Won't you take a seat?" She sounded calm and matter-of-fact, as though having a man like Lord Mandeville in the house was an ordinary occurrence.

"That would be most welcome," he said.

This would necessitate her sitting, too, away from the hearth and the bonnet-ridden Barkley. She bent to undo the dog's bonnet, hoping she wasn't drawing attention to herself, but the knot was stuck, so she gave up. Thankfully Lord Mandeville was occupied taking in the baskets of darning by the sofa, or maybe it was the sofa itself, in all its threadbare glory.

Celeste finally found her voice. "To...to what do we owe this pleasure? Our father is in town, I'm afraid."

Mrs. Pike chose that moment to return with a tea tray and the last of the oat cakes. Daphne had hoped to sell enough perfume today to buy more supplies, but alas. She poured the tea and handed the cup and saucer to Lord Mandeville, happy her hands were steady.

Hugh took the tea, and settled more comfortably into the sofa. "Indeed?"

"Indeed," Daphne replied firmly. "He has been there these past four months between trips to India. He is still attempting to rebuild his business after your father put him in debtor's prison. You understand." *You have no idea.*

He stiffened and his expression shuttered. "What I understand is that my father is dead, and I am left picking up the pieces." He looked around the room. "Much the same as it seems you are."

Never were truer words spoken, even if it felt wrong to be in sympathy with him.

Both she and Celeste missed Father, but the brunt of responsibility had landed firmly on Daphne's shoulders. How she wished he were here to take this interview and run the household.

Sometimes it felt like he didn't want to return. Not now that mother was gone.

Lord Mandeville's gaze returned to Daphne, and energy jolted between them. Her heart skipped a beat and her breath hitched. Or perhaps she imagined it, because he broke the gaze easily. He crossed one long leg over the other, heightening the impression he was too big for the delicate sofa.

The sheer masculinity of him was dizzying. And his clothes looked more expensive than all of their belongings put together.

His coat fitted his shoulders to perfection, so unlike the open linen shirts he used to wear in India.

Perhaps she could withstand all that male perfection if it weren't for the alluring smell that came with it. And even that might be bearable if she hadn't been so close to him mere hours ago, breathing him in, trying to identify the many layers of scent he exuded and only identifying one—Hugh.

It teased her again, and made her wish she could bottle it.

She looked at Celeste, who cleared her throat but said nothing, looking dumbstruck. It was understandable. Lord Mandeville was unlike her young beaus. He was a proper man.

He leaned back into the sofa, looking relaxed and yet oddly predatory. "Herein lies my quandary. In town, they tell me your father is here in the country, and when I visit the country, you tell me he has been in town these past four months. Which should I believe?"

Daphne straightened. "I suppose you should believe the young ladies who have received correspondence in his handwriting. Although what business you can have with Father after all these years eludes me."

Thanks to Hugh's accusations, she now suspected what business he had, but did he come here looking for thieves, or just for information? With his exquisite blue coat and ruby twinkling from a snowy white cravat, Hugh looked more likely to ask you if you'd like a ride in the park than take you to the nearest magistrate. But looks could be deceiving.

He leaned forward, his deep blue eyes pinning her with such intensity that she held her breath. There was a hardness in those eyes now that hadn't been there before, and when combined with the fierce straight brows above, it made him look dangerous. Made her pause.

He had changed.

"I have a small problem," he said, his deep voice vibrating with a tension that suggested there was much feeling behind the words. "There are anomalies in the stock of Oriental Spice and Fragrance. Large anomalies of the kind that only happen when criminals are at work. In fact, entire shiploads are missing. My investors have given me a small fortune and now I have no goods to show for it."

"Not exactly a small problem," Daphne said faintly. Her hands started to shake so she pressed them together. If Father was involved, it would be a hanging offense.

He nodded. "They only steal the most expensive items. Neroli, ylang ylang, rose, frankincense, Indian sandalwood and, worst of all, Persian Essence. Whoever stole them knew exactly what they were stealing."

She used all those oils in her perfumes. It must have been the connection that sent him after Lady Spellwater.

Lady Spellwater had to disappear—and fast.

"I would assume most thieves do," she said.

Hugh steepled his fingers and stared at the fire, his eyes narrowed. "I have two leads. Firstly, an anonymous lady could be making perfumes using the stolen goods. She calls herself Lady Spellwater. I found her this morning but am unconvinced of her involvement."

Daphne's heart beat so fast she was sure the entire room could hear it. Now would be the perfect time to tell him she was Lady Spellwater, but until she found out what Father was up to, talking could condemn him to a hangman's noose. It was better to hold her tongue, at least for now.

"Is that the perfume called By a Lady?" Celeste interrupted with convincing naivety. "We purchased a small vial at our local haberdasher! Would you like to sample it?"

Daphne barely knew where to look so as not to give them away.

"No, thank you," Hugh said, somewhat dismissively. It seemed he was the first man in England not to be enchanted by Celeste.

Celeste lifted her chin; a clear sign she'd taken his lack of adoration as a challenge.

"The other lead is your father. He worked closely with us for so many years—"

"Before you set your lawyers on him."

"He owed us a debt, I believe? A debt he could not pay?" Hugh shrugged.

Daphne clenched her fingers against the sudden urge to reach out and throttle him. How *dare* he dismiss their plight so easily when his family was the cause of it? "He could not pay the debt because your father took his customers, leaving him with no income. Your father stole our business and many more."

She had wanted to say none of that, but the words tumbled out.

His expression froze, and his body stilled. "As to that, I was not involved. But your father may know things about the business my father took to his grave. I'd like to ask him."

"But you said my father was a lead. That suggests you suspect him."

"A lead to more information only." He looked around. "Anyone thieving our stock would be living a little more affluently."

The very thing she was loath for him to see made him less suspicious. Thank goodness for small mercies.

"As long as you don't think Father had anything to do with it," Celeste said, smiling. "Everyone knows he can't even buckle his shoes without falling over."

Thank goodness for young, beautiful sisters who said precisely the right thing at the right time. Especially when their elder sister wasn't quite so convinced.

HUGH TRIED to keep the anger out of his voice. "That I can well believe."

26

Seeing their genteel poverty, it was hard to fathom why he'd thought Edward was the thief. No one stealing the vast quantities that had gone missing would leave his daughters alone in the countryside with no relatives, no chaperone, and dare he say it, no funds in evidence.

And not a whiff of perfume on the air at all, just a faint smell from the dog lying in front of the hearth, for some reason wearing a bonnet. He'd tried to make sense of why, but gave up.

The idea that Daphne herself could be Lady Spellwater was gone. When oils were mixed consistently over a period of time, nothing could hide the layers of fragrance. The house would be filled with it. Even the air outside in the courtyard would smell of it faintly. It would be ever present, even if she locked herself in the attic to do it.

And, if he was at all honest, there was no way the run-down young lady in front of him could have spat the fire that Lady Spellwater had in the lane.

He must look elsewhere.

But these girls were also his childhood friends, and they were moldering away in a freezing house with bare walls and threadbare rugs, warming themselves with a tiny fire built with twigs that smoked.

And to see how they savored their oatcakes as if they were the finest macarons...well, it made him feel ill.

Edward Davenport had been prosperous before the Mandevilles had decided, in so brutal a manner, they no longer needed him as a middleman. He must help.

Though born a gentleman, Daphne's father had decided his family's welfare was more important than their position in society. His business purchased all Mandeville stock once the cargo arrived in London and then sold it around the British Empire. It kept the Mandevilles one step removed from trade, which had suited Hugh's father perfectly. That was, until his father realized how much money Davenport was making and cut him from the loop to plow the money into his peerage ambitions.

Would the Davenports be in this situation if it weren't for his father's greed?

Within two years, Lord Alfred Mandeville, Baron Tintern, was Earl Mandeville and Edward Davenport was in debtor's prison. Who would blame Daphne for hating him? She didn't know that Hugh was working his way down the list of people they had stood on. He just hadn't reached the Davenports yet.

Well. He was here now.

He kept himself calm with great difficulty. "How long did you say Mr. Davenport has been in London?"

Daphne's expression became uneasy. It was as though she didn't want to confirm how long they had been left alone, knowing how neglectful it made her father look. But Celeste had no such qualms.

"Almost four months," she said.

"He corresponds regularly," Daphne said evenly.

"I'm sure he will be home soon," he found himself saying, as if he were the person to comfort them.

She shook her head. "It's unlikely, I'm afraid. Starting an enterprise from scratch with no funds is difficult. His visits are stretching further and further apart. But we don't blame him. He misses Mama terribly."

The hollows under her cheekbones and wary expression spoke of a woman who'd endured hardship far beyond her years. What a tragedy. The Daphne he knew in India had been annoying and mischievous, trying every way she could to goad him. She'd been full of life. In fact, he'd often thought she would grow to be lovely. This Daphne had curbed her tongue but had lost so much along the way that it was hard to recognize her. Perhaps that was within his power to fix. Or more precisely, make amends for.

He rose and walked to the fire, being careful not to stand on the dog's tail. Or its bonnet ribbons. "I know we treated your family badly; my father was a man of small scruples and inflated ambition."

Daphne's only response was to lift both eyebrows as if to say 'is that all you offer by way of an apology?'

He raised a hand. "It's not enough. I know. But I can try to make it up to you."

He would still like to question Davenport, even if it was clear that he wasn't the culprit.

"You don't owe us anything," Daphne said primly.

But he did owe them. All the years he'd turned a blind eye to his family's ruthless ways, all the years of saying things would be different when he inherited their business dealings, didn't mean anything when the product of those years sat before him as incontrovertible proof of Mandeville wrongdoing.

He would do something, damned if he wouldn't. The responding surge of satisfaction at the thought was all the convincing he needed.

He turned to Celeste. "Come with me to London. You'd like some time in town during the Season, wouldn't you?" And if he were honest, the chance to find Edward Davenport through his daughters may have come into his reasoning.

But a girl like Celeste could surely secure a suitable match. The Davenport name had to be worth something. Her great-grandfather had been a viscount, for heaven's sake. The fact her father was in trade now would be difficult to overcome, but perhaps with his mother's entrée it was possible.

Celeste closed her mouth, which had been shaped into a small *o*, and nodded.

"You can stay with us at Curzon Street." The more he thought about it, the better the idea sounded. Daphne and Celeste could live in luxury for the Season, perhaps both forming an attachment, while he kept them in his house, ensuring Edward Davenport's help with his inquiries.

Daphne drew in a sharp breath but he forestalled her comment by swiftly adding, "It's not much, but if my mother can see you both settled, I know it will go a good way toward making amends for your shabby treatment by my family."

"Why we'd love to!" Celeste said and then looked at Daphne, whose expression was that of someone offered an stay with the devil himself. "At least, I think we would. Whatever is the matter?"

"It's just, my love, we aren't equipped for a trip to town." She motioned to her dress, a hideous thing of brown and yellow pattern that looked like a congealed curry.

She was so far away from the girl who dressed up in bright saris, pretending she was an Indian princess. But everyone had to grow up. Heaven knew he'd had to. And sometimes life didn't give one the fairy tale.

"Think nothing of it. My sister purchased an entirely new wardrobe after her recent marriage and left all else behind. I'm sure they could be made to fit. Mother loves nothing more to launch young ladies into society. With Lily married and living in the country, she's woefully underemployed."

Daphne shook her head. "We couldn't. Really. Your mother would never agree." And the wary look in Daphne's eye suggested she didn't trust him.

He could have sworn he heard a slight groan coming from Celeste's direction, and the look that passed between the sisters was all pain on Daphne's side and all pleading on Celeste's.

"My mother would feel exactly the way I do," he said, wondering briefly if it were true.

He was sure Daphne needed only the tiniest push to succumb. Could she have changed so much not to want this adventure? In India, she'd been daring and mischievous. Surely that girl was in there somewhere still?

CHAPTER 3

IN WHICH THE DEVIL DUELS WITH A DEEP BLUE SEA. THE DEVIL WINS

Every sensible part of Daphne screamed that they should not go to London with Hugh. He had surely only offered it to make finding Father easier rather than for any altruistic reason.

And yet, there was Celeste, her gaze an imploring mix of longing and hope that broke her heart.

Daphne closed her eyes. She needed to locate Father and bring him home. If she could no longer earn money as Lady Spellwater, he'd have to do his duty by them. They had given him ample time to establish his new business. Now he could find an alternative way to support them.

"I say we let the dog in the bonnet decide," Hugh said. "What's her name?"

"His name," Daphne replied stiffly, "is Sir Barkley." And if he expected her to let a dog decide such an important issue, he was madder than she first thought.

"Oh, poor chap," Hugh said to the dog. He squatted and gave the dog a scratch under the chin. "What have they done to you?"

Celeste laughed, and Sir Barkley lifted his brown eyes in sorrow.

Daphne cleared her throat. "How can a dog possibly decide?"

"Simple. We will all call him. If he goes to Celeste or me, you come with me to London. If he goes to you, you stay here and continue with your darning."

Celeste clapped.

Daphne quirked an eyebrow. "Considering there are two of you and one of me, the odds are stacked in your favor." But perhaps that wasn't such a terrible thing. Maybe the best way to convince Hugh she wasn't Lady Spellwater was to allow him to check on them for a few weeks. And this was the best chance Celeste had of enjoying a Season. If ever anyone had enough charm and grace to make up for lack of dowry, it was her sister. She would quash her suspicions about his motives so they could eat well, even if it was only for a few weeks.

Hugh picked an oatcake off the plate and waved it in the air, gaining Barkley's undivided attention.

"I think that would be called cheating," Daphne said.

"Pass me one, too," Celeste said urgently.

"On the count of three?" Hugh handed Celeste a biscuit.

The excitement in the air was hard to resist. But then, Hugh Mandeville always had a way of lighting up even the dourest room. The fact he put the fear of God in her today didn't change that. Daphne sat back and folded her hands on her lap.

Hugh's smile was wickedly lopsided. He got down on his knees and waggled the oatcake in front of Barkley. "One..."

Really, you'd think an earl would behave with more dignity.

He glanced up and winked at her. "Two..."

Although, a man who knew how to play *was* appealing.

"Three!"

All three of them created a chorus of "Barkley, Barkley, come here bo—."

Barkley hoisted himself off the floor and had those oatcakes in his mouth and swallowed before they could even finish their sentence.

Daphne sighed. "I knew I didn't stand a chance against oatcakes."

She looked up. Lord Mandeville's expression was one of utter satisfaction.

"I think I shall bring Sir Barkley along for future decision-making," Hugh said. "Excuse me while I find my man." He bowed. "I will return soon."

Hugh had barely left the room when Celeste launched herself at Daphne and wrapped her in a joyful hug. "You are the best of sisters. Thank you."

Daphne closed her eyes. "This is the worst idea we've ever had."

There was no way they could travel into the lion's den and survive. Even if she was on her best behavior and left Lady Spellwater behind, something was bound to go wrong. It always did.

And yet...how could she deprive Celeste? Her sister deserved a season, however fleeting it might be.

Celeste released Daphne from the hug, holding her at arm's length. "We're going to London! What could be better?"

"Bed and a blanket over my head? Seriously, Celeste, I don't know if Lord Mandeville means to make amends to Father or hunt him. We haven't seen him in over ten years and suddenly he wants to take us to town? You need to be more wary."

"But you heard him. He feels terrible about what his father did to Papa. If he's making amends, I'm happy to let him. Anything that gets me away from here."

Before Daphne could respond, Lord Mandeville came back into the room, dusting off his hands. "Come now, Miss Davenport. Don't frown. Look upon this as a blessing. Trust me."

He didn't know what he was asking. She should *not* trust him, and he most definitely should not trust her. They were not friends anymore, and it was unlikely they ever would be again. The only thing they had in common was finding Father. Hardly the basis for a friendship.

But then, didn't they say one should keep one's enemies close? How better to see how much danger she was in than to live in his house and be privy to family conversations?

"Very well." A sense of impending doom struck even as she said the words.

Sir Barkley padded over to Hugh, nuzzling into his hand in a most disloyal way. "I will send word to my mother that we will set out tomorrow morning. Do you have some parchment?"

Daphne went to the bureau and found a piece of foolscap. She had paper. What she didn't have was a way for Lord Mandeville not to discover they might be precisely the thieves he was hunting.

HUGH LEFT SOON AFTER, and Daphne slipped out the back door to take the well-worn path over the fields to Ayah's cottage.

She should make this trip to see Ayah triumphant with an empty basket and a pocket full of silver coins. Now she had to tell her to stop making perfumes posthaste. Heaven knew how she would take it. To say her old nurse was outspoken was an understatement, but she had always been more mother than nurse and was now more friend than mother. England would be unthinkable without her.

Daphne lifted her nose to the warm spring day. The gentle breeze brought with it the smell of her own creations long before the thatched roof of Ayah's cottage came into view. She must be making more of the new perfume, because the heady scent of jasmine danced around on the breeze like a carefree sprite.

She reached the outhouse that had served as a dairy before they started using it as a stillroom. The closer she got, the louder the voices became until she could hear the rhythmic Hindi of Ayah's daughters, chatter and laughter that sounded like bells pulled on a string. Three bells to be exact.

Daphne stopped in the doorway. The four women worked at a long wooden bench, each with their own task. Nupur blended the low notes, Tapi measured the middle blend, and Ayah only trusted herself to heat the beeswax to the perfect temperature to take the perfume. Then her eldest, Ramita, poured the mixture into the snuff tins. The bevy of small vats, oversized droppers, and measuring spoons were all as familiar to her as embroidery stitches were to other ladies. She loved to work right next to them with her sleeves rolled up and a large dimity apron covering her gown.

Ayah was silent, her brows drawn together in concentration as her hand hovered over the beeswax to gauge the temperature. Her long black and silver braid rested on her shoulder, and glimpses of a yellow sari peeked through her large white apron. They worked hard for their share of the profit, but Ayah said it kept the family busy while her husband was in London working at a coffeehouse. This business was supposed to create freedom for both families. They'd hardly started, and it was all going to end.

When they noticed her at the door, the girls stopped working, and gathered around to listen to another installment of "Did Daphne Sell any Perfume?" If only she could sell it as well as they made it.

Ayah looked up. "Come. Come. Sit. Sit. How did it go?" The hope in her voice made Daphne's stomach flip.

Daphne picked up a tin from the workbench and lifted it to her nose. As always, she was transported to the Maharaja's walled garden, lying on the grass looking up into the leafy haar-shringar with its closed white blossoms, waiting for darkness to fall open. Night Jasmine. Hot, so very, very hot—but happy and lazy, with the sound of bees from a nearby hive in the air. Every blend was a step closer to India, but it never took her back completely, no matter how tightly she shut her eyes. Sometimes she hated England so much she wished it would. A little voice reminded her that India wasn't perfect when she was there, either, but she squashed it.

She opened her eyes abruptly. "How did it go? Not well. Lord Mandeville was waiting for me in Reading."

Ayah paled, not an easy feat with her complexion. She remembered Hugh just as surely as Daphne did. "Does he know you're Lady Spellwater?"

"He knows nothing." Daphne quickly relayed the happenings of the morning.

Ayah's expression darkened when she heard that Hugh had warned Daphne to stop making perfumes. "No. We cannot let him." She thumped the table with her palm, and the tins jumped. "If we want to make perfumes, who is he to stop us?"

"Well," Daphne said. "He can if we are using his goods. If Father truly has stolen them and left them here. Tell me if you know anything I don't."

Ayah shook her head. "No. I don't."

"Then going with him to London is the best way I can think of to get him off our scent, and to ask Father directly."

"No. That is no reason to go to London."

There would always be an argument. "Then Father should be here to take care of us. In his absence, I decide, and my decision is to go to London and help Celeste find a husband."

Ayah grumbled in Hindi, as she was prone to do whenever anything truly annoyed her.

"Pardon?"

She pulled on Daphne's arm. "I said do not fall in love with him again."

Daphne felt the blush bloom in her cheeks. "I was never in love with him! A slight fascination, nothing more. He was dashing and four years older than me."

She could have kept going on with her defense, but Ayah held up a hand. "Fool others, but not me. Trust me, little one, do not go to London."

It was enough to make her think twice. It was hard to rouse Ayah into any temper, and yet Daphne could see the flush on her cheeks.

"I may not want to go to London, but I am going. And if I can introduce Celeste to society as Hugh plans, then so much the better."

"Oh, 'Hugh' is it?" Ayah raised an eyebrow as if that small slip alone proved her point.

"Lord Mandeville," Daphne amended. "But it will be 'darling Hugh' if he helps Celeste marry. The Mandevilles used us abominably and now they want to make up and be friends." Not that she truly believed it, but perhaps it would make Ayah sleep better at night.

"He is not your friend and you are not his." Ayah wrung her hands on her apron. "He will betray you just like his father betrayed yours. They were the best of friends, too."

"I will not give him the chance to betray me. I will be on guard every minute of every day."

Ayah's responding expression suggested she didn't believe a word of it.

Daphne left the cottage soon after, but Ayah's ominous words remained with her all the way back to the house, like storm clouds on the horizon.

CHAPTER 4

IN WHICH A LUXURIOUS CARRIAGE BECOMES CLAUSTROPHOBIC

The following morning the ladies found themselves bundled into a town coach just like the ones she used to ride in as a child. The air smelled of beeswax; the leather was as soft as old velvet, and there was a cashmere blanket on her lap, even though it was early spring. But there was one large, insurmountable problem, and he was sitting across from her, riding backward.

Daphne had always counted her exquisite sense of smell as a blessing. But in this moment, in this carriage, with this man, it was more akin to torture. His fragrance still hit her like a nip of brandy, creeping through her veins on a luxurious undulating path. Sandalwood, leather, and clean man. It made her feel things she should never feel. Not if she wanted to keep her head.

He sat there, ignorant of his effect on her, trying to draw her into conversation time and time again when she could barely string two coherent words together.

And then there was the necklace in her pocket, rubbing against her leg with the swaying motion of the carriage. Her mother's ruby necklace, given to her by the Rajaputrah. The last of the

Davenport treasures, and the one she and Celeste had sworn never to part with after the sapphire engagement ring disappeared. Celeste knew she'd brought it along, but not that she intended to sell it as soon as they reached London. Lady Mandeville would not want to give her daughter's wardrobe to them, she was sure of it.

Hugh stretched his legs, and Daphne tucked her feet farther under the seat. If he accidentally touched her, she would probably swoon. It was most vexatious.

Her hope had been to make enough money selling perfumes to give Celeste a season in London, hiring a house and maybe even a chaperone, no gem-selling required. But then life had whittled away all the money. Now the string of rubies in her pocket were all they had left. The thought made her sad and drew the unwanted attention of Hugh.

"A penny for your thoughts," he said.

Why couldn't he try to sleep or be content to watch the rolling green hills and cows like Celeste? Then she wouldn't have to worry about inadvertently saying something that would make him see Lady Spellwater and not dull Daphne Davenport.

"Surely they are worth more than a penny," Daphne said. "I wouldn't want you to think I undervalue myself."

Her breath caught. It was the kind of spirited thing Lady Spellwater would say.

But he merely raised an eyebrow, as though mildly surprised. "Very well, a pound."

She leaned forward and tried to pry open the window. "Now how can I possibly give you a pound's worth of thoughts?" The window was stuck, so she slumped back in her seat. "I'd be here until we reach London." Just like she was stuck until London with his glorious scent.

"I have the time." He opened the window with ease, then he settled back into the corner, keeping a steady eye on her. She shifted uncomfortably. Nobody ever looked at her. She kept herself as exciting as a puddle. But he didn't look away, and he was waiting for an answer.

She glanced sideways at Celeste, whose jaw had slackened. A delicate snore fluttered the ribbons of her bonnet, and her neck was bent at a most uncomfortable angle. She could sleep anywhere and at any time of day, and her snores sounded like a kitten's. It would be annoying if Daphne didn't love her so much.

"You can tell me," Hugh said in a conspiratorial hush. "She's fast asleep."

Daphne smiled slightly. "If you must know, I was thinking about how I must sell Mother's necklace."

"Surely you don't have to." There was incredulity and pity written on his face, which was not the way she wanted him to look at her.

Daphne lifted her chin. "Of course I must. I cannot depend on your mother to provide for us; that would not be fair. Unless you think Celeste's dress is suitable for London?"

The dress in question was a yellow-and-white-checked morning dress Celeste had cut from old curtaining they'd found in the attic. The right sleeve puckered at the seam, and now, sitting in the luxurious coach, it looked shabby.

He didn't say a word, just glared at the dress as though its very existence was an insult.

Reaching down, she turned her pocket out and tipped the necklace into her hand. It was so dear, old, and beautiful. She dropped her gaze so he couldn't see the tears gathering in her eyes. Once they were under control, she held the necklace up to the light.

He took it from her, his thick dark eyebrows pinched together. A few moments later, he looked up. "I'm afraid someone may have pawned it already. These rubies are most definitely paste."

The safety of that last valuable item dissolved before her eyes.

It seemed she couldn't stop blinking, looking from Hugh, to the necklace and back again. "How can you possibly tell?"

He rubbed his finger across the largest gem. "The facets have little chips and scratches. They are, after all, only glass. I'd wager your mother wore this for quite some time not realizing. The actual gems would be much sturdier. The only thing that could scratch a ruby like that would be a diamond."

"Oh, dear." With a shaking hand, she took it back from him.

"I'm truly sorry." He did sound sad for her. Why did he have to be so considerate? It would be easier to think of him as the enemy.

She wanted to hurl the necklace out the window, but there was a chance the setting was still the original gold one, so she put it back in her reticule, feeling a little more foolish than she did before.

"You don't need it," he said. "A new gown or two, and you'll have your pick of beaus."

His kindness made her want to tell him the truth—that she could love no man more than she loved crafting perfumes. If each person had only one grand love in their life, she had already found hers. Because one thing she knew for certain, no man would allow her to continue her obsession once married. It was one or the other.

The problem was that she'd never before felt a twinge of sadness about it. But to tell him she couldn't marry would echo Lady Spellwater's sentiments, the very thing she was trying not to do. She needed to be the opposite of Lady Spellwater in every way.

She schooled a dreamy look onto her face. "Do you really think so? I had long since given up hope."

"Never give up hope, Miss Davenport." He leaned back and pinned her with his fathomless dark blue eyes. His scent enveloped her once again. It was both exciting and threatening. Just for a moment, time slowed and the horse's footfalls faded into the background. There was just Hugh and a moment that was almost perfect. Then she connected the burning in her chest with the fact she'd stopped breathing and took a deep, shaky breath.

Enough.

"Well." She cleared her throat and shifted uncomfortably. "I'm sure I don't know how to attract a gentleman's attention."

There. Lady Spellwater would never have uttered such nonsense. She would say that no man was worth giving up her entire world. That independence was more important than matrimony. He would have to be a hero, an Adonis, and everyone knew they didn't exist beyond the walls of the British Museum. And even then, they were normally missing an arm or a foot.

"I remember a certain girl who asked me to dance at the Monsoon Ball, even though she was supposed to be in bed. It seems you knew, once."

She closed her eyes against the memory, but it was too strong. The balmy night air and lying flat on her balcony where she could just spy the goings-on of the ballroom below.

"You were alone on the balcony beneath my bedroom." Daphne's sad smile was very real. "And that girl is long gone. I left her behind in Bombay."

There was a flash of pity in his eyes before he covered it with a bland smile. "That's a shame. That sprite was very entertaining."

Now she was on more certain ground. "I found sprites have a hard time in England, Lord Mandeville."

"How so?"

"Well, sprites have to live in the same world as everyone else. They have to go to church on Sunday, buy tea and bread, and try not to take offense when people cut them direct on the streets and in ballrooms."

"This happened to you?" It was said with the disbelief of a man who had never suffered a moment's rejection.

"Initially." She tried to ignore the sting of hurt the memory brought. "I arrived in Reading, accustomed to wearing bright colors, singing as I walked, and saying exactly what came into my mind."

"The English women of Bombay do enjoy great freedoms."

"They told me," she continued. "They all told me that things would be different in England, but I was too silly to believe them. How could anyone not love me? I had been cosseted and loved my whole life. Yet the people of Reading whispered behind their hands and never returned my visits."

"Oh dear," he said, but his eyes smiled. "Could it be that you were bossy? You did have a tendency toward imperiousness in those days."

Celeste snickered, showing she wasn't as asleep as she pretended.

Daphne frowned. "Why would you say that?"

He laughed and crossed his arms over his chest. "You even tried to boss me around back then. 'Hugh, this bolt of muslin is inferior, take it back.' Ring any bells?"

Good Lord, perhaps she had been vulgar to the townsfolk. She certainly did remember nothing being to her liking in wet, dreary England. "In any case, they drummed it out of me quick as a flash."

"More likely you just learned to hide yourself a little better. Biding your time, shall we say? The real you is in there somewhere, Miss Davenport." His gaze briefly searched her face. "We'll find her."

No, he wouldn't. She straightened. "Daphne, the sprite, is better left in India. She'll only vex me here."

"Not necessarily," he said. "Some of the most enchanting women of our age are sprites. Mischievous and witty. Or like Lady Spellwater, mysterious and keeping society enthralled with her next perfume."

"I daresay that the same society would hound her into the ground if they knew her identity," Daphne said, unable to help

43

the bitterness in her voice. "So I won't use her as my model, if you please."

"No," Hugh said. "You're right, of course. No respectable man would marry her while she continues in trade. Perhaps if she stopped and created perfumes as a hobby? Then it would not be out of the question, I suppose."

"That sounds rather insipid."

Hugh shrugged. "Unfortunately, ladies do not sell their goods at shops. She has effectively taken herself off the marriage market. It is one or the other."

Daphne shrugged. "If anything, she has just provided herself with a dowry. I think a gentlewoman can conduct herself properly when engaged in matters of business, just as a gentleman can."

Hugh frowned. "Gentlemen should not engage in business, either, from what I can gather."

Daphne tilted her head to one side. "But you do."

"Only until I find these thieves, then I shall return to being removed from trade."

The thought of him toeing the line of the proper English gentleman made her heart clutch. "Oh. What a shame. I always remember your grandfather—it must have been your maternal grandfather—being a wonderful business man. He visited us many times. He once boasted how, at thirteen, you had shown him a better way to load the ships to maximise space. I'm sure he would want you to continue his legacy."

"I will," he ground out. His eyes flashed and Daphne knew she had hit a sore spot.

Before she could respond, Celeste straightened in her seat and shot her a warning glance. "I think we should agree that everyone deserves love, whether they are in trade or not. There is a perfect match for everyone, you know. Lady Spellwater's beau will love her and her perfumes so much that thoughts of anything else will disappear."

God bless Celeste for hoping her sister could make a love match. It was endearing, if totally naïve.

"I'm sure you are right." Hugh's expression suggested he doubted it. "Someone, somewhere may find a lady of that notoriety appealing. But in the upper classes? Breeding and accomplishment are the yardstick for making a good marriage."

He took some papers out of his bag, ending the conversation and consigning all women of less than good breeding and reputation to the bonfire.

"Then I definitely won't make a good match as I have no accomplishments to speak of," Daphne said with a smile.

Celeste was too young to understand the other path taken by women who didn't meet society's marriage standards, but Daphne wasn't. They were fun for men to play with for a while, but not for the serious business of begetting an heir.

Hugh had not changed so much, after all. Still the arrogant princeling Father had once called him. If only he was ugly to boot, it would make sparring with him that much easier.

She stared out the window and tried to control her annoyance—at herself just as much as him. "The lady you marry will be something very special indeed, my lord. I wonder that she won't topple over under the weight of her own goodness."

"Lady Johanna can well handle her virtue," he said smugly, rifling through the papers.

Shock held Daphne still for what felt like an eternity. She could only stare at him. Of course he had an intended. Men like Hugh Mandeville didn't swan through life without attracting a bevy of admirers. She was a fool twice over.

"In fact," he continued on, "she can probably give you both some pointers about how to go on in Town. We'll call on her. I'm sure you'll like her as much as I do."

Daphne closed her eyes against a wave of unaccountable sadness. "I'm sure we will. How long have you been betrothed?"

He thought for a moment. "Not betrothed as yet, but we have been courting almost three years now."

"Three years!" Celeste said.

"Yes, I know it is quite a long courtship. But it was the last thing my father wanted of me before he died. Then he did die, and we went into mourning. When I came out of mourning, Lady Johanna was most unfortunately back in for her mother and then her uncle." He shrugged. "I'm sure we will get to the altar, eventually."

Daphne frowned. "You don't seem overly concerned." It was beyond her how men could consider marriage as just another task.

"I have learned that marriage is more of a transaction to begin with, and that those gentler feelings only come after years spent together. And I am quite busy at the moment with the thefts. But we are all out of mourning now, so that is something."

Daphne patted her chest like she was aflutter. "Oh, to hear one's beloved speak of your betrothal as 'a transaction.' I vow you make my heart leap."

His lips pursed together, his expression annoyed. "I once heard Lady Johanna tell her mother my estates were more important than my character, so I assure you, I am not wrong. It is neither here nor there. Children will be made, dynasties assured, promises kept. And by the time we are both old and gray, I'm sure there will be a marked affection between us."

"Then we can only wish you happy," Celeste said with an expression that suggested she had no words left other than *good grief.*

∾

THEY STOPPED for an early afternoon repast. Hugh installed Daphne and Celeste together in a private dining room, as they had no chaperone, and took himself off to the taproom where he ate lunch with his confidante and coachman, Mr. O'Keefe. He pushed a tankard across to him. "If you found nothing, then there is nothing more to say, I suppose."

He'd instructed him to make a quiet but thorough search of the Davenport premises while he interviewed the Misses Davenport.

O'Keefe pulled on his magnificent gray moustache. "Oh, I found things. Pigs, chickens, a pretty litter of kittens in the barn." He raised both shaggy eyebrows at his employer. "Not what you had in mind?"

Hugh smiled at the dry tone. The O'Keefe patience had obviously been stretched too far. But the bedrock of their relationship was his bluntness. "I was hoping for oils and spices as opposed to barnyard animals."

O'Keefe rubbed his eyes. "None of those. Not a whisker. Not even a sniff of a whisker."

Hugh had known it was unlikely when he'd witnessed their poverty, but with so few leads, striking Edward Davenport off his list was a blow. But the feeling of relief that accompanied it could be easily explained. After all, investigating Davenport would make things deuced uncomfortable while Daphne and Celeste were living in his house, while the thought of telling Daphne her father was a criminal would make him feel criminal himself.

Was it the guilt that caused the painful awareness whenever she was near? As though he'd been jolted awake and suddenly saw clearly that the only thing he needed to do was make everything good in her world. That doing this would make up for all the wrongs. He'd found himself talking about Lady Johanna just to admonish his brain for constantly thinking of Daphne. Wondering what was going through her mind as she stared out the window, wanting to feed her another biscuit to chase away the hollows under her cheeks.

Stupid sense of honor. He took a bite of the thick bread. It must have something to do with memories of how she was in

India, because he didn't feel the same way about Celeste. She looked like an angel who had fallen on hard times, and any man in his right mind would want to save her. But all Hugh could see was Daphne and those night-dark eyes and cherry red lips.

Where had that come from? Cherry red lips? He rolled his eyes. He'd barely even started his own ale and this was the kind of thoughts he had?

O'Keefe leaned back into the chair with a groan that spoke of his age. "What do you do with the ladies now? They're useless to you if Davenport is innocent."

"But if he's innocent, I owe them recompense. Their poverty can be laid directly at our door."

O'Keefe snorted. "Moonshine."

"You disagree?"

"You take your pity too far. You never saw Davenport at work. A more slimy agent you'd never find. Always looking for a shortcut. He doesn't deserve your pity."

"But perhaps his daughters do. He may have taken the wrong path, but they are still the great-granddaughters of a viscount. They deserve to take their place in society no matter what their father has done, no matter how he earned his living."

Hugh didn't want to feel pity, but when he'd watched the sisters savor every mouthful of the cheese and biscuits in his carriage hamper, he not only felt pity, he finally felt like he was doing something important and right. But it certainly complicated matters.

O'Keefe pushed his chair back from the table and stood. "If you're going to descend into thinking you have to save the Empire and all those in it, I'll wait outside."

Hugh shrugged. "It can't be helped. I have to sort this out."

"And continue thinking of all the ways your father was a rascal. He was, and I don't deny it. But so was Davenport. The spice trade when you were young was a brutal place and no place for a gentleman. Don't you convince yourself you should marry one of them by the time you get to London. You don't owe them a farthing."

O'Keefe had been his father's coachman too and probably knew more than he'd ever let on. "It's time to tell me, old man. I've found the files, and I can see that Father cheated many people out of a great deal of money. It is hard for me to equate that with the man who played chess with me and took me trout fishing. What did you see? Don't worry about darkening his legacy. What I'm imagining is worse than the truth."

The old man shrugged. "I've always believed 'least said soonest mended' and don't want to besmirch your father's memory." He chewed on his thumb, as he always did when he was thinking. "But your suspicions are true. He was the best of men to his family and to his staff. But anyone beyond that circle was fair game. He used all and sundry to achieve his goal, that being the earldom. If I could count the number of times he told me 'that's for our ears and eyes only, O'Keefe,' I'd be a rich man. He and Davenport were in it up to their ears together until your father dumped him." He exhaled loudly. "But that's all done now. You have the earldom as your father wanted, and nothing can take it away from you. You don't have to make up for his sins."

O'Keefe pushed his chair in, shot Hugh an expression designed to make his employer take a good hard look at himself, and left the room. It used to work when he was a lad, but it wasn't quite as successful now. Only Hugh knew how he'd turned a blind eye to his father's ambitions, how he wasn't as innocent as he'd like to be.

Hugh collected the Davenport sisters from their private room where they had made very good work of the cold collation the inn had provided. The lemonade pitcher was also empty.

Daphne looked up with a guilty expression, while Celeste surreptitiously took a bread roll and dropped it into her reticule.

"I see lunch was acceptable. Are you ready to take the final leg of our journey to London?"

CHAPTER 5

IN WHICH LONDON MAKES A DUBIOUS FIRST IMPRESSION

I t was a good day for traveling, and the clear roads should see them in London by late afternoon.

Hugh opened the carriage door for Daphne and Celeste. Celeste looked as fresh as the spring afternoon they were about to set out in, but Daphne's eyebrows were drawn together, and she had a habit of chewing her lip that only drew his attention to her mouth more than it should.

Was she worried for her father? And did that mean she knew something she wasn't telling him? She should confide in him, but that was easy for him to say.

He offered his hand to help her into the coach. The jolt of energy when she took his hand made him blink and drop her hand quicker than manner would dictate. What on earth was that?

She smiled brightly—though it did not quite reach her eyes —then settled her skirts and patted the lace fichu she had tucked into her bosom. "Thank you for the most excellent repast."

Obviously, she had not felt that jolt. She would also not be looking at his lower lip if he bit it. Get hold of yourself.

He jumped into the coach and sat opposite the ladies. The footman closed the door behind him.

"You are welcome," he said. "I hope I find you both refreshed and ready to arrive in London?"

Celeste's eyes lit up, but Daphne just pursed her mouth and looked out the window. She was concerned, probably about her father. What a fool he was for thinking of flirting with her when she obviously had weightier matters on her mind.

"Miss Davenport, if something concerns you, I do hope you will confide in me."

She seemed to collect herself and said, with a small smile, "Thank you, I will. But everything is fine."

Everything was most obviously not, but he couldn't make her share her problems. And he couldn't spend the rest of the trip to London staring at the sprinkle of freckles across her nose or the way a long dark curl had escaped her coiffure and sat on her shoulder. What he needed to do was plan his next move in London to find the thief.

The moment they landed back in town, he needed to start the chase.

On the way home they would drop a message at Bow Street for his Runner, Richard Wolfe, to visit Mandeville House to provide an update. After the meeting, they could track the elusive Davenport down together. He was no longer a suspect in Hugh's mind, but he might know the person who was. If luck was with him, he might even know Lady Spellwater.

He'd lost precious time traveling to Reading when the man he'd been looking for had been in London the entire time. Immediately after Daphne was settled, he would seek her father's direction. In fact, why wait?

He cleared his throat. "Where does your father stay in Town, Miss Davenport?"

Her gaze flew to his, her expression alarmed. "You still want to see him?"

"I'm sure you understand my need to apprise your father of your whereabouts." He tried to be reassuring.

"We can do that," said Celeste. "Surely you are too busy."

He shook his head. "It would be better coming from me. After all, our families have a checkered history. I need to assure him of my good intentions and see if there is any knowledge he may have to help in my endeavour."

Daphne seemed to consider it and then nodded. "Yes, of course. He stays at Limmer's."

"Thank you." He let out a breath he had not realized he was holding. "I shall call on him after I see you settled."

Finally, a proper answer and a bright new lead to follow.

DAPHNE KEPT her smile fixed and pretended to enjoy the journey. What did Hugh mean when he said he had to apprise Father of his intentions? He couldn't be going to see Father because of concern for them, but the little spark of joy inside argued otherwise.

He did not need to hand her into the carriage with such care, like she was the finest of ladies, but that could be attributed to his gentlemanly manners. It was the way his eyes kept getting drawn to her lips that intrigued her most. Did he think of kissing her? She certainly didn't want to think of kissing him, but the well-worn path from her previous tendré was very alluring. Indeed when she was sixteen she'd spent hours, maybe even days, dreaming up scenarios where Hugh would kiss her. Those dreams were obviously barely buried and being so close to him brought them all back to life. It was distracting and annoying; more so now when she knew he was as good as betrothed. At least back then he was unattached.

She sighed.

Instead of looking at him for the whole trip, she should strike up some conversation. With luck he might say something that would disgust her. One could live in hope.

"What are you thinking, my lord?"

He snapped out of his reverie and regarded her as though he'd forgotten she was there entirely. It was a deflating moment. "Just business matters."

She picked up her book and began to read, only sneaking peeks at him when she knew he was looking the other way. His eyebrows, drawn together in concentration, long dark eyelashes fanned out over his cheeks as he stared down at his papers. He had relaxed into the corner of the seat, one arm resting near the window, the other holding a sheaf of documents covered in numbers. Maybe they were the ledgers that showed the thefts.

It took some time for her to realize her book was upside down. She hurriedly righted it and forced herself to concentrate on her poetry.

He lifted his gaze, catching her staring squarely at him, and smiled, lazily

Fire bloomed in her cheeks and she dropped her gaze to her book.

Dratted man.

After a while, she gave up the pretence of reading and instead stared out the window. The forests turned to fields, then market gardens, and then mile by mile, the outskirts of London itself. The place where she would find out if Father was a thief or not. Nerves made her pulse skitter.

If only the carriage would slow its cracking pace to prolong their proximity, but the Spring day was fair and the roads clear of all but the occasional coach.

The carriage moved on, into the heart of London. Daphne frowned. It may have been years since she'd visited the city, but the Earl of Mandeville's townhouse was definitely near Hyde Park, and they'd long since left the green stretches of the park behind.

"Have you changed address?" she asked Hugh.

He shook his head. "No. We travel past Bow Street so I can have a message dropped to my man of investigation."

"Is he a Runner?" Celeste asked with relish.

Hugh nodded. "Indeed. Although far above your average kind. He commands a small fortune."

Daphne shivered. A professional thief-taker. It was the stuff of nightmares.

The carriage slowed as they entered a less reputable part of London. Buildings crowded along the street's edge, throwing the road into shadow while urchins played in the dust and dubious ladies ambled with no apparent direction. Covent Garden.

"Bow Street," Celeste breathed, showing far too much relish for a young lady. Daphne frowned at her but Celeste just shrugged. "What? It's exciting!"

Hugh frowned. "Yes, but we will barely stop. I'll have you home directly. I apologize for this small delay."

His tiger jumped from the back of the carriage and opened the door to take the message from Hugh.

He was back within the minute, and the carriage set off again. But it was slow going, and there was a knot of carriages, horses and pedestrians ahead. Chanting and excitement filled in the air, the noise almost deafening and alarming.

"Is it a mob?" Celeste asked, peering out the window.

Carriages and horses inched forward, passing through the throng one at a time.

"Nothing you need to see." Hugh closed the curtain with a swift sharp movement, but not before Daphne glimpsed the crowd spilling into a small laneway and the gallows soaring into the gloomy sky like macabre maypoles.

"Oh my," she said, leaning back. Father could go to those if he was stealing from the Mandevilles. Nerves erupted, churning her stomach. They were thirsty, those gallows, like the people that loved to watch them. She must have paled because Hugh briefly put his gloved hand over hers. It didn't comfort her in the least.

"Not the first thing you should see when you visit London," he said. "I should not have come this way."

"It's part of life." She closed her eyes briefly. "If you break the law, you pay the price. It's times like this I thank the Lord I am law abiding."

Hugh nodded and seemed happy with her comment. He removed his hand and the small comfort it gave her. "It's not an end to life I would wish on anyone."

"Not even the thieves stealing from you?" Would he happily see her father up there if he was guilty?

"Not even them. But you need not worry. It's not your world. Your world will be shopping, dance instructors and balls."

I wish. But the truth was, Newgate could be her world. She closed her eyes, the stark vision of the gallows against the blue sky etched in her mind.

If Father was involved, he needed to quit right now, before he got caught. She had to get word to him as soon as possible. She thanked heaven she hadn't given Hugh his true location. The sound of the cheering and leering throng filled the cab until Daphne wanted to put her hands over her ears to make it stop. Instead, she lifted her wrist to her nose and concentrated on the pure Damascus rose she'd rubbed there until the carriage picked up pace. Such a gentle and innocuous scent, and one that would lead no one to suspecting her to be Lady Spellwater. It brought her comfort and the feeling that everything was going to come around.

She would make it come around.

They entered Curzon Street at just past four in the afternoon, gliding to a halt in front of a pair of imposing wrought-iron gates. Behind the gates stood a white mansion, its tall Doric columns soaring three stories high. Chimneys too numerous to count sprouted from the gray-shingled roof.

Grooms swung open the gates, and their carriage swept along the circular drive, coming to a halt under a portico.

Hugh alighted from the carriage and held out his hand to Daphne. "This is home, ladies. At least for the short term."

She put her gloved hand in his. The touch shot sparks within her. With a deep breath, she stepped out and waited for Celeste, perhaps holding on to his hand a moment too long.

A servant, liveried in the deep red she'd come to associate with the Mandevilles, opened the door, his face blank as his gaze swept over them standing on the flagstones with their luggage at their feet.

"Welcome home, my lord." He clapped his hands and within moments, the footman had picked up their luggage and carried it off inside.

But she couldn't seem to move and noticed Celeste hadn't either. It was a very grand house. Crossing the threshold seemed a declaration that they belonged in a house like this.

"A case of 'careful what you wish for' isn't it?" Celeste murmured. "How many times did we wish we lived in a house like this, and yet here we are, about to do just that and scared out of our wits."

But they did belong in a place like this. Well, perhaps not quite as grand, but at least a cousin of a house like this. And it was the Mandevilles who had stolen it from them.

"Pooh," Daphne said, grabbing Celeste's hand and following Hugh up the stairs. "I am not even slightly scared."

They were led into a magnificent entry hall with a checkered marble floor. A staircase circled up to the domed ceiling that was so high Daphne could barely make out the cherubs painted on it.

A maid came to join them, curtsying to the group. "If it pleases you, my lord, Lady Mandeville has asked me to take the ladies to their rooms when they arrive and provide refreshment. She will see them when she returns."

Hugh smiled. "Thank you, Marie." He turned to Daphne. "Mother has already taken care of things. Marie will take you to your room so you can recover from the journey, but is there anything else I can get for you before my man of investigation arrives?"

Daphne shook her head. "No, everything will be perfect, I'm sure." It was obvious he was keen to prepare for his meeting.

Hugh bowed deeply and strode away.

They were shown to their room, which was an oasis of calm green with a plush Turk carpet and two beds.

"Can I have the bed farthest from the door?" Celeste didn't wait for an answer, but went to it and sat on it, bouncing lightly on the edge. "It's so soft! Almost as soft as the way Hugh looks at you." She smiled like a person in possession of a great secret. "He stole glances at you all the way to London. If I had Father's penchant for gambling, I would say he holds you in high regard."

"Hush," Daphne said, looking out the open door. "Lower your voice. He is just being gentlemanly."

She couldn't admit that all the feelings she'd had for him in India had come back in a rush, despite the danger they were all in. Her heart had not grown an ounce of sense in all the years that had passed. Even now, the thought of him stealing glances at her just as she had been at him had heat rushing to her face.

Celeste's eyes widened. "Oh dear. That didn't take long, did it? You always did have a soft spot for him. I mean, I understand it, he is dashed handsome, but Daph..."

Daphne held up a hand, cutting her off. "I know. My heart is foolish; it cannot be helped. But it will be ignored."

Celeste shrugged. "Oh, well, don't feel bad. If he looked at me as he looks at you, I would likely be a simpering mess, too."

Daphne picked up a cushion from the bed and threw it at her sister's head.

Celeste ducked, but it still clipped the side of her head. "Ow!"

Daphne smiled and looked past her sister to the escritoire that was thoughtfully stocked with parchment, an ink bottle, and quills. "Let's write Father a note."

Celeste frowned. "And how would we deliver it? Use a Mandeville messenger? You know how that would end."

"Surely I can make it vague enough not to arouse suspicion."

"You would also send it to where Father actually is instead of Limmer's. Hugh will find out as soon as you've sealed the wax."

Daphne frowned. "True. But how will we find Father if we can't send messages?"

"I'll tell you what. You write that note, and I will find a way for us to go for a walk by ourselves and find a boy to deliver it for us. We have a few pennies. What say you?"

"That I almost forgive you teasing me." Daphne took a piece of parchment from the drawer. "Almost."

Even if the threat of the Bow Street Runner and Lord Mandeville weren't so strong, she could hardly accept Mandeville's hospitality if Father was stealing from them. And it was a distinct possibility, no matter how much she'd like to deny it. One way or the other, she had to discover the truth.

But it was hard to be both vague and cautioning at the same time.

Dear Father,

Imagine my surprise when Lord Mandeville arrived on our doorstep looking for you! He would hear of nothing but that we travel to London with him so he could reunite our family. We are staying at his house on Curzon Street.

Please send me word that you have received this note as soon as you are possibly able.

I await your reply.

Your loving daughter, Daphne.

. . .

THERE. That was vague enough to escape notice if a servant read it and yet pointed enough to get her father's attention.

She hoped.

Celeste read it over her shoulder. "Do you think you should mention the Bow Street Runner? He needs to know how serious this is. If we can find him, we should advise him to leave London."

Daphne folded the letter and sealed it with the basic seal and blue wax she found in the top drawer of the escritoire. "If we both thought he was innocent, we would be trying to find him so he could clear his name, not to advise him to run, wouldn't we?"

The anguish in her sister's eyes was hard to ignore. "We are not acting as though he is innocent, though, are we? And if he's not, Daphne, we have no right to interfere with the Crown trying to bring him to justice. No matter how much it would ruin us and our future."

Daphne nodded. "True, but I can't think that right now."

"So much for coming to London to go to balls and see the sights! I vow we have the worst luck—" Celeste stopped midsentence. "I hear someone."

She was right; there was a deep male voice along with Hugh's coming from downstairs. They both went to the door and leaned forward.

"You said midday," the visitor said by way of greeting.

"I bet it's the Bow Street Runner," Celeste said in an excited whisper, her eyes bright. How she could be excited by such an event, Daphne would never know.

"As I told you in my note," Hugh said, "I was unavoidably detained."

"Can I meet your detainees?" The man laughed, as though he'd made a good joke.

Daphne looked at Celeste. Her expression was as horrified as

Daphne felt. "Are we detainees?" she said, in horror. "Have we stepped into a trap?"

"No," Daphne said, and wished she felt as confident as she sounded.

"May I meet them?" the visitor's voice was as polished as any peer.

Daphne stepped into the hall and crept toward the stairs, hoping to catch a glimpse of the man. Unfortunately, he was facing the stair and her movement caught his eye. Their gazes locked, and, for a moment, Daphne felt like a deer caught in a hunter's stare. He was tall, dressed in unrelieved black, and unshaven, with eyes as dark as a moonless night. She shivered and gooseflesh rose unbidden on her arms.

"Ah," he said. "Is this the lady in question?"

Too late now to run back to the safety of the bedroom. She plastered a smile on her face and started to walk down the stairs.

"Please stay where you are, Miss Davenport," Hugh said. He turned to Mr. Wolfe. "I do not have Miss Davenport's permission to introduce you and will not subject her to your interrogation, no matter how politely you couch it."

Hugh was giving her the choice. Her heart warmed to him.

It was her chance to escape, but Daphne continued toward the two men and executed a shallow curtsey. "You have my permission, Lord Mandeville." She knew, as Hugh did, that Bow Street was infamous for getting the information they required, one way or another. She might as well appear to be compliant even if her every instinct was to run the other way.

Hugh took a deep breath and exhaled it slowly. It was a frustrated sound. "Very well. Miss Davenport, may I present Mr. Wolfe, who was raised on a property near to ours in Surrey but currently undertakes the occupation of Bow Street Runner for reasons none of us understand."

Mr. Wolfe bowed, but Daphne didn't like the speculative gleam in his eyes

She, however, had no intention of showing her fear. "How long have you been a Runner, Mr. Wolfe?"

"Long enough, Miss Davenport. And we prefer the title Principal Officer." He smiled at her, but there was no warmth in it.

"Or thief-taker?" she asked innocently, only to receive a bark of laughter in return.

"Definitely thief-taker, Miss Davenport." He sobered instantly. "I do love to take a thief. Do you think your father could be one? I promise to make this as painless as possible if you cooperate."

Her heart thumped so hard she could barely hear herself think. Pull yourself together, Daphne. She instinctively stiffened her spine. She would not show him her fear. "No, I do not think my father is a thief. I begin to wish I had not been so brave as to want to make your acquaintance. And as for making it painless, you are already paining me!"

"Now see here, Wolfe—" Hugh began, but Daphne stayed him, with a hand on his arm.

He looked at her questioningly, and she knew then if she'd asked him, he would throw Wolfe out of the house. "He is but doing his job. No harm taken."

Marie walked past with a tea tray.

Hugh nodded. "Thank you, Miss Davenport. I suggest you follow Marie to your room and relax after our journey."

"With pleasure." Daphne curtseyed again and followed the maid up the stairs.

She took a deep shuddering breath. That was far too close. They were in deep trouble. Wolfe was a man who always caught his thief.

HUGH STOOD AT THE WINDOW, his gaze focused on distant Curzon Street. It was either that or strangle Wolfe for his forwardness. "What news?"

"Another theft," Wolfe said from behind him, cracking his knuckles.

He turned, Daphne forgotten for a moment. "But how? The warehouse is locked down."

Wolfe fished a cheroot from his pocket and met Hugh's gaze. "Apparently, we should have sent the deliveries with a team of outriders."

"Between the ship and the warehouse?"

"Brazen, eh?" Wolfe lit the cheroot and inhaled deeply. "We lost two hundred pounds of stock."

Hugh's stomach fell. It was the largest theft yet, and on top of the others, put his operations in a vulnerable position. How many thefts could he endure without having to sell off land to counter the effect? "And the thief proved he can take the goods from right under our noses. What of our suspects?"

"I tracked Langley down to a pub in Cornwall, Richards of Yorkshire died last year, and Rodwell I haven't found. And you? What of Davenport? Did you find him, or did you bring his daughters to town to lure him out?"

"I struck Davenport from the list the moment I saw the way his daughters live. A bare house and larder. Surely if he were responsible, there would be some luxuries, some spending." He grimaced. "I brought them to London just as much to save them from the way they are living as to lure Davenport out."

Wolfe carelessly knocked ash into a gilt and blue Sevres bowl that was never intended as an ashtray. "Don't be a fool."

"You think it foolish to want to help them? I call it my duty. Any honorable man would've done the same." Hugh removed the bowl and passed Wolfe an ashtray. "Heathen."

Wolfe grinned. "Then I must be without honor, because I believe it foolish to strike Davenport off the list merely because he's wily enough to hide the proceeds of his crime. Take a look at this."

Wolfe drew a sheaf of papers out of his satchel.

Hugh moved around the desk to stand beside him.

"What you see before you," Wolfe said, "is five years of stock-taking from the company. I have cross-referenced the losses against the times when the manager, Mr. Lacey, has been absent from the office. More often than not, goods appear to go missing at that time."

Hugh scanned the figures, saw the validity of what Wolfe said, and nodded. "So, we have a thief who knows when Lacey is not there and takes advantage of the situation. Or it's Lacey himself."

"And worse, this pattern has continued even with staff changes. Lacey had a complete staff change when he first noticed the discrepancies—it made no difference."

"So perhaps someone who has previously worked for the company and has some inside knowledge."

"Precisely," Wolfe said sombrely. "The list grows longer. And perhaps there is a team. You cannot strike Davenport out quite yet. He might just be part of something bigger."

Hugh shook the thought of Daphne's too-slim body out of his head. "No man would leave his own flesh and blood to starve. We should continue to look elsewhere."

"You may look elsewhere, my friend; I will continue to look at Davenport and his lovely daughters."

Hugh shook his head. "I'd be surprised if you found ladies of quality to be anything other than horrified at the thought of their father being involved."

"I looked not for horror, merely for her attempting to disguise her horror."

"Meaning that if she tries to disguise her upset, she's trying to hide her reaction to protect her father? That could be true." He paused, remembering how she had done just that moments before. Why did he automatically leap to her defense rather than suspect her? "But from what I saw at their house, Miss Davenport is very proud. She would consider any display of emotion as a failure on her part. It was badly done."

63

Wolfe shrugged. "I will do many bad things in the course of finding you justice. You pay me well so you don't have to do those things yourself, so spare me your outrage."

"You don't think I could do them myself?" In truth, it was simply safer to have Wolfe handling the inquiries, as he wasn't so sure he'd be able to stop himself from dispensing his own rough justice. He didn't want to end up hanging from a noose himself.

"Let's test it then. We need to know everything about Davenport's history since you last saw them in India. Any detail about Davenport's life could be a clue, any pastime, any interest. Are you dirty and desperate enough to learn all of Daphne's secrets, knowing you'll be using them against her?"

"I think the point is that I won't have to use them against her. And yes, of course I can. Don't you think family comes before all else?"

"We shall see." Wolfe picked up his cheroot again, and blew smoke that curled like a ribbon. "I don't think Miss Davenport is actually stealing from you, but she is hiding something and often a lady with her ear at the right door can be the link that brings down an entire criminal scheme. I will find that weak link whether you approve or not."

Hugh raised an eyebrow. "Not if you want your exorbitant bill paid. You will stay away from her while she's in this house, whether you like it or not."

Wolfe held up both hands. "You have her all to yourself. Just ask yourself why that idea appeals so much. Because it does, doesn't it?"

Hugh sat at his desk and waved Wolfe off. "If you've finished your games for today, you can make use of the carriage and go find Davenport where Miss Davenport said he'd be—Limmer's."

Wolfe snubbed out the cigar and picked up his hat. "Don't hold your breath."

CHAPTER 6

IN WHICH DAPHNE STRIKES A BARGAIN

One hour later, when Daphne and Celeste would normally be planning their dinner, Lady Mandeville requested their presence for tea. As they dutifully made their way down the stairs, Celeste squeezed Daphne's hand. "What if she doesn't like us?"

Daphne smiled. "How could she not like you? It's impossible. Just pretend we are meeting Mrs. Erskine." Their old friend from home always had a kind word and a hot meal at the ready in exchange for whatever the girls grew in their garden.

Celeste exhaled. "Oh, what a good idea! Thank you."

Daphne wished they truly were meeting Mrs. Erskine. Her only memory of Lady Mandeville was of a bevy of attendants fanning her so hard that visitors were buffeted by whirlwinds from five different directions and ended up with their hair blown to Jericho.

The footman met them at the door, then knocked and entered. They followed him and stopped still, Celeste gasping softly. The enormous room was painted eggshell blue, and covered with so many oil paintings that it looked like an art gallery. Chairs and sofas—all upholstered in blue and gold fabric

—were scattered about the room. In the middle of the room, there was a round table with a large vase of flowers on it. If the Mandevilles were suffering from the thefts, their living conditions showed no sign of it.

Lady Mandeville reclined on a sofa near the far window, a shaft of afternoon sunlight illuminating the pages of the book in her lap.

The footman stopped in the center of the room and introduced them. The only indication Lady Mandeville gave that she'd heard him was a nod as she kept reading. Once the footman had left, she closed the book and, with a small sigh, sat up and beckoned Daphne and Celeste to her.

"Do come forward, ladies."

They made their way to her, weaving around the pretty chairs and tables. She wore a dress of deep mauve that suggested she still mourned her husband. Her silver hair was drawn back from her face in an elegant sweep.

She remained a handsome woman. Her strong jaw was thankfully not as strong as her son's, but she sported the same thick eyebrows. A waft of rosewater and something musty, like old parchment, reached Daphne. In India, Lady Mandeville had always smelled like lemons and soap, like she was trying to clean off the dust and heat. Daphne was more likely to dive into it.

Daphne dipped into a curtsy. "It's a pleasure to see you again, Lady Mandeville. May I present my younger sister, Miss Celeste Davenport?"

Celeste curtsied. Daphne knew she would not speak until she was spoken to.

"Very prettily done, my dear," Lady Mandeville said to Celeste. "I'm sure you'll take quite well. Now tell me about your trip to town."

They spent the next few minutes in small talk about Reading, the weather and the recent wedding of her daughter.

The tea arrived and Lady Mandeville poured with the grace

one would expect of a countess. The cakes were small but delicious. Celeste took a few more than was perhaps polite, but Lady Mandeville pretended not to notice. It was kind.

Everything seemed very amicable and Daphne let herself relax just a little and took the last sip of her tea. Celeste did the same and no sooner was her cup rattling on its saucer than Lady Mandeville put her own tea cup down and smiled at Celeste.

"Now run along up to your room; our footman James will show you the way."

She was sending Celeste away? *No!*

The footman stepped forward to take her. Celeste curtsied again and took her leave, shooting Daphne a look of obvious relief.

All very well for *her* to be happy about this turn of events.

"There now, just the two of us having a coze."

Daphne nodded, although it felt anything but cozy, the chair pushing her into rod-straight posture and the safety of servants listening to every word, gone. She took a deep breath. Lady Spellwater spoke to strangers every other week, persuaded them, cajoled them; why couldn't she talk to Lady Mandeville? She may no longer be making perfumes, but perhaps her alter ego would come in handy during the visit to London.

"I'm sure you're wondering why I've sent your sister away." She paused, frowning slightly. "I wanted something understood before you unpack your bags."

Daphne held her breath, waiting for her to continue. Lady Mandeville seemed to be searching for the right words, which could only mean it was something difficult for her to say.

"You see, I remember you from Bombay. Or more to the point, I remember your mother being very amused at how in love with my son you were."

Daphne drew in a sharp breath. Betrayed from the grave by her mother! "I assure you, that was *many* years ago."

"Many years ago, but we both know that love knows not the

bounds of time." She fingered a locket around her neck and raised her eyebrows, as though daring Daphne to deny that she still had a tendré for her son.

"I am a grown woman now," Daphne said, somewhat stiffly. "I'm not given to flights of fancy."

Lady Mandeville nodded. "Exactly. You are a grown woman, and while I admit that your attire and complexion leave a lot to be desired, it appears you have grown into the looks you promised."

Truly? She'd never thought herself as beautiful—how could she when compared to Celeste—but the compliment nevertheless had a happy smile tugging at her lips.

"I have heard Lord Mandeville is all but engaged."

Lady Mandeville's gaze met Daphne's. Her eyes were deep blue and so like Hugh's it was disconcerting. "Perhaps, but my son has a penchant for saving anyone he feels his father has wronged, and he feels his father has wronged *you*."

Hugh made a habit of it? Perhaps he truly had brought them to London with good motives.

Daphne hesitated, knowing what she was about to say would annoy the older woman. "Righting the wrongs of the past is something all good men do."

Lady Mandeville's cheeks darkened and her lips thinned. There was something in her expression that suggested she was barely keeping her anger in check. "My husband gave *everything* to improve our standing, both financially and socially. Hugh thinks too much."

The last seemed to slip out without Lady Mandeville meaning it. But it was interesting that she did not deny that Hugh was right.

The older lady briefly closed her eyes, then pinned Daphne with a hard stare. "All I ask is that you don't set your cap at him."

She made Daphne sound like an adventuress, which wasn't *so* far from the truth, but only in the realm of commerce, not luring a poor man into matrimony by taking advantage of his good nature.

That was an interesting thought—did she now believe Hugh had a good nature?

"I hardly think I'm a damsel in distress. If anything, I think Lord Mandeville brought us to London to aid him in his search for my father. I think you'll find he's not in the least interested in me."

Lady Mandeville blinked, and Daphne had the impression she'd said something that surprised her. "Nevertheless. I want your promise you will not flirt and simper."

Daphne straightened. "Flirting and simpering, if I were even capable of such, does not a marriage proposal make, especially not when the man in question is almost betrothed." It was starting to annoy her, the way Lady Mandeville thought she had any power at all over Hugh. Perhaps there *had* been guilt in his eyes when he inspected their house, but who would offer for a lady just because he felt sorry for her? It was ludicrous.

She looked at her hands, tightly clasped in her lap. They were rough from the hard work real ladies did not do. If Lady Mandeville had paid any real attention, she would have realized that Daphne was a long way from being countess material.

Lady Mandeville exhaled a short sharp breath. "Very well. Let me make this easier again. Hugh's upcoming betrothal is the most important one this family has seen for five generations. I do not need Lady Johanna crying off because Hugh is paying attention to you. The future of the Mandevilles depends on your promise. I am happy to use my own funds to pay, not just for one or two dresses, but for an extensive new wardrobe for you and your charming sister. And not just any seamstress, but my own, Madam Le Favre. In addition, I will launch you into society to the best of my ability in return for your promise."

Daphne stared at Lady Mandeville unable to believe she was serious. She smiled and shook her head. There was no decision to make. Hugh may have already offered to buy them some dresses, but an entire wardrobe would be so much better.

"Thank you. I accept your kind offer and promise not to make calf's eyes or set my cap at your son. I appreciate you honoring his offer to introduce Celeste to society. I have no intention of souring that kindness."

The older lady smiled, obviously relieved. "My thanks, Miss Davenport. You show superior understanding."

Daphne couldn't feel insulted when suggesting Hugh might marry her was more of a compliment. Of course, had Lady Mandeville known she was Lady Spellwater or that her father might be in receipt of stolen goods, then that opinion-and her generous offer-would no doubt be withdrawn.

"Lovely. That is all." Lady Mandeville picked up her book, indicating that the interview was at an end. She waved her hand over the tea tray. "Would you like to take these up to your room to share with Miss Celeste?"

Oh, Heavenly Father, thank you.

"Yes please, how kind."

Lady Mandeville motioned for the footman to carry the tray away. "Take these up please, James." She turned back to Daphne. "We have a dinner engagement this evening, so I will order the kitchen to send supper trays for you both."

Daphne would never argue about receiving an entire plate of cakes.

"Thank you, Lady Mandeville." She bobbed a curtsy, happy with the turn of events. They would both have new dresses, pelisses and bonnets. Even better, now she had cake without having to sit with Lady Mandeville and pretend she wasn't interested in eating.

She followed the footman up the stairs. Only she knew how unlikely, how impossible it would be for Hugh to offer her marriage. It felt almost sinful to take the wardrobe from Lady

Mandeville, but the old lady's peace of mind must be worth a lot to her.

Her promise not to flirt with Hugh was a small price to pay for having Celeste launched into society not looking like someone's country cousin.

Lady Spellwater would approve of the bargain.

CHAPTER 7

IN WHICH LORD MANDEVILLE IS STUNNED INTO SILENCE

L ady Mandeville could move at lightning speed when she chose to, for Daphne and Celeste had an appointment at the modiste the very next morning.

They were sent with a footman, then deposited outside a charming shop with *Madame Le Favre* painted on the window in crisp gold lettering.

"I'd hoped to buy you this wardrobe myself," Daphne said, grabbing hold of Celeste's hand and squeezing.

Celeste gave her a quick hug. "Don't be daft. If someone else will pay for it, so much the better."

"True," Daphne replied. "But doing this is all I worked for, and that the Mandevilles should provide it…" She trailed off, aware she sounded ungrateful but not knowing how to stop herself.

"Oh, admit it," Celeste said, dragging her toward the door. "It's more that the Mandevilles, and especially one handsome Mandeville in particular, aren't the monsters you thought they were."

Daphne smiled. She had not told Celeste about the bargain she'd made with Lady Mandeville or what the true cost of the dresses were. "Perhaps."

Celeste laughed, and they entered the shop. Daphne's sour mood evaporated when she saw the small, expensive jewel box of a boutique. There were swaths of red fabric draped from ceiling to floor, and huge gilt looking glasses. It smelled so strongly of full-blown roses that Daphne studied the room until she found them, packed into a vase on a table in the room's corner. Would the dresses smell like roses too?

But there was something else—a smell so familiar that her nose was slow in realizing the fragrance was out of place. It was the gentle scent of her first perfume, By a Lady.

Daphne carefully turned until she found the source—six bottles standing proudly on a silver platter. She walked casually over to them, picking one up. "Look, Celeste," she breathed. "How did these get here?"

"By magic?" her sister replied, eyes wide.

Or, more likely, the tinkers that Ayah often sold the perfumes to had made their way to London. She could think of no other explanation.

A very young, thin lady dressed in black stepped into the room, a measuring tape around her neck. She smiled when she saw them standing near the perfume.

"It is called By a Lady. Isn't it lovely? Those are my last six bottles, and there are no more to be had. If you would like a bottle, best get it today!"

"Oh," Daphne said. The fact she could speak at all was a miracle, with the wash of excitement and pride she was experiencing. "Do your customers like it?"

"Adore it! And everyone is trying to discover the identity of the creator. I have been told she calls herself Lady Spellwater. So far, she has eluded us all." She waved her hands around, as if to punctuate the elusiveness. "But tell me, my dears, you are the Misses Davenport, are you not?"

"We are." Excitement thrumming through Daphne's veins. *People love my perfumes.*

This could be her best and only chance to have a proper London supplier. But she had to do it without risking either herself or Celeste. It was still a risk, but her hammering heart told her it was worth it. Worse still, she knew she would regret it forever if she did nothing. This was about more than just herself and Celeste. Ayah and her family needed this too. She chose her words carefully.

"I must tell you that I am in a unique position of correspondence with Lady Spellwater. I could write to her and see if there is more to be had, if you like?" She shrugged a shoulder as if Madam's answer were nothing to her either way.

Madam Le Favre's eyes lit up. "Never say it."

Pride filled her. "I cannot promise anything, of course, and she is quite protective of her identity."

The modiste crossed her hand over her heart. "I would never breathe a word."

Since dressmakers were a hotbed of London's gossip, Daphne took that statement very lightly.

"Daphne..." Celeste said, a note of warning in her voice.

Instead of listening to her sister, Daphne pulled the snuffbox from her reticule. "She gave us this sample before we left for London. What do you think? Of course it will be different on each lady's skin."

Madam Le Favre took the small container, rubbed her finger on the beeswax and then onto the skin of her wrist. She then lifted her wrist to her nose and inhaled, a look of utter pleasure on her face. "Oh, my," she said, her French accent entirely gone. "Heavenly. I am transfixed."

Daphne glanced at Celeste in triumph. *That's more like it.*

"I would love to sell this and..." She searched Daphne's face, then looked around the empty shop. "Tell Lady Spellwater that I also am in a unique position. I would commit myself to making her perfumes the most popular in London. That is, if she allows me to buy directly from her instead of buying it from tinkers."

"How would you make it popular?" Celeste said, her usually gentle voice with an edge of sharpness. "You know she does not want to be identified. We do not want to be the reason she is exposed. It will ruin our friendship."

Madam was quiet for a moment. Then she smiled. "I am acquainted with Joseph Sadler, you know, the famous aeronaut? My mother worked in his family bakery in Oxford." They must have had a slightly shocked look on their faces for Madam rolled her eyes. "Yes, yes, I am not French. But French modistes command the best prices, so for the purposes of my business, I am as French as a croissant. But, you see, this is why I feel kinship with Lady Spellwater. We are both hiding our true identity to make our way in the world. I assure you, I would never betray her. I have been making his mother's dresses since I started in business. He has offered many times to take me up and he has an ascension next week, I believe. Lady Spellwater might be interested? She could throw scented cards from the balloon to announce her arrival in London. Joseph will most certainly do this favor for me."

Daphne sucked in a shocked breath. He was one of the most famous people in England. Thousands watched his balloon ascensions and thousands more read about his exploits in newspapers and magazines. Lady Spellwater would indeed be a famous name. But the risk was too great. How would she explain her absence? How would she get back to London once the balloon landed?

Daphne shook her head. "I do not think she would do that. But perhaps if *you* wore a heavy veil, you could assume her identity for the purposes of the balloon flight?"

Madam clapped. "Oh what fun! I would love to. No one will recognize me if I have a thick enough veil."

"Very well, I will send word to Lady Spellwater today. With luck I will have an answer for you by our next fitting."

Madame Le Favre clasped Daphne's hand. "I am beside myself

with excitement. Leave the press to me. But now, let's order you the wardrobe Lady Mandeville is set on. It will be my best work, I assure you." She turned to Celeste, looked her up and down in appraisement. "Bon, bon." Her French accent was back. "With my creations you shall both turn the Ton on their heads."

"We would be happy just to be presentable," Daphne said lightly, but Madam just brushed her aside with a wave of her hand.

"Nonsense. Each of you seat yourselves at a lounge. My assistants are gathering designs and fabric and will be out in a moment."

"But how will they know what suits?" Celeste said.

"Ha! They had each of you pinned by the time you'd exited your carriage. This is our profession, our art. What Lady Mandeville was thinking, suggesting I put you in canary yellow, I'll never know!"

Daphne knew—it was an effort to make Daphne less attractive, for the yellow would make her skin sallow. Madam Le Favre left them, gliding out of the room with more elegance than her plain black dress should have afforded.

Daphne settled on the lounge, feeling like the cat that got all the cream in England. "Oh, what a day."

"Careful now," Celeste said in a whisper. "We did not plan to bring Lady Spellwater to London." Celeste's grimaced. "She is a myth, a phantom. Let her remain one."

"Everything will be fine. I am quite removed from the risk. This is the perfect solution." The statement was mostly bravado. They were relying on the generosity of others with each step here in London and that was always risky. But what if they never found Father? Then she would kick herself for not doing everything she could to secure their future.

Celeste frowned and Daphne pulled her into a hug. "Lady S is here now and there's no sending her home. I will write to Ayah this afternoon and have her send as much Scandal as she has for Madam Le Favre to sell."

"Heaven help us," Celeste muttered. Thankfully the assistants strode into the room, carrying bolts of beautiful silks, laces, and muslin. It distracted Celeste almost instantly.

Annalise—the young lady assigned to help Daphne—had more sophistication in her left earlobe than Daphne could ever hope to attain. With her dark hair, pale skin, and hazel eyes, she was almost an exact match for Daphne's coloring. Then Daphne noticed Celeste had a fair assistant. Madame Le Favre was no fool. She was master of her own world, making astute decisions to secure her future. It was enough to make one sick with envy. Imagine if she, Daphne, could run a business like this in London, but for perfumes. She wanted it so badly that her stomach ached.

Annalise sat next to Daphne, her smile shy. "Miss, if we do nothing else today, we should make a decision on the ball gown. The seamstresses need time to construct our creations, so we should get started."

She pulled a gown in a late stage of completion across her lap. "This is a new design Madam is toying with. Something similar would become you. Shall we?"

Daphne touched the gown reverently. It was too beautiful. Yards and yards of rich, light mauve silk, with a diaphanous overlay of lace shot through with silver. It was finished with a golden-corded belt around the waist. Daphne drew in a slow breath. It wasn't a debutante's dress, because it wasn't white, but it was perhaps close enough that nobody would notice.

"I fear it won't suit me." Daphne said, pulling her hand back, frightened her roughened fingers might catch the delicate material. It likely cost more than an entire year of rent on their cottage. That had to be wrong.

But Annalise ignored her, pulling Daphne up by the elbows and toward the change room. "You are afraid it will suit. I have seen this many times. Go, try it on. If you hate it, I will eat my shift."

The front door opened, and a young woman, dressed in an elegant blue walking ensemble with a foot-wide ruffle hem, entered the shop with her maid trailing behind her. She looked around, her expression demanding immediate attention.

Daphne expected Annalise to drop her dress and run to the new arrival, but she merely nodded at the lady and guided Daphne gently toward the change rooms.

"Pardon me," the lady said, addressing Annalise, "I need to see Madam Le Favre." She stabbed her parasol at the ground.

"She will be out shortly, Lady Johanna. I can hear her coming now. I am serving Miss Davenport."

Lady Johanna! This was who Lord Mandeville was destined to marry? Intrigued, Daphne took her in from head to toe in one quick glance. She was tall, with long graceful legs and small bosom. She moved with the upright carriage of a trained lady, her chin lifted, her glance taking in all around her and probably judging it inferior.

"Davenport, you say?" Lady Johanna strode forward. "Miss Daphne Davenport, currently staying with Lady Mandeville?"

Daphne curtsied. "The very same. But I'm afraid you have the better of me."

Lady Johanna dipped a tiny curtsey in return. "Lady Johanna Wilcox of Somerdale Manor. We are the Kent Wilcox, you understand. My father is Strathdale." Her light blue eyes flashed with pride. But Daphne could not help thinking those bulging eyes were just a little frog-like. It may not have been a kind thought, but it allowed her to ignore her imperious tone.

"Ah," Daphne said, without a clue what it meant to be a Kent Wilcox as opposed to any other sort of Wilcox. Much less a Strathdale.

"Lady Mandeville sent me a note asking me to help you make your way into society." Her gaze lazily scanned Daphne and appeared to be unimpressed. "Of course, I will assist you in any way I can, although vouchers to Almacks will be out of the question, I'm sure."

Celeste groaned from her change room.

"I'm sure there will be plenty for us to do without the rarefied surroundings of Almacks." Daphne curtsied. "Thank you for your help. If you will excuse me?"

This time, she prodded Annalise, hoping they could go to the change room. Before they could leave, Madam Le Favre rushed out to greet her customer. "I was sure we agreed you would come this afternoon, Lady Johanna? My seamstresses have been up all night, but the dresses are not quite finished." She wrung her hands as though this were a tragedy and not the slight inconvenience it was.

"Very well," Lady Johanna replied with a bored shrug. "You can wait on me this afternoon with your assistants and the dresses then," Lady Johanna declared, arching a pleased eyebrow at Daphne. "Miss Davenport, I will wait on you tomorrow to draw up a plan of attack."

"I look forward to it." *Beside myself with excitement, in fact.*

The door slammed, and Lady Johanna was gone.

Annalise looked apologetic. "She is a difficult, but good customer. Her father is the Duke of Strathdale." Annalise stepped inside the change room.

Hugh had not mentioned he was courting the daughter of a duke. But then, at his social level, perhaps that was normal. She rather thought it wasn't, though.

Daphne was set to follow when a rider leaped from his large black horse directly outside the shop. She watched with fascination as Lord Mandeville had a short conversation with Lady Johanna and came toward the shop. What a sight he was. It was hard not to admire the graceful way he jumped the steps and swung his cane in the air before landing with catlike precision right before the entry.

Oh, but he looked angry.

He opened the door. The silver bell tinkled a warning, and he descended on her.

"You!" he said. Then he spotted Madam Le Favre. "I need to have a private word with Miss Davenport."

Madam Le Favre and her seamstresses left the room. Daphne reached out and held on to Annalise. "Stay, please?" The seamstress nodded and went back into the change room.

Her heart leapt in her throat. *Merciful heaven, had he discovered her secret already?* And how like the way of the world that discovery would come just as she was about to get a lovely dress. It was too cruel.

"Me," she replied, letting the curtain fall fully closed behind her. "And hush, Celeste is in the next room."

"Don't you 'me', me," he said, his expression harsh. "You know what you did."

She shoved her shaking hands underneath a bolt of checked muslin and tried to stare at him evenly. She'd made a decision long ago that no matter how intimidating a man was, he'd never know she was cowering. Lord Mandeville was no exception.

"I'll 'me' you anytime I want to 'me' you," she said, and then, because the argument was so silly, smiled.

That made his face stormier, if that was possible. "Madam, this is no jest."

His anger was very contained, and that was somehow worse than her father's blustery outbursts that spent themselves quickly. Lord Mandeville's anger was the kind that could likely boil quietly for months, probably years.

But no matter how fearsome he was to behold, he was also, unfortunately, quite delectable, in a green coat tailored to fit his form perfectly. It made his shoulders look so broad and strong. Tight buckskin breeches disappeared into the most beautiful pair of black leather riding boots she'd ever seen. The intervening years had put no dent in her longing for him, it seemed. She swallowed and dragged her errant thoughts back to the matter at hand. Whatever troubled him—whatever he thought she'd done—she could take heart from the fact that he hadn't brought Mr. Wolfe with him. Perhaps all was not lost.

She forced a smile and patted the lounge to have him sit by her. "It may not be a jest, but it could be called a farce without too much imagination. What troubles you?"

He refused the invitation, preferring to stand. "What troubles me, as you so politely put it, is the fact that you lied to me."

"In saying what, precisely?" She was pleased the words came out evenly rather than reflect the tremors she felt inside.

"Your father's whereabouts. Limmer's Hotel? They haven't seen him there for *six months.*"

She held up a hand to stop him. "Careful, my lord. I may not be a gentleman, but I still have my honor. Any man would call you out for that."

Even though she *was* a liar, heaven help her. She could promise herself never to lie again, but her whole life was a lie, so what would be the point? One day, perhaps she could live a blameless life, but that day was not today.

"So, as far as you knew, he was at Limmer's?" His deep blue eyes were flinty and hard, but there was a hint of a question in them, as though he wanted to believe the best of her.

She nodded. "It's where he has always stayed. Could we please discuss this when we get home? I was having a perfectly lovely time until you arrived."

How could she tell him that she was just as confused about where her father was? That the hotels she had sent her letters had responded the same way---her father was not there.

"I will find him, you know." There was determination in his voice.

"I hope so. Tell me when you do. I have a bone to pick with him myself." She eyed him with impatience, then stood and walked to the change room, drawing back the drape. "Please excuse me, I have a dress to try on."

"You told me only yesterday that you had letters from London. How could he not tell you where to reach him?" His voice was still harsh, but there was a pleading note to it now. "I refuse to believe a parent would leave his only daughters unchaperoned and with no way of contacting him. I want to believe you, but you're making this very difficult."

She entered the fitting room and closed the drapes with a snap, hoping he would take the hint to leave. As Annalise helped remove her pelisse and untie her dress, she added, "And you're ruining what should be a perfectly wonderful experience for me. I will ask you again---can we please resume this later?"

The new dress floated over her shoulders. Once Annalise had pinned the silver sheath over the silken dress, she turned and studied herself in the mirror. The dress was beautiful, and the assistant was right---it suited her to perfection.

It was a dress that exuded the confidence and allure of Lady Spellwater and everything Daphne wanted to be. The silk was smooth against her stocking legs, the very luxury of the fabric making her feel special.

"I don't know what to think," Hugh said abruptly.

The sudden sound of his voice on the other side of the drapes made her jump and Annalise squeak. "Excuse me!"

In one of the other rooms, Celeste giggled.

"I want to believe your father has nothing to do with this," Hugh continued gruffly. "It amazes me how quickly I feel responsible for you and Miss Celeste. I think it must be our shared history, but you already feel like sisters to me."

Sisters. Trouble was, he certainly didn't feel like a brother. Not to her. But for the sake of what she'd promised Lady Mandeville, it was probably for the best. "I'm afraid I have no idea what it would feel like to have a brother."

She met Annalise's eyes in the looking glass, and they both

smiled. It was the color, she decided. It had been too long since she'd worn anything but the dullest brown that didn't show the dirt, or pale green that turned her skin sallow. The glorious purple made her complexion glow.

"Even if you don't help me" he went on, "I will continue to have your father investigated until I get to the truth."

Would the man never leave her alone? She snapped back the drape. "Do what you will."

His eyes gaze traveled slowly from her slipperless feet to the expanse of bare skin at her shoulder where he couldn't seem to shift his gaze away. "Ah... you look..."

What a delicious feeling, to know she affected him so. The tips of her ears burned.

He closed his eyes, against what she had no idea.

When he finally opened them, the anger replaced by an emotion she couldn't place. Confusion, perhaps?

Daphne smiled. "I look, ah, what exactly? Like a bag of rags? Like a vagrant?"

"Not like a sister," he said simply, and gave her a crooked smile that made her heart lurch.

He caught her hand and drew it slowly to his mouth, brushing the lightest of kisses across her knuckles. Then he turned her hand over and pressed another kiss into her palm. Even through the gloves, she felt the heat of it, and gasped.

"I look forward to dancing with you at the ball," he said, his voice far more casual than the heat in his eyes.

Then he was gone as quickly as he came, leaving Daphne at a loss. It was going to be very hard keeping him at a distance if he was going to look at her as though she was a delicious morsel.

She turned to Annalise, who beamed from ear to ear. "And that, Cherie, is the power of the right dress."

"I will take it," said Daphne. *And five more like it.*

Perhaps the days of drab Daphne Davenport were over.

~

THE FOLLOWING DAY, as they took the stairs down for luncheon, Daphne was aware that Celeste was regarding her intently.

"What's wrong?" Celeste asked eventually. "You don't look well."

"I'm not well," Daphne replied. She pulled a note she had received from Mrs. Pike after lunch and handed it to her sister. "I was going to keep this from you, but you must know what is happening."

Celeste scanned the letter and then lifted her gaze to Daphne, her eyes wide with horror. "They took everything? How can they do that?"

"A warrant. They have somehow obtained our address in Reading. Poor Mrs. Pike must have been beside herself."

Celeste winced. "But does this mean Father has run up yet more debt?"

"I think so." Daphne handed Celeste the second page. "Mrs. Pike tried to list what they took. I think we will barely have any furniture left and all of the paintings and silverware are definitely gone."

"We are truly on our own." Her brows drew together and she looked like she was about to cry. But for Daphne it just felt like a foregone conclusion. Perhaps nothing had the ability to shock her any more.

"They have apparently left the kitchen table and chairs behind, which is generous of them. Mr. and Mrs. Pike said they will remain until we return but they are actively looking for a new position."

"Oh."

Daphne took Celeste's hand. "This trip becomes more important than ever, both from the perspective of you finding a match, and me launching our perfumes. It is not just a hobby any more, it is our independence."

Celeste nodded. "You are right. I heard Lady Johanna's voice in the entry earlier. I really don't feel like meeting her now, but I suppose I must play nice."

"She has agreed to help us, so we must do our best." Celeste was taking the news in her stride and once again Daphne felt ashamed for thinking she wouldn't. She may look fragile, but she was made of stern stuff.

Celeste linked her arm in Daphne's. "And with our new wardrobe, who knows what might happen! We must *make* it happen."

Daphne regarded her sister's dress. "I'd like to see any dressmaker do as well as you did!"

They had dressed in their best matching short-sleeved dresses, made from their last bolt of muslin from India. With Celeste's skill with a needle, Daphne thought the dresses were lovely.

That was, until the footman opened the door and Daphne saw Lady Johanna, sitting across from Lady Mandeville in a cornflower blue silk and gauze morning dress that seemed made entirely of pintucks and pleats. Her hair was elegantly piled on her head, and a cashmere shawl was draped around her shoulders. She was the perfect lady.

She darted a glance at Celeste, who was taking in the ensemble like she was filing it away for future sewing reference.

Lady Mandeville stood. "Come, come, my dears. Lady Johanna has just told me how she is delighted to show you around town."

"Prepare yourself," whispered Daphne to her sister.

"I'm sure it is difficult to come to London from the country," Lady Johanna said—kindly, if Daphne was to be fair. Lady Johanna picked up her tea and took a dainty sip. "London is sophisticated, busy, and bustling. If you are used to a quiet country life, it can be overwhelming to one's sensibilities. It often is to mine."

It was so sweetly said that Daphne couldn't bristle, even if London did not overwhelm her. Perhaps she had been wrong about Lady Johanna. Lady Mandeville nodded, as if encouraging her to agree.

"Assuredly," Daphne said. "Although I have enjoyed these few days thus far."

Lady Johanna's gaze swept their dresses. "And what charming gowns you are both wearing. Do you always match?"

Just for a moment, Daphne caught the glint of malice in Lady Johanna's gaze. She had to be aware that their circumstances meant they had no choice but to have matching dresses, but to point it out was the height of rudeness.

"Well, no," said Celeste, looking anguished. "But we do the best we can."

Daphne put her hand over Celeste's. "Our best is generally good enough. But never fear. The dresses Madam Le Favre will deliver will ensure we are not countrified."

"Too true, although I would suggest"—Lady Johanna turned to Lady Mandeville—"that for the first few weeks, you limit your social interaction to small things, perhaps a visit to Gunters or a museum. The girls will not be ready for balls or the opera or Vauxhall, so it would be nice to take it slowly. And as you have just mentioned, Lady Mandeville, that Lord Mandeville will be unable to squire us around, that is just an additional reason to keep our adventures modest."

Daphne understood at once—both Lady Mandeville and Lady Johanna thought it more prudent to keep Hugh and Daphne away from each other. She heartily agreed. The farther they kept Hugh and his sticky questions away from her the better.

Lady Mandeville nodded, looking thoughtful. "That would be for the best, I believe. Although Hugh has already sent our acceptance of Lord Devlin's ball next week."

"I hardly think my sister will find beaus at Gunters," Daphne said politely. "We are perfectly capable of carrying on in society without fainting at the prospect and will be unobjectionable in every way."

"We will start with Gunters and then Astley's theater," said Lady Mandeville as though Daphne hadn't spoken. "What a wonderful time we will have!"

Celeste gripped Daphne's hand tighter.

And what could Daphne say? They were guests and could not invite themselves to more exciting entertainments. But she would find a way the moment an opportunity arose.

Lady Johanna stood. "I must be going. I have promised Lord Eldridge that I will take a turn around the park with him this afternoon."

It was said lightly, but everyone in the room knew Lady Johanna was telling Lady Mandeville that she had other, loftier options with which to replace her son if need be.

CHAPTER 8

IN WHICH OUR HERO FINALLY CATCHES ON

Days later, at an unspeakable hour in the morning, Hugh stepped into the back garden, of all places, hoping to continue the conversation he and Daphne started days ago. His mother obviously had a plan to keep him away, for the ladies were forever out at various entertainments. If he was lucky enough to partake of dinner with them, Daphne was seated as far away as possible. After dinner, he might play a round of whist with her—but his mother was there too, adjudicating the conversation. For her part, Daphne seemed happy to be led away.

He hoped she had not taken him in dislike after his display of anger at the modiste, but the skip in her step and secret smile as she avoided him suggested this was more a game of cat and mouse.

The identity of the cat was up for debate.

The frustration only made him strain for the warm sound of Daphne's voice. He told himself it had nothing to do with finding her company entertaining and everything to do with losing precious time in discovering where Edward Davenport was. It was just that he longed to hear what she thought of London.

But every minute that passed meant Edward Davenport was still not questioned, and Hugh was no closer to having Daphne tell him where the man was. His gut told him Davenport knew *something*.

He visited the kitchen for some early coffee, and Mrs. Branshaw, the cook, informed him that his quarry had been in the garden since just after sunrise. She then handed him a still steaming slice of bread with butter. He took a bite. "Delicious, as always."

The morning light was soft and golden when he spied her in the garden. Triumph stabbed through him. *Alone at last.*

She was crouched by a straggly plant, in a mint green dress, looking like she was part of the foliage herself. Her hair was artlessly braided into a long plait, falling in a thick silk cord over her shoulder. It almost reached her waist. How would it look untied and free? Curls sprang from the braid, attempting escape, and the temptation to reach out and unknot the white ribbon at the end of it was cursed strong.

He seemed to be spending a lot of time thinking about her, even if she looked at him like he was nothing more than an amusement while she enjoyed her time in London. She was intelligent and witty, true, but she also held secrets, even if he had no idea what they were. Nor would she ever tell him.

It was intriguing. It was infuriating.

Denying her allure would only make it worse. Better to indulge in the harmless attraction and simply not act on it.

She must have heard his footsteps, because she straightened abruptly, surprise crossing her face. Her brown half boots were wet with dew, and her cheeks were rosy. "Oh. I didn't expect anyone else to be up at this hour."

He walked to her, watching as her expression moved from surprise to wariness.

"You like the garden in the morning, Miss Davenport?"

"Yes, oh yes."

With a grimace, she handed him the leaves she'd picked from the plant. "Could you hold these a moment?"

She twisted her hair into a bun, displaying her too-slight figure as she lifted her hands to the back of her head. He crushed the leaves in his fist without thinking, and a waft of peppermint surrounded him. She turned and took the leaves back, looking askance at the mangled heap he'd made of them.

"I said hold, not obliterate," she grumbled.

"Sorry." He watched—with far too much interest—as she closed her eyes, lifted the leaves to her nose and inhaled deeply.

She smiled, seemingly lost in the scent, but soon opened her eyes and regarded him with none of the alarm he'd first spotted. "Have you been looking for me?"

"Perhaps I have. It has been so hard to speak to you that I wondered if I'd have to get a letter franked just to have a word."

She arced an eyebrow. "Well, here I am. What can I do for you?"

Direct, as always. But he had no intention of being the same. Rather, he wanted to lure her into confiding everything. Somehow.

"Shall we walk?" He motioned toward the path.

She nodded and they moved on through the garden. Patches of soft morning light created halos of gold around everything it touched, including Daphne. It was easy to believe the best of her right at that moment, that she'd help him if she had any information.

"Oh my," Daphne said. The sun had broken through the clouds and bathed the house in light making the walls take on a mystical glow. "It never ceases to amaze me what the early morning sun can do."

"It's a lovely old house. It's a shame we'll have to sell it, but I see no alternative." Not quite true, but she need not know that. He hated the necessity of manipulating her emotions but couldn't see an alternative.

She stopped in her tracks. "Sell it?"

The alarm in her eyes almost caused him to renege on his fib.

He continued walking. "But of course. I have customers and investors who funded the cargo ships, but no goods to show for it with all the thefts. Circumstances dictate the sale of a large asset, and I can't possibly sell the estate in Surrey. This is our only alternative."

"Just sell a few of those paintings in the blue room. That should cover it." She sent him a sly smile that suggested she saw right through him. Then she bent to examine some thyme that had crawled its way into the paving. "In any case, I thought you'd caught yourself a wealthy lady?"

Did he detect a note of jealousy? Or was he imagining it? "This problem is mine, and not for my future bride to bail me out of. I can fix it."

She looked up, her dark gaze sharp and intelligent. "Noble, but perhaps a touch silly? The money is there, after all." Then she smiled. "Oh, I see. You haven't actually *told* her about the thefts, have you?"

"Why would I bother her with my business dealings?"

Both her eyebrows shot up in surprise. "Any husband of mine who didn't involve me in such a large problem would be having a larger problem in his marriage."

She'd be a handful, that much was certain. "It will all be resolved before we marry."

"What about your mother? Does she know?"

He shook his head. "No. She doesn't need the worry."

Her expression was shrewd. "Or perhaps you don't want her to think you've failed."

She was right. He might not be about to lose the house, but how could he tell his mother that only three years after her husband died, their fortune had been eroded?

"Men always underestimate women. She may support you in ways you haven't dreamed of."

"Unlikely given she feels, like my father did, that I should concentrate on my peerage and not our commercial endeavours," he replied. "I am supposed to remove the talk of 'shop' around the family for good. She would expect me to leave it all this to the authorities and go to my club to make the aristocratic contacts I'll need in my parliamentary career." *He could think of no worse fate.*

And why was he saying any of this to her? He was supposed to be getting secrets from *her*, not the other way around.

She frowned and scrunched her nose a little. "I am confused. I remember your grandfather in India being very involved indeed."

She remembered correctly. "It was the classic example of my father marrying beneath him for money, then everyone trying to forget where the money came from. Grandfather built Oriental Spice and Fragrance, and I'm sure he thought I would be running it or he wouldn't have taught me so much while he was still with us. I find it frustrating to have my hands tied." He shrugged. "But I didn't come here to tell you my woes; I want to help you with yours. Do you need anything my mother has not provided?"

She shifted from one foot to the other, looking uncomfortable. "No. Everything has been taken care of. Your mother has been most generous. Not just a few dresses, but an entire wardrobe for us both."

"Pardon?" He must have misheard. Why would his mother do that? Especially after she'd left him in no doubt as to what she'd thought of him bringing Daphne and Celeste to London.

He motioned her through the next arch and then rejoined her. "Why would my mother buy your wardrobes?"

Daphne's expression turned mischievous. It brought out a dimple near her mouth that was enchanting. "She believes you have a penchant for saving poor wretched creatures, and I'm just poor and wretched enough to be a great temptation." She laughed as though it were a great joke, though she winced. "She wouldn't listen to reason either, not that I protested long, I must admit."

For a moment, he couldn't say anything, astonished his mother saw him so clearly. She was right, too, about Daphne being a temptation. But it had nothing to do with her wretchedness and everything to do with something as simple as the way she looked at him. Teased him. As though she actually saw *him*. Not the earl, not the wealthy suitor, but him. It was disarming.

"Then I suppose if you're to keep your dresses, you'd best stay away from me. Do you think it's possible?"

"Oh, entirely," she said without pause.

"But what if I came to this garden every morning? Would you give up your daily walk to please my mother?" He said it in a teasing tone, though it oddly annoyed him to think she could take or leave him so easily.

"I could find another time of day to come. I do prefer early morning, but the dresses are exquisite, and you..." The way the rest of the sentence was left to trail off led him to believe he didn't compare to a good ball gown.

But then she shot him a teasing glance, undoing everything she'd proclaimed. Perhaps she was just trying to stay true to the promise she'd given his mother. He could admire that kind of discipline.

He smiled back, and there was a small moment of understanding between them. "Very well. Since I'm dispensable, I suppose I'll allow you to continue your morning visits unchallenged."

She nodded, her gaze moving from his. "I like exploring your garden. There are five different types of mint here, did you know? One of them smells distinctly like cocoa. I haven't even made it into the flower garden yet."

He knew. This garden was his grandfather's. Each time he returned from his travels, he had brought home a new variety of plants to show his daughter and grandson. His son-in-law was not so interested.

Then, when his grandfather stopped traveling, the garden was their classroom. Sometimes when he visited the garden, he could still see the ghost of his grandfather bending over the plants, much like Daphne was. He was never afraid to get his hands dirty and always had time for his grandson. There was a small potting shed down the back where it felt like Hugh spent most of his childhood, listening to his grandfather's stories of far-off lands.

His father may have been absent and distant, but his grandfather made up for it in spades.

He'd died just before Hugh's twentieth birthday, and Father had encouraged other pastimes, like riding and opera. Things that would further their social ambitions. It had felt very grown-up at the time, but now he wondered if he would have been happier among the dirt.

He took her arm and guided her through the garden his grandfather had loved so much. "Wait until you see the wild-flower garden. I studied botany with my grandfather, so I'm qualified to be your guide. You'll find me quite knowledgeable."

They walked in silence to a brick arch that divided one part of the garden from the next. It had a wisteria trained across it that was starting to bud. Daphne let out a satisfied sigh. "How beautiful. Dear heaven, it's like putting my head in a bouquet."

She was right. Spring had visited the garden and painted it with color. Hugh bent to a green bush with shiny fragrant flowers. "Here we have the prized…" He searched for the right name and came up blank.

"Gardenia jasminoides," she filled in. "From Southern China. And next to it, abutilons. Chinese Lanterns."

He picked the bud of a strange orchid. "What of this one?"

Even in the pale morning light, he could see the blush rising up her cheeks. She turned to him and said, matter-of-factly. "Venus's Slipper. The flower of love." There was a challenge in her eyes, the knowledge that she knew he wanted to flirt with her, but that she didn't want him to.

He released her and stepped onto the dewy grass. "You seem

to have an intimate knowledge of flowers. Perhaps *you* should tour *me* around the garden."

Her bright smile told him she was pleased. The morning light revealed a smattering of freckles across her nose.

"My knowledge is of the secrets of flowers," she said, with relish. "They all have secrets."

The secrets he knew were more like noxious weeds than flowers, like the list his father kept of people he had blackmailed. But she was confiding in him, so it was a step in the right direction. "What kind of secrets?"

She bent down and cupped a pink flower in her hand. "We see them for their beauty, we adore their fragrance, but we never study the effect they have upon us. When we lived in India, Father brought Mother a box full of vials filled with the oils of exotic flowers and herbs. Each vial made me feel something different. Peppermint would clear my mind so I could think. Lavender calmed me when I was anxious. I was entranced."

If it was anything like her entrancement with his garden, he could picture it quite clearly.

"So, when you crushed the mint earlier you were trying to clear your mind?"

She nodded. "Definitely."

He'd never expected to find a woman who led such an interesting interior life, even while her exterior life seemed so desolate. Daphne might think the flowers had secrets, but the bigger secret was Daphne herself. No wonder he found it hard to reach her. She was in her own world.

His mind flashed back to Lady Spellwater, running down an alleyway with an incomparable scent trailing behind her. A woman using stolen oils that would lead him to his thief.

His gaze snapped to Daphne, her face full of wonder at something as simple as a handful of mint. A woman who loved perfume above everything else.

Would such a woman use the love of the things she knew best to try and save her family from ruin?

His entire being rejected the idea that she could lie to him so effortlessly.

And yet...

He drew in a breath, fighting the urge to immediately confront her. Because she would just deny it. Even if she *wanted* to confide in him, she had to know it would make things worse for her father. The last thing he wanted to do was alert her to his sudden suspicions.

But if Daphne *was* Lady Spellwater, he would discover it, damned if he wouldn't.

But he floundered for a reason *why* she would be using stolen goods.

Of course, she might not have known the goods were stolen, but surely *now* she had to be questioning that.

"As much as I *do* love this garden," she continued, an edge of wistfulness in her voice, "it also makes me sad."

"If I could hazard a guess," he said gently. "You miss India."

"With all my heart. Or perhaps I lost my heart when we left there, I'm not sure which." Her gaze met his, her dark eyes shining. "Do you ever dream about a place and awake with the smells and tastes on your mouth? Sometimes it makes me so homesick I want to cry."

Home was India? To him, home had always been England, even when he was more familiar with the streets of Bombay than London. His childhood had been there just as hers was, when they based themselves in the Indian city to run the business. Or did she just long for India because it was the last time her family had been happy?

"All I remember is overwhelming heat and never being able to keep the starch in a cravat." He took an involuntary step toward her and caught her hand. "I'm sorry it's been so hard for you."

Though he hadn't intended it, he drew her close and wrapped

his arms around her. She leaned into his embrace, fitting there like the missing piece of a puzzle, her head tucked under his jaw, her shoulder snug under his arm. He knew a moment of wonder as he inhaled the fresh lemon and thyme of her hair.

"Perhaps England would be better if you had a family of your own. If your father weren't so unreliable." He stopped, searching for words. "Life here can be full of joy and color, too, if you want it to be."

"No."

Her voice was muffled by his jacket but the vehemence of her tone surprised him.

"Just 'no'?" He brushed her hair with his hand, not able to help himself.

She pulled back and looked up. Deep sadness shadowing her eyes. "Do you think I choose this for myself? I long to be free. Free of my father and his money problems, free of trying to make ends meet, sometimes even free of Celeste, although I love her more than anything. No more problems. Just free. Run in a field with my hair down kind of free."

He would love to tell her to be free, but he understood all too well the restraints a family could place on one. "It is never too late to find happiness, surely?"

"I've accepted what life has dealt me; indeed, I've tried my hardest to make the most of it. Let's just leave it at that."

"It's not too late." He bent his head and kissed the corner of her mouth. She tasted of honey and desire and all the things he shouldn't want. Without thinking, he murmured, "Where is your father, Daphne?"

She gasped and pulled away from him. "I...I don't know."

He let her go. *Damnation, he had alarmed her. So clumsy.* "Where does he like to go? There must be something. You can't be free until you find him. And *I* need to find him before Wolfe does."

"You do?" she said. All he saw in the dark depths of her eyes was suspicion.

"Of course! I don't want to see him exposed to Wolfe any more than you do." But if he was guilty, and if Daphne *was* Lady Spellwater and using stolen goods, Wolfe would arrest him, and Daphne would be caught up in it. He couldn't allow it.

"Very well," she said, voice a little too brittle. "He likes the fireworks at Vauxhall, the theater, and the opera. He also enjoys going to balls whenever he can procure an invitation. He found his best business contacts in the ballroom. Whether he currently enjoys those entertainments, I have no idea. But if he is in a room, Celeste and I will be able to spot him very quickly. He is our father, after all."

Coincidentally, all the activities two young ladies would love to attend. He didn't believe a word of it, but he'd try anyway. Because somewhere, at some ball or opera house, someone would know of Edward Davenport. London society just wasn't that big.

CHAPTER 9

IN WHICH LADY SPELLWATER HAS
AERONAUTICAL ASPIRATIONS

Three days later, Daphne sat at the breakfast table, still keeping her distance from Hugh. Since their morning discussion in the garden, he'd dogged her with all manner of innocent questions about her favorite pastimes. She knew he was not flirting but waiting for her to slip up again. Hopefully, her innocuous and confused answers deterred him.

In the meantime, a fitting of their new dresses revealed the perfumes had arrived at Madam Le Favre's shop. Today was the day the good lady herself would go up in the balloon and throw samples of Scandal to the thousands of people in attendance. Nerves bloomed in her stomach at the thought of Madam taking such a risk for their benefit. She hoped all the perfume sold would make it worthwhile. She would love to watch, but the entrance fee was far too expensive for the small amount of coins she had left in her purse.

Hugh alternated between staring out the window, drumming his fingers on the tabletop, and scanning the pages of his newspaper. Finally, he threw the latter down with a growl.

Lady Mandeville frowned. "Whatever *is* the matter? It's

impossible to have a peaceful breakfast with you throwing things around."

Celeste giggled. "Indeed, do tell us, my lord, before you hurt the poor newspaper."

In truth, if she'd been able to throw something, she would have. She'd still not found Father. She'd sent notes to all his usual haunts but they had come back negative. The gnawing, terrified feeling she'd woken with this morning was still there and it was getting worse.

Hugh took a deep breath, then exhaled loudly. "It's Lady Spellwater," he said. The look he shot Daphne was filled the suspicion. "The *Times* says she is going up in Mr. Sadler's balloon ascension this morning at Burlington House courtyard to celebrate her new perfume, the one in which she uses *our* ingredients."

"The one in which you *allege* she uses your ingredients," said Daphne, unable to help needling him.

"Yes, yes. As you say." His expression suggested his agreement was little more than politeness. "But here is the worst part— listen to this 'rumour has it Lady Spellwater paid one hundred guineas for her seat in the balloon.' She must be making a fortune to afford that!"

"If Lady Spellwater wants to be part of history, I'm sure that comes at a price." And hopefully it dissuaded him from thinking *she* was the lady in question. He knew she didn't have two shillings to rub together. "You need not be concerned for her."

"But I am! Each day, the paper has tantalizing stories of her, half of them not true, I'm sure. Having met her, I am worried she may be mobbed. Bow Street will surely be there to question her. If *I* was enough to make her tremble with fear…imagine what they will do!"

He continued tapping his fingers on the table. His concern was touching…and unexpected.

But thank goodness it was not actually her going up in that

balloon. The other day in the garden, his gaze had narrowed after she'd declared her love of fragrance. Being with him while Lady Spellwater went up in a balloon was a perfect way to divert him.

Celeste bit the corner of her piece of toast. "Since Bow Street is investigating at your request, perhaps you should call them off?"

Hugh shook his head. "I can't ask them to investigate and then hamstring them. They must be allowed to conduct their duties as they see fit, or I'm wasting my money."

Lady Mandeville cleared her throat. "Why was I not told that you have employed Bow Street on our behalf?"

Hugh met his mother's gaze evenly. The only thing betraying his alarm was a muscle twitching along his jaw. "It is a trifle, Mother, I assure you. We have had cargo thefts from our warehouse. I will brook no criminal activity in the company that belonged to your father, and protect it just as I would Mandeville Hall."

She nodded and pressed a hand to her heart. "Your grandfather would be proud of the care you take with what he created. I know what lengths your father went to, to ensure you never had to engage in trade, but it was my family's legacy that enabled the purchase of so much of what we own. It deserves our respect."

Hugh briefly looked taken aback. "Thank you, Mother. I agree entirely."

Daphne looked at him with a crooked eyebrow that she hoped conveyed *see? I told you.*

Hugh smiled at her. "It would be in our best interests for me to visit the ascension today. I would not want to miss the chance to question our best witness again."

Celeste almost jumped out of her chair. "May we come, too? Daphne, wouldn't you love to see Lady Spellwater?"

Daphne clapped her hands in excitement. "Yes, I would love to. Can we come, too? Please say yes."

He tilted his head, studying Daphne for too many uncomfortable moments. Then he smiled like she'd just passed a test. "That would be perfect."

The footman came in and stood next to her, offering her a small plate that had a wax-sealed note on it.

"Thank you." *What could this possibly be? Hopefully not the creditors saying they've taken the only thing we have left. Sir Barkley.*

She broke the seal and opened it.

Dear Miss Davenport,

Please come to the dressmakers at ten this morning. There is a problem that I must fix or you will not receive delivery of them before the ball.

Yours faithfully,
Madam LaFavre

Daphne's shocked intake of breath caught the attention of everyone.

"What is it?" Celeste said. The entire table had the question etched on their faces, too.

Daphne turned the note around so that Hugh could read it. "Madam Le Favre needs us to come for a fitting this morning. Otherwise, our dresses will not be ready for the ball." She frowned. "Lord Mandeville, I know it is not what we planned, but could you drop us there on your way to Burlington House? Would it be too much out of your way?"

He nodded. "I would be happy to. Although I am sad you will not see the ascension."

Daphne exhaled in relief. The note that alarmed her and she wanted to visit Madam at the earliest convenience. Something may have happened to the perfume while it was in transit to London. The last thing they needed were willing buyers and no perfume to sell.

Daphne glanced at the paper now open on the table. The title of the article was "Lady Spellwater, Aspiring Aeronaut." Underneath that, a smaller line read "Should we let our ladies take to the skies?"

Daphne shivered, wondering that herself. She prayed Madam Le Favre would be safe. "Please excuse me. I must go and ready myself."

"I, too." Celeste pushed her chair out. "Wait for me, Daphne."

Daphne paused by the door for Celeste to catch up, then they climbed the stairs together.

"What is really in the note?" Celeste whispered. "You seemed concerned."

Daphne handed her the letter. "There must be something wrong with the perfume."

She scanned the letter. "We'd best get there quickly if there's something we need to fix. Thank goodness you didn't agree to go up in that contraption. Did you see the way Hugh looked at you? And he seemed so relieved that we wanted to come along."

"I know, I know. Thank goodness for Madam Le Favre. She's braver than I."

"She's a braver than all of us put together."

Daphne and Celeste arrived at the modiste to discover that something *was* wrong, but it was not the perfume.

"No, no, my dears, there is nothing wrong with the perfumes. They're beautiful." Madam ushered them to a small room behind the main shop where there was a simple wooden desk with two chairs. "Sit, sit."

They sat, both with their hands clasped in their laps, waiting for the bad news to fall. "Don't keep us in suspense, what is the matter?"

"I had a visit."

Daphne's stomach fell. This felt eerily similar to the 'visit' Mrs. Henderson had just before she rejected her entire basket of perfumes. "Oh?"

"A Mr. Wolfe. He has discovered I am selling your perfumes and decided that I myself am Lady Spellwater."

"But why?" Daphne asked.

"Probably because I could show him no receipts for the perfumes I purchased. I got them off a peddler. Apparently that makes me look very suspicious."

"Oh." Daphne thought hard. "I gather this means you do not want to go up in the balloon today."

Madam closed her eyes. "I'm sorry. I cannot. My reputation cannot be tarnished by Bow Street. I am only just making a profit and it would see all of that gone. You understand?" Her expression was pleading.

Daphne nodded, her mind whirling with possible solutions. The only thing she would not accept was abandoning their plan entirely. "I truly believe you mean that. But unfortunately *someone* must go up in that balloon because we *must* start selling perfume. Will any of your girls do it?"

"I asked and they are all too lily-livered." Madam's mouth was a disappointed flat line.

With a tremor in her heart, Daphne made the only decision she felt was available. "Very well. I will do it."

"Daphne," Celeste said slowly, a note of warning in her tone.

"I must," Daphne said. "How hard can it be? I shall just close my eyes if I am scared."

Madam Le Favre exhaled and her shoulders slumped. "Oh good. I didn't want to let you down, but if you can do this our plans can still go ahead."

"I'm not worried about you being scared, Daph. What if *you* get caught? What if Mr. Wolfe comes to the ascension? This is too big a risk."

It *was* too big a risk. But it was also the launch of the new perfume and their one shot at having Londoners buy that perfume in the large numbers she needed to start again now that all had been lost in Reading. This wasn't a time for holding one's cards. It was a time to put everything one had on the table and stake the lot.

"We must trust that I am up to whatever Mr. Wolfe and the big balloon have to throw at me. I will get this done, we will sell all of Lady Spellwater's perfume and all shall be right with the world."

Madam Le Favre put a hand over her heart. "You are a woman after my own. So brave. Wait until you see the beautiful gown I was to wear, I'm sure we can make it fit. You will look like an angel."

Celeste groaned. "And how am I supposed to make excuses for you to Lady Mandeville if you land in the Channel?"

Daphne shrugged. "Say I have a megrim?"

Her eyes narrowed. "A darkened room won't fix that kind of megrim."

Daphne took her sister's hand and squeezed it. "I'll be fine! Stay here until I return. I'm sure Madam will let you learn some tricks from the seamstresses you will love, then we will just say we've been about town together. Or, if I'm not back by dark, enter the house quietly, and then later on, say I have taken to my bed unwell. Lock the door, and nobody will be any the wiser."

"You hope." Celeste sighed. "Very well," she said. "I will try my hardest to make sure nobody discovers you. And if you're not home by nightfall, I will make sure the back door is open. But Daphne..." Celeste paused. "You had better not die in that thing, or I will kill you."

CHAPTER 10

IN WHICH LORD MANDEVILLE GIVES CHASE

After dropping the Misses Davenport at the modiste, Hugh went back home to collect his horse and then rode it to the large courtyard in front of Burlington House. If the ladies were not with him, he had a mind to see just how far that balloon went today. At least he couldn't deny their disappointment at having to stay behind. Daphne actually had tears in her eyes.

He dismounted and handed the reins to the footman who accompanied him. "Wait for me here. I'll be back before the balloon ascends."

He'd purchased his ticket with the man at the entry, who was armed and large. Nobody was getting in who hadn't paid, but that didn't stop people clambering up nearby walls and standing on any roof or balcony they could access. Londoners would always find a way. The silk balloon was surrounded by fabric walls to stop people who hadn't paid from getting a glimpse of it. It was still being filled, with the help of special ticket holders who paid dearly to be part of the set up. A few of them were inspecting the gondola-shaped basket and the sacks of ballast that hung from the side.

At least Lady Spellwater had plenty of protection from the crowd. She didn't need him.

Despite the large patches of blue, the clouds moved across the sky at a brisk pace. Not exactly a good day to take a piece of silken fabric and float yourself across the city.

Outside the fence, the throngs waited. Vendors carried baskets with pies and tarts, a shilling each. Everyone who was anyone, from ladies to opera singers to dandies, milled inside the fence. There were also more than a few men and women with sketch pads, eager to illustrate the event for display in tomorrow's print-shop windows.

Each one of them there to glimpse Lady Spellwater and Mr. Sadler in a balloon.

He took a deep breath. No sign of her yet.

His goal was to talk to her rather than be a spectator like everyone else. But looking around at the crowd of thousands, that was unlikely.

He was about to take off when he felt someone stand next to him.

Lady Johanna.

His heart sank a little, because life had run away from him, and he hadn't paid her as much attention as he ought.

Daughter of a duke, she came from the old-world connections that Hugh's new earldom needed. She had shown nothing but perfect manners and the gentle grace one would expect of a lady of her calibre. His valet had let drop that she had embarrassed Daphne and Celeste over tea last week, but he was sure she had not meant to. Sometimes the London crowd could be acerbic, and she was no stranger to holding her own in that world.

She gave him her hand to clasp, which he dutifully did. "Lord Mandeville. I see you could not keep yourself away either. I am here with my father." She was dressed in a dashing red military-style coat with epaulets in gold braid, complete with a tall hat with white feathers. Dressed for battle and he wondered why. But it was nice to see her out of her mourning attire.

"How did you know I would be here?"

"Your mother may have mentioned it when I called this morning. Since I intended to come myself, I thought I would look out for you."

"I'm glad you did." *There goes any chance I had to question Lady Spellwater.* "These things are always more fun with company."

She tilted her head up to him, a sparkle in her light blue eyes. "I am always available for company and fun. I do miss our backgammon games. I'm sure I had the advantage."

He smiled. How much simpler life was when all he had to do was to visit his clubs in the morning and play backgammon with Lady Johanna in the afternoon. "Then you must allow me to recoup my losses. Let's play again soon."

He didn't commit to a date because his time was not his own as he looked for Davenport and took care of his daughters.

She nodded, her pursed mouth indicating she wasn't quite satisfied with his answer. She had every right to hope for a proposal from him, and soon. Despite her being in mourning, they had spent so much time together over the past year, so many walks, rides, that she must wonder what held him off.

"I suppose having the Misses Davenport has upended your calendar. Come, give your regards to my father." She took the arm he proffered and led him to the very front of the mansion, a place reserved for the most important people. Which the Duke of Strathdale was. He was a man of about sixty, with a strong physique and gray mutton chops that reached down his jaw. Today he was dressed very much like Hugh, in what looked like a Weston creation of dark gray superfine and light pantaloons with braid up the side. No old-fashioned clothing for the duke. He could walk past the window at White's with no risk of being teased.

Hugh bowed. "Good morning, Your Grace."

The duke greeted Hugh with a solemn nod. "Mandeville. My daughter requested me to invite you and your mother for dinner later in the week. Are you available?"

Hugh nodded. "Of course. We would be delighted." His mother adored any invitation to the duke's house.

"Good, good. I have some friends it would be beneficial for you to meet. Never hurts to know as many as possible when you take your place in the House of Lords."

Hugh nodded. "A sound plan." Strathdale was always looking for numbers in parliament, and any man marrying Johanna would definitely be counted on to take his responsibilities in parliament seriously.

Not go gadding about the country chasing thieves or perfume makers once they were married.

Johanna clasped his arm. "Oh my, look, there she is!"

The focus of the spectacle emerged from a carriage at the front door of Burlington House. The crowd cheered, and she waved. Dressed in billowing white muslin, she wore a large straw hat covered in red flowers and a white veil draped over her face.

"She truly never shows her face," Lady Johanna mused. "I find that suspicious. But the dress is lovely."

Hugh nodded in agreement. "Indeed. Although that is not the dress for a balloon ascension. She will freeze."

In good news, dropping Daphne and Celeste at the dressmaker put Daphne out of the running as possible Lady Spellwater. That along with the hundred guinea seat this flight supposedly cost.

Because if that were Daphne up there, no number of armed men could stop him getting her away from the balloon and into his carriage. It definitely was not safe.

"Why should you care if she freezes, Lord Mandeville?"

"I...uh." He found himself lost for words. "An observation, nothing more." Hugh shrugged one shoulder. "Would you wait for me here? I'll be straight back."

He pushed his way through the crowd so he could talk to Mr. Sadler. The guard checked his ticket and allowed him through.

The silk balloon was suspended from two large poles and was almost inflated to its full capacity. Soon it would be in the air like a wingless bird.

He introduced himself to one of the most famous men in London. "How are the conditions today?"

Mr. Sadler, a gray-haired man of around sixty, shook his hand. "The best conditions, Lord Mandeville. I'd take my grandchild up on a day like today."

"And if it's windier than you envisage, drop as soon as it is safe."

Lady Spellwater joined them, her stride brisk and business-like. If only he could rip the veil from her face but what sort of monster would do that with thousands of people watching? "It is heartening to see you are not indifferent to my safety, my lord, despite your convictions."

"*You* seem to be." He turned to Mr. Sadler. "Where will you land?"

Mr. Sadler shook his head. "My lord, we go where the wind takes us. I have no way of knowing where that is. But I always find villagers willing to assist."

"Villagers! How far will you fly?"

"With today's wind? Around eight miles; further if the wind is stronger. I expect to be up around an hour today." There was a little more impatience in his voice now. "The wind is south-westerly, so head north-east." He looked between the two of them. "If you were intending to follow us."

Lady Spellwater let out a shaky breath, and before he could help himself, he took her hands in his. They trembled through her gloves. "You don't have to do this." All his plans to ask probing questions were gone. "This is not worth risking your life over."

"I'm braver than that, my lord." Her voice was deep and

slightly husky, the same voice he'd last heard in Reading. It was definitely the lady herself and not a stand-in as he'd half expected.

"I'd be happier if you weren't suspended a thousand feet from the earth in a wooden box." He took off his coat and handed it to her. "Put this in the balloon, or you'll freeze. There are a few guineas in the pocket; use them to get yourself home if you need them." He paused, feeling mischievous. "I shall see you soon to get my coat back."

She took the coat from him, folding it over her arm. "I will return it soon. I'm not sure how." She turned to look at the balloon, which was inflating to a gargantuan size. "Why are you being so kind to me?" she asked, head tilted to one side.

"I need answers," he lied. "In any case, good luck Aspiring Lady Aeronaut. I hope it goes well."

She looked past him, her eyes widening in alarm. He turned to see Wolfe at the ticket box arguing with the guard stationed there. "Best be quick about it, though. I have a notion trouble is about to descend just before you ascend."

~

THE TERROR in the pit of Daphne's stomach was a crawling black Medusa of a thing. As if the thought of the flight wasn't enough, Mr. Wolfe snapped at her heels. It was just as Celeste had foretold.

Mr. Sadler and his team had finished the preparations. It might be a very scientific object but it was also beautiful, the gondola painted royal blue and gold, while the yellow satin of the balloon itself was something she would love a dress made out of. Six men stood at the ready to untie the tethers that kept the balloon earthbound.

"Almost ready, Lady Spellwater. Get your bag of goodies."

"I have it right here." Daphne lifted the bag of five hundred little favors she had attached to miniature silk squares to make them float. Madam Le Favre had certainly been busy. She wanted to sell the perfumes just as much as Daphne did. The new stock now took pride of place in her shop, ready for an influx of customers.

Someone tapped her shoulder and Daphne turned to see Lady Johanna, looking imposing in an all-red ensemble and a militant gleam in her eye.

"Lady Spellwater," she drawled. "I'm pleased to make your acquaintance. I am Lady Johanna Wilcox."

"How can I help you?" Daphne looked over her shoulder at Hugh's retreating form. "Let me guess, you'd like to warn me away from the man you have designs on."

Lady Johanna nodded. "Clever. And you admit you are acquainted with him. Interesting."

Daphne sighed loudly. "I hardly know the man and I assure you he has no interest in me."

"He gave you the coat off his back. And I know he was annoyed to see me here. When he was looking at you, he wasn't listening to me. At all. Early stages, perhaps. But I mean to nip this in the bud."

Daphne shook her head. "Can't we just acknowledge that a man is entitled to live without interfering women trying to influence the outcome?"

Lady Johanna smiled. "Surely you jest? Women have manipulated these situations since time began."

Daphne considered her 'rival' and shrugged. "Frankly, if you can't hook Lord Mandeville now with money, beauty, and connections on your side, I'm not sure you ever will."

Lady Johanna gave an outraged huff. But before she had the chance to reply, Daphne held up her hand. "Now, if you'll excuse me, I have a balloon to float majestically away in." She bobbed a slight curtsy and turned, feeling exhilarated and suddenly less nervous about the ascension.

"You don't want to make an enemy of me, you know."

Daphne shrugged one shoulder. "Why not? I like an adventurous life."

"Everyone back!" Mr. Sadler shouted. His guards ushered all but his team from the vicinity of the balloon. And not a moment too soon, as Mr. Wolfe had just managed to push his way through. Probably without paying. *Please don't follow the balloon.*

He strode past the guard and came to a halt a few feet from where she stood in the gondola. "Seems a shame to apprehend you in front of this glorious crowd. But the Crown's needs, my dear, are greater than yours." He turned to the aeronaut. "Wait a moment, Mr. Sadler, your passenger is alighting."

A jolt of anger hit her as she realized he fully intended to apprehend her in front of thousands of people. *Not today, Mr. Wolfe.* "You are odious," Daphne said. "I can't imagine how you sleep at night."

He shrugged. "Like an angel, I assure you. Step out now."

"You, sir, are no angel," she said.

He just laughed. "Or, at least, not yours. Now out you come."

A strangled cry escaped her and she was about to comply when Mr. Sadler yelled for the ropes to be released and the balloon lifted into the sky to a roar of the crowd.

Ha!

The last thing she saw was Mr. Wolfe's receding face, eyes narrowed, fists clenched by his side.

LADY JOHANNA RETURNED to Hugh's side, sporting twin blotches of red on her cheeks. "She *is* headstrong."

Hugh laughed, watching the balloon rise. He felt his heart soar with it. "She must be, to go up in that contraption." The gondola itself was painted like a ship, while the brilliant yellow balloon was a fifty-foot orb that took his breath away.

"That is not a good quality in a lady." She turned to him, waiting for him to agree with her.

He noticed Wolfe step away from the launching area. *Missed again, Mr. Wolfe.* "Not for a lady, but for a woman of enterprise, it is not a bad one." He really should stop siding with Lady Spellwater, but the sight of her bravely floating off in the balloon moved him.

She looked down on the crowd, waved, then put her hand into the large bag she carried. She threw tiny packages that floated to the ground where people cheered and scrambled to pick them up.

Then he could swear she looked straight at him, smiled, and threw a parcel his way. He caught it with his left hand.

"Oh, well done!" Lady Johanna said. "Pray, what is it?"

Hugh handed it to her with as much unconcern as he could muster. "Open it and let's see." The minx had thrown it directly at him.

It felt like a challenge. One he was more than happy to accept.

Lady Johanna unwrapped the parcel, which had a small square of silk attached like an umbrella to slow its descent.

A small wooden flower sat inside the parchment. "Oh, how pretty," Lady Johanna said. She lifted it to her nose and inhaled. "Goodness, if I ever take leave of my personal fragrance, I might buy this. Would you like to try it?"

"I am aware of it."

Her eyes brightened. "Do you have some kind of trade connection with Lady Spellwater? I know speaking of business with me is distasteful, but you can tell me if you are."

"I am, of sorts. Without intending it."

She looked both instantly relieved and satisfied. He could only wonder what conversation she'd had with the perfumer.

He took the parchment from her and read it out loud.

· · ·

Hello London,

Do you love a good scandal as much as I?

My new perfume is called Scandal. Take this flower in memory of me. Let its fragrance inspire you to a scandal of your own.

Your devoted servant,

Lady Spellwater

LADY JOHANNA WATCHED HIM CLOSELY. "I'm sure under that veil she is the most mundane of creatures."

He took the small wooden flower from her and lifted it to his nose. It was the same as the solid wax fragrance he'd smelled in Reading. "Could a mundane creature make a scent like this?"

He looked up as the rising figure drifted ever higher. He must guard himself a little better. Because Johanna was right, the lady in that balloon could have him follow her with a crook of her smallest finger.

He and all the other men here.

"I think not." He gave her back the flower, although it cost him a pang to do it. "I'm off now, I shall see you soon, I'm sure."

"You're chasing the balloon, aren't you?"

He quirked a brow at her, annoyed by her insightfulness. "I do need to get my coat back."

CHAPTER 11

IN WHICH LADY SPELLWATER SETS HERSELF FREE

With the roar of the crowd beneath them and the ominous creaking of the gondola, the balloon lifted farther and farther from the ground.

She soon ran out of parcels and contented herself with flying the sky-blue flag on the end of a pole as Mr. Sadler instructed. She tried to thank him for ignoring Mr. Wolfe, but he had just replied "Who?", so she left well enough alone.

Mr. Sadler kept himself busy with the gas pipe and the level of hydrogen in the balloon until he was finally happy and pulled up a bottle of brandy with a flourish. He found a glass, poured a finger, and handed it to her.

"For your nerves, my dear."

Daphne laughed and took off her hat, not caring that Mr. Sadler would get a perfect view of her face. *To Hades with it.* She refused to see this bird's-eye view of the world through a veil.

She took the small glass of brandy and drank it one swallow, coughing as it lit a trail of fire down her throat. "Thank you. I think."

Mr. Sadler laughed and put a smaller amount in his own glass. "It will keep you warm."

Daphne picked up Hugh's large navy coat from the bottom of the gondola and wrapped it around herself. It was still warm from him and smelled like an embrace of cedarwood and leather. *I wish you were here.*

In a few moments, she felt brave enough to look over the edge. "How small the carriages look," she said.

They sped across entire city blocks in mere moments, Mr. Sadler pointing out the British Museum and then the Foundling Hospital as they headed north-east over London. All the while, the balloon rose and the gondola swayed and creaked like an old man's knees. All that separated them from the air below was a thin layer of wood. But it was impossible to be scared. The air smelled salty and smokey, which mixed well with the brandy on her lips. It was the smell of freedom.

Flying in a balloon wasn't like being a bird; it was a graceful glide through the sky, like a leaf on the breeze. The gray buildings of London got smaller and smaller, the tops of the trees were green circles and the pathways that crossed the gardens yellow ribbons. They passed a clock tower chiming the quarter hour, a flock of pigeons fleeing from the sound.

Then they were in the clouds, and then just as suddenly, they were above them, and there was blue sky above and a carpet of scooped clouds below, like meringue on a cake. She pulled the coat around her, enchanted with everything except the way the wind made sharp whips of every hair on her head.

The wind took them north-east, just as Mr. Sadler predicted.

They drifted along over fields and farmhouses, sheep and rivers, at the mercy of the breeze. Much like her life had been at the mercy of forces she had no control over. She was forever trying to judge where the winds of her life would take her. Like her father. Or what society would do to a woman in trade. Why did she allow that? How would it feel to just throw all the ballast over the side and fly as far as the wind would take her?

If she could just get Celeste settled, maybe she could try.

"How long have we been up?" she shouted at Mr. Sadler after a while. They had traveled so many miles in such a brief time and she somehow had to be back in London before night fell.

"Almost an hour." He motioned down with his hand. "Shall we descend? It takes time."

She nodded.

"Very well. I'll let some gas out and won't jettison any ballast." He inspected the valve just under the balloon and made some adjustments.

Slowly, slumberously, the balloon came down. But the wind took them to the left, where a copse of tall trees stood. Daphne drew a horrified breath. They would crash. They drew closer, and all she could think of was Celeste and Hugh and how much she would miss them.

How much she loved him and wished she had kissed him, just once.

"Throw the sand!" Sadler threw out some ballast, and Daphne joined him, untying a bag and letting it loose. The balloon jerked up and over the trees, scraping the topmost branches. She wasn't sure if the sound of cracking wood was the tree or the gondola.

"That was close." Mr. Sadler looked over the side keenly. "I am trying to judge the best point. An open field is best. A hedgerow is not so good. Those oak trees would have been a disaster." He was almost jovial, as though this was far from the worst thing he'd encountered.

He waited until they were clear of trees. "Right, now's the time. Brace yourself."

They sped toward the ground.

Be brave, be brave.

Daphne clung to the side with all her might as the balloon bounced across a grassy field toward cows standing on a dirt mound. All she could hear was her beating heart and the cows mooing at their intrusion.

The gondola hit the ground three times before it stopped

with an earth-shattering thud and tipped onto its side. The balloon deflated behind them, the silk rustling in the breeze. It lay like a discarded blanket, still attached to the gondola by the netting.

"Climb out and wait under that tree, Miss," Mr. Sadler said. "I'll head out to the road and find some locals to help us."

"Lovely." Daphne picked up her hat and put it on her head, then crawled out of the gondola, only getting her foot caught in the netting once.

The cows came to investigate. They were brown with beautiful almond-shaped eyes that showed no alarm and only curiosity.

Mr. Sadler didn't have to find the men because they found him—a group of eight converging on the field from different directions.

Daphne put her veil in place.

"Where are we?" she heard Sadler ask them.

"Just south of Wanstead," one replied. "We'll have this packed up in no time, Mr. Sadler." Such was the level of his fame that he didn't even need an introduction.

"Is there a posting house you can recommend in Wanstead? I must take myself and my lady aeronaut back to London this afternoon."

They all turned to look at her, not having realized she was there at all.

Daphne pulled the veil over her face and waved, making no attempt to join the group. The men followed Mr. Sadler's instructions and carefully folded the balloon and fit it as best they could into the gondola. The sun rode low in the sky by the time it was all done, and not that she wasn't grateful for the adventure, but she needed to return to town. One hour up in the balloon and likely hours to get home by the time they found a carriage and horses.

Daphne shivered despite having Hugh's coat wrapped around

her. Her stomach rumbled because she'd walked out on breakfast early and hadn't had lunch.

After time enough that her toes were going numb from the cold, a new man jumped over the stone fence and strode toward her. His carriage was by the side of the road, an old red thing that at least signaled the new arrival was not Hugh.

But something about the man, even so far away, triggered her awareness and as he came into focus she was left with no doubt.

Hugh. How had he found them? She supposed the balloon put a large target on them. He must have left directly after they spoke.

He certainly looked good, striding over the field in his long boots and breeches with only his waistcoat, which was navy, with gold buttons that glinted in the sunlight. His dark hair blew around in the breeze and looked ridiculously romantic.

"Well met, Lady Spellwater."

Damn her traitorous heart for being so relieved to see him. It skipped a few beats and then settled on drumming madly in her ear. She wanted to leap into his arms but held herself back.

"Goodness, the lengths you'll go to get your coat back," she drawled.

"Or alternately, get *you* back." He turned and waved an arm to take in the men sitting in a group listening to Sadler retell every ascension he'd made thus far. "Shall I take you away from this muddy field?"

Daphne smiled. "I'm not the kind of lady who abandons her original party. I will stay with Mr. Sadler."

He nodded. "Shall I ask Mr. Sadler if it would make his life easier to take you off his hands?"

She shrugged. "I cannot stop you."

He would, too. He would use his charm and title to get what he wanted. But she wasn't about to spend a carriage ride with him figuring out her identity, when part of the reason for this balloon trip was to dissuade him she was Lady Spellwater!

She walked across the field. Mr. Sadler greeted her with a salute. "Lord Mandeville has offered to take you back to London."

"Thank you, Mr. Sadler. I am, however, happy to return to London with you."

The older man glanced around at the excited group of men. "No need for that. If I don't have to scarper back to London, I'll stay overnight here and enjoy the fine Wanstead hospitality."

The pub. He definitely meant he planned to have a fine night at the pub and if Daphne went with Hugh, he could have it. He had been kind enough to allow her to ascend with him.

She stepped forward and offered him her hand to shake. "Very well. Thank you again."

There was nothing for it. She would be two hours in a carriage with Hugh and his questions. She didn't have any more answers than the last time he spoke to Lady Spellwater. He could ask all he wanted. She had nothing to say, except for the fact that she was a little less convinced she wasn't using stolen goods, considering Father had disappeared off the face of the earth.

He didn't begin straight away, allowing time for the carriage and horses to find their rhythm.

"This is not your carriage." It could not be his carriage, because the upholstery had holes and stains.

"No. Apologies for the condition, I did not have a great deal of choice in Wanstead." He looked at her with a lazy gaze and a small smile playing around his mouth. It was like sitting with a large black panther, sleek and graceful while it indolently planned your demise. Then he surprised her.

"How was the flight?"

She could only see genuine curiosity in his expression.

"Beyond my wildest imaginings. I was petrified to start with, but then the clouds were like flying through fog and I could see the world like a bird…"

"Breathtaking?"

She nodded. "Yes. We were only up for an hour, but it seemed like forever. I am so grateful."

"To who? Because the young lady I met in Reading would not have the connections for a balloon ascension. You are in a rarefied club now, Lady Spellwater."

She shrugged. "I would remind you that you know little about me." He actually knew far more about her than he realized, but it was all in bits and pieces he luckily had not yet put together. She hoped.

"I don't need reminding." A slight smile played around his mouth.

"For all you know, I am bosom buddies with the Prince of Wales himself."

"Highly unlikely." He rolled his eyes.

She bristled. "Why?"

"You have better taste than that."

She smiled despite herself. "So, you admit I have good taste, then. This feels like a victory. Considering all you know of me are my perfumes, you must hold my skill in high regard."

"You are a master perfumer. I have smelled the many facets of both Scandal and By a Lady. Tell me how you do it."

She was quiet for a moment, trying to come up with an answer. "Nobody has ever asked." She looked down at her hands. "For me, perfume-making is strongly influenced by places. By a Lady is from our garden in spring, layers of flowers, but Scandal is from somewhere much more exotic, as you know. I take my memories and then experiment with the extractions, writing down my findings over and over until I have it just right. Each perfume could have a hundred variants." She peered at him through the veil, but it was impossible to see his expression. "It's quite an obsessive pastime. I have quite the collection of full journals."

"I am intrigued." His tone suggested he truly was. It gave her a small thrill. "Do you have other perfumes?"

"Only in my mind. At the moment, I am working on a more masculine concoction. All leather and liquor. Every scent should offer a journey." She stopped abruptly. "If I can manage it. One never quite knows."

"You are doing an excellent job. I can only imagine what you could achieve with proper distribution."

The air rushed from her in a giant exhalation. "I had thought you would be disgusted by industriousness. Your kind dislikes honest hard work."

"You do not know 'my kind.' My maternal grandfather, who I like to think I resemble, built and led his own enterprise. I find myself thinking there is room for the modern peer to extend his capabilities."

She blinked. Was this the same man who had said Lady Spellwater would never marry because of her trade?

"But what of the modern gentlewoman? Surely you still consider me beyond the pale for being in trade."

He stared at her for a long moment, then looked out the window. "I respect your abilities, but I do not know what kind of lady you are."

"I am a lady who works. For money."

He winced. "I would prefer ladies not to work for their living. We gentlemen should take care of all things so they could indulge in whatever art form they chose, without needing to sell it."

"Life is not always so accommodating."

The silence drew out between them.

He took a deep breath and ran an exasperated hand through his hair. "I wish you would show me who you are. I am looking for the thief of my perfumes, not for you. And I may have asked you to stop selling perfumes in Reading, but I accept it is your prerogative to continue, no matter how foolhardy it might be with Bow Street involved."

He was trying to convince her he posed her no threat. But until she spoke to Father, she could give nothing away.

She didn't turn to look at him, just continued looking out the window. "I see no point to stopping. If I am using stolen goods, then I have already used them and would do well to recoup as much money as I can to pay you back. If I am not, then I have no reason to stop, do I?"

She stole a look at him.

He nodded and blinked slowly. "*I* will count it as a triumph that you are accepting that you may be using stolen goods."

She turned fully to him, trying so hard to keep her voice deeper than it normally was. "I am no fool, Lord Mandeville, whatever you may think. I, too, am trying to find the provenance of the oils I am using and once I do know, you can be sure you will be the first person I tell."

"I appreciate it," Hugh said.

"And now I would prefer to sit quietly since you have a way of making me tell you things I had no intention of telling you."

He smiled as though quite happy with himself. Soon enough, the country fields turned to market gardens and dwellings came closer together.

They were on the outskirts of London.

"Now, where can I drop you?"

"Covent Garden will suffice. I can catch a hack home from there."

He considered her. "Interesting."

She shrugged herself out of his coat and shivered when the icy air hit her bare skin. She rubbed her hands up and down her arms.

There was a light in his eyes she didn't trust. Or maybe it was the look in his eyes that made her shiver. Like he could see right through her. "Don't follow me."

"I have no intention to. I am just looking forward to speaking to someone when I return home myself."

She didn't need to be told that person was her, sans veil.

Good Lord, what had she done to give herself away?

~

TRIUMPH FLOODED THROUGH HIS VEINS. Ever since the garden, he'd thought there was a chance Lady Spellwater was Daphne, only to be dashed when he dropped her at the dressmakers on the way to seeing the elusive figure at the balloon ascension. There was no way she could have arrived there so fast after him.

But then in the carriage, when she spoke of not being certain anymore, when she spoke of perfume-making and being a lady, her voice had lost its deepness, and it was just Daphne talking to him, he was sure of it.

But not one hundred percent sure. However, there was no way she could beat him home after dropping her at Covent Garden.

He arrived at Curzon Street to find both Daphne and Celeste still out. The staff assured him they had seen neither Daphne or Celeste since he left with them that morning.

It was now after five. Where were they?

There was a note, written in Daphne's hand and delivered at four, asking for a carriage to collect them from the dressmakers.

That was certainly a long time to spend at the dressmaker. But delivered at four? At that time Lady Spellwater was still in the carriage with him.

"Get me a fresh horse," he barked at whoever was listening.

He rode to the dressmaker, which coincidentally, was only two blocks from Covent Garden and arrived to see Daphne and Celeste laughing at the sheer number of boxes that were being stacked into the carriage.

He drew up alongside. "Well met, Miss Davenport" he said, in a deliberate echo of his earlier words to Lady Spellwater.

She looked around, clothed in a brand new dress of patterned blue muslin with dark blue fringing. "Mandeville," she greeted him, delight dripping from her voice. "Do you like our new dresses?"

"You have been here a long time. Almost seven hours by my reckoning."

Celeste laughed. "No, silly. We have been up and down Bond Street, had lunch at Gunters—"

Daphne interrupted her sister. "Which, I might tell you, was comprised entirely of cake."

Her cheeks were suspiciously red, like the wind had been buffeting her face.

"And then topped it off with a visit to the Circulating Library." Celeste held a red-bound book aloft. "Madam Le Favre told us that if we returned at four, with some final alterations, we could collect the first part of our wardrobe."

"And here we are!" Daphne finished off. "Our gowns are beautiful and will make us feel like we belong in London."

Hugh frowned. What could he say to that? Accuse them of being liars after such a delightful scene?

He rolled his eyes inwardly. "Very well. Make your way home then." Hugh saluted them and nudged his horse to join the crawl of carriages on the road, but he didn't go home. Rather, he went slowly around the block and returned to the dressmakers. Their carriage was gone, so he tethered the horse to the post and opened the front door.

Madam was at the fabric counter. "May I help you, Lord Mandeville? Is something wrong with what we have supplied?"

"No, no," he said. "I was just wondering what time the misses Davenport returned to your establishment this afternoon."

She squinted as though thinking. "Around four? They had walked the entire city from the look of them. But don't worry, I made them rest and gave them both a strong cup of tea."

Hugh nodded, thoughtful. There was no reason for the dressmaker to lie.

CHAPTER 12

IN WHICH THE OPERA IS ENTERTAINING FOR
ALL THE WRONG REASONS

Daphne snapped open her fan against the heated air of the opera house and wondered for the fiftieth time why she'd lied to Hugh about her father's pastimes. The opera was the last place on earth anyone would find Edward Davenport, who was more likely to frequent a cockfight than *The Marriage of Figaro*—and the entire thing was in Italian, of which she had no knowledge.

But Hugh was nothing if not determined.

The more she grew to like Hugh, the more Daphne found the lies mixed with an alarming dose of the truth. Like a magician, he seemed to conjure it from her, until surely one day, she would just tell him everything he wanted to know. Perhaps she should just confide in him and be done with it, but that trip past the gallows still put the fear of God into her.

But here at the opera, she could pretend, just for a few hours, that everything was normal. If only all she had to think about was the little note Madam Le Favre sent her earlier telling her how many perfumes had been sold. She had done a little dance—already five bottles and eleven tins of Scandal.

Their box was like a plush little cabin looking out onto a sea of people. A hidden and dark place where she could close her eyes and swim in the sea of scents surrounding her.

On the way into the box, they'd woven their way through the throngs where threads of her own perfumes wound themselves around her. Heated on different skin, they took on their own life. It was dizzying.

Lady Mandeville had erred, because Hugh sat next to Daphne, dressed in dark evening clothes, a ruby twinkling in his cravat. He leaned forward against the rail, scanning the audience, ignoring the stage and the players on it. He looked elegant and powerful, ready to leap into action. A hunter with a scent of his prey.

But since he wasn't going to find anything, she could afford to sit back and enjoy the evening. For once she didn't feel out of place. In her cream silk gown with Spanish mantilla, she belonged next to the likes of Lord Mandeville. She felt elegant and perhaps a trifle pretty.

He'd taken her arm entering the theater, found her champagne, and procured a pair of opera glasses. Indeed, he was making himself so agreeable that it took a great deal of self-control to remember he was only there to catch Father.

All else was just a means to an end. At least that was what her mind told her, while her heart told her to trust the heated look in his eye when he'd first seen her trailing down the stairs in her silks.

But she had promised Lady Mandeville she would not flirt, and apart from that woeful scene in the garden, the promise had been kept. She only had a short while not to give her heart to him again. For his heart was not his to give in return.

He turned to her, catching her staring at his thigh. "Have you stopped looking?"

It took a moment to realize he meant looking for Father. She smiled apologetically. "It's so dim. I can hardly see the stage, much less my father in the audience. I thought to look out in the corridors after the show."

Hugh nodded and sat back in his seat. "I think it's another wasted effort. I can't see him anywhere, even though this is opening night. You'd think an opera aficionado would be here."

Daphne felt a momentary pang for what the tickets must have cost, but then, his mother was enjoying their outings this week, so perhaps all was not lost.

On stage, the Count flew into a rage after finding Cherubino hiding behind a chair. The Italian was very hard to follow. If she closed her eyes and ignored the sublime music and the roar of polite society gossiping, she could feel the heat emanating from Hugh. If she closed her eyes, there was only him, only this moment, and everything was perfect. The world hushed to a whisper. It was easy to pretend everything was fine, Father wasn't missing, and she was just a lady at the opera.

"Mandeville," Lady Mandeville said loudly from the other end of the box. "Pass my reticule. I would like to use my opera glasses again."

The sound of Lady Mandeville's voice brought Daphne down to earth and made her remember the promises she needed to keep. She pressed herself to the back of the seat as Hugh passed the reticule over her to Celeste and then finally on to Lady Mandeville.

"Even if we don't find Father," Daphne said to him. "I'm very much enjoying the opera."

He smiled lazily, leaning back into the chair. "Happy to oblige."

Her cheeks bloomed, so she picked up the pace of her fan against the sudden heat. He seemed to have moved beyond friendliness, but then, it could just be her active imagination. She must ignore it. But as long as he sat close and waves of his spicy and yet fresh scent washed over her, she could believe, for just a moment, he truly found her alluring.

A man coughed loudly in the stalls downstairs, and Daphne lurched forward, dropping her fan in her lap and lifting her opera glasses to see better. *Father?*

Hugh leaned forward too, suddenly at attention, his keen eyes trying to pinpoint where she was looking. "What is it, Daphne?"

"Nothing," she whispered, barely registering the use of her Christian name for the first time. It couldn't be. What on earth would Father be doing at the opera? He coughed again, and she found him easily, three rows from the center aisle, in a gold waistcoat. Her heart leaped to her throat.

Hugh raised his opera glasses and scanned the crowd, resting his arm next to hers on the wooden railing. Even him touching her long gloved arm sent shivers through her. "By Jove, it's him. Well done, Daphne!"

Well done, Daphne, indeed. And even more shocking, the lady sitting next to Father, in a lurid purple and green dress, rested a hand on Father's thigh and squeezed.

Daphne drew in a sharp breath. Father had another woman?

Her world spun, and a million questions rose in her mind without an answer among them.

"I gather you don't know the woman he accompanies?"

She didn't lower her glasses. "Never seen her in my life." She was a large woman with a florid countenance. "Perhaps it's not Father, after all."

"Then it looks *very* like him." He rose, and after making excuses that she needed some fresh air, pulled her out of the box.

She was so lost in thought she didn't notice him take her arm, but she did notice the way he held on just a little too tightly. Did he think she would try to escape? Or was it just the excitement she could feel bouncing off him? She'd led Hugh straight to Father, but why was he at the opera of all places, and why did he look so well-to-do?

130

The corridors were empty but for servants. The sounds of the stage and crowd dimmed, but that only made the sound of her steps all the louder.

They made it to the stalls and stood at the back of the throng.

"This will get crowded when the performance finishes," he said. "If I lose you, meet me by the front doors."

She nodded, but all of her focus was on searching the crowd for the familiar head. On one hand, she wanted Father to escape, but on the other she had too many questions of her own. She stood on her tiptoes. "I can't seem to see him now," she said. "Where did he go?"

"He's still there," Hugh said. "Don't fret."

She was fretting, but not for the reason he thought. "Lift me up," she said, wanting to assure herself it was him.

"Very well." He lifted her onto the base of a nearby column, and if her heart raced that bit faster, surely it wasn't because his hands fit so snugly around her waist. "The end won't be far."

The end of the opera and of her.

She strained to see, even though now she was the same height as Hugh. "He had better have a very good explanation," she said, trying not to notice that Hugh held a protective hand in the small of her back. "What on earth am I going to say?"

"This is not the time or place for conversation."

"Very well," she said reluctantly. "But if we lose him, the blame falls squarely on you."

The problem with being the same height soon became apparent. Hugh blew gently on her neck, raising tiny hairs right into her scalp. No one had ever done that before. The warm breath with the hint of champagne on it was as intoxicating as the bubbles themselves. Her knees weakened.

"No one can escape me once I set my mind on it," he whispered.

She shivered. This was it, then. Everything had come down to this. Part of her wanted to rush to the man she thought was her father, but an equally strong part wanted to delay the evil moment as long as possible, to give Father time to escape so she could find him tomorrow and figure out what on earth was going on.

CHAPTER 13

IN WHICH A DARK CARRIAGE IS AS GOOD A PLACE AS ANY TO CRY

Hugh never thought about what effect finding Edward Davenport would have on Daphne. Her jaw was clenched, probably to stop the uncontrolled shivering that racked her body as they stood at the back of the stalls. But despite the shock, Daphne was on her toes, trying to catch another glimpse of him.

That bounder Davenport was well fed and prosperous, his round belly pushing his green and gold waistcoat out like a billowing sail. The moment he saw him, Hugh knew he was guilty. It was the opulence he'd expected to see when he'd gone to their house near Reading. That Daphne and Celeste still attacked every meal like famished orphans made him itch to pull Davenport's cork.

But what would Daphne do if he arrested him? Rather than helping her as he'd told her he was trying to do, he would be blowing her world completely apart.

The thought shook him to his toes. He didn't *want* to hurt her in any way, but it already felt like that was going to happen.

The chatter of the crowd and warbling of the opera singers dimmed as a rush of blood went to his head.

She took a step toward her father. He took her by an arm encased in white satin gloves and pulled her back. He leaned down and whispered in her ear. "No."

The sophisticated sweep of her coiffure allowed him close enough to smell the sweet mix of rose and orange blossom in her perfume. He imagined her standing in front of her mirror, dabbing the soft fragrance behind her ear, her long neck stretched, her skin warmed by candlelight.

She gave a delicate shudder as his lips brushed the velvet soft skin of her earlobe, bringing him back to the present. The headiness of finding Davenport must be affecting him.

Pull yourself together. If he didn't follow Davenport back to his hiding hole, he'd escape again like the wily fox he was.

He cleared his throat. "We'll just follow him tonight. See where he goes. We don't know how he will react to seeing you, and I can't afford to lose him again. There will be plenty of time to ask him questions tomorrow."

She turned to him, awareness of his closeness written in her rosy cheeks and flustered gaze. "A prudent plan," she said. "I don't trust myself to face him at the moment without doing him some violence."

"Precisely." He straightened. "Wait here, while I make our excuses."

"What will you say?"

"That you're unwell and would like to go home." With the blush still on her cheeks, she was the picture of good health. Heaven knew if his mother would believe him. He was sure Celeste had spotted him from the opera box just as Daphne had, if her shocked expression was any indication.

"Very well." She watched him go as though scared he would disappear.

Celeste turned the moment he entered the box, her brows raised in question. His mother turned, too, and fixed him with a hard stare. "Celeste and I wondered if that was Mr. Davenport in

134

the stalls."

He sometimes forgot his mother was so sharp. "It is. Daphne is distraught and begs to be excused for the evening. I will escort her home."

His mother rose. "We should leave, too. This is just as painful for Celeste as it for Daphne."

The last thing he needed was his mother on the chase after Edward Davenport. She had no idea he suspected Davenport of the thefts. He threw Celeste a warning glance that she thankfully interpreted.

"Oh, but I would like to stay till the end." She turned to his mother. "Would you mind?"

Mother looked unconvinced.

Celeste took her hand. "Please, Lady Mandeville. We shall be fine in the carriage, just the two of us."

Mother gave him a curt nod. "Mind you get Mr. Davenport's direction before you leave, Mandeville. Miss Celeste just told me they have struggled to locate him."

"Of course. We'll take a hack and leave you the carriage. I'll see you at home." He bowed out of the room.

When he returned to Daphne, she still had her eyes locked on the back of Davenport's balding head as though trying to get answers from the shiny bald pate. She looked forlorn and so lonely that he wanted to pull her into his arms. He knew how hard it was to discover a parent had feet of clay.

"Come," he whispered, with none of the ferocious triumph he was feeling. "We'll find a hack." He led her into the lobby and onto the street. "That way, we can follow him as he returns home." He tried to keep the excitement from his voice.

He hailed a hack, sending two on their way before finding the third clean. Once, last century perhaps, the hack had been a small gentleman's coach, although whatever color the leather had once been, it was now blacked over and cracked with age.

He handed a gold coin to the driver. "We wait here until the opera finishes. Then look out for a man in a green and gold striped waistcoat. We'll follow him, and double the fare for you if you don't lose him."

"Yes, sir," the driver said. "John Wright's always up for a challenge."

Hugh relaxed into the sadly dipped seat.

And so, he found himself in yet another dark enclosed space with Daphne. The opera box had been only just bearable, with his leg brushing up against hers while the music flowed over them. But at least the noise and commotion had dampened his awareness somewhat. Now, with the excitement of finally finding Davenport, the temptation to kiss her was potent. She looked even more delicious by moonlight. Her attention was firmly focused on the front of the opera house.

"It will be at least a quarter hour," he said idly.

"I cannot bear the wait." Her voice shook with indignation. "I'm so angry. Attending the opera while I make the most of the bones we have in the cupboard." She sat back, crossed her arms over her chest and frowned.

"Don't frown," he said. "As long as we've found him, it makes no difference what he was doing, does it?"

"I thought he was working as hard as we were. Not enjoying London's delights with a new lady." She put her face in her hands. "I'm sickened."

"He wasn't sitting in very good seats, if that makes you feel better." He smiled, glad the darkness covered it.

"Not particularly. I'll feel better when I throttle him." She was shaking with anger as though she finally understood that her father was a scoundrel. Indeed, seeing Davenport looking so flush with funds meant it was more and more likely he was their culprit.

"Calm, Miss Davenport. We'll have him locked up soon enough."

She dropped her hands from her face and regarded him with

wide eyes. There was an awkward silence. "I beg your pardon? At what point did you gather any evidence that he is behind your crimes? This is about Celeste and I." Then she peered closer at him. "Goodness, you're ecstatic, aren't you?"

"Sad the thief is your father, but happy to find the thief, yes."

He glanced out the window, very aware he was getting caught up with her and could well miss his quarry. "I assure you, his possible guilt does not affect my regard for you or your sister."

But she just raised an eyebrow. "It all amounts to the same thing at the end of the day. Actions show your regard and by having Mr. Wolfe arrest him before I've even had the chance to speak to him–" She broke off, shaking her head.

It was anger speaking, the need to lash out and blame someone for her disappointment.

He could make it up to her in a hundred ways, but not the only way that satisfied his honor as well. He could not offer her the protection of his name. Lady Johanna was waiting for his proposal. No gentleman would do that to a lady after leaving her to dangle for so long.

"I wish there was a way to convince you that I mean you and Miss Celeste no harm," he said. "I hold you in high esteem."

DAPHNE FELT BATTERED by the conflicting emotions. "You are as good as betrothed. I'm sure I do not need to know anything about your high esteem." Her pulse was already skipping from the close proximity to him, despite the horrible situation. Her pulse was as traitorous as he was.

"You are right. Even if it feels a little more wrong every day." He sighed and it sounded like the sigh of a man cornered but resigned to it. "I just..." He left the sentence unfinished.

She strained to read his expression as he sank back into the shadows.

She sat ramrod straight, wringing her hands. She took a deep breath to steady herself. The hack smelled like an old boot and whisky, but Hugh's scent weaving through made it bearable. Musky, sweet and almost edible.

"Be still, Miss Davenport," he said, eyes hooded and amused.

"I can't." Father was leaving the opera with no idea what was about to rightfully descend on him. If not tonight, then definitely tomorrow. And Hugh sat across from her, moonlight slanting through the carriage window and sculpting his face into something cool and unattainable.

"Your hands are shaking." He took off his glove and picked her hand up off her lap, drawing it into his own. She leaned forward, unable to pull away, her attention held by his heavy-lidded gaze.

His unique fragrance wove around her, more potent the closer she was.

What was he doing?

The heat of his hand burned its way through her satin gloves, sending a trail of gooseflesh up her arm. Time slowed, and the moonlight threw its silver light on his hand holding hers. Agonizingly slow, he tugged one finger at a time, until her glove was entirely in his hand and the cool air hit her skin like a caress. She exhaled and drew a shuddering breath. His essence filled the cab like a heady incense.

She knew what he was doing. Distracting her. She could only hope it worked. Perhaps if she just stayed in this carriage, she'd never have to face her father at all. Good Lord, she was losing her head. She couldn't let it happen.

She tried to draw her hand away. "We'll miss him."

It was a weak reprimand, and by his smile he knew it.

"I have the driver looking out for him. Rest easy," he said mildly, rubbing his thumb into the cradle of her palm. Rubbing in delicious circles that led to larger circles of sensation all over her body.

Just when she thought she might swoon with the exquisite

feeling, he lifted her hand to his lips. His breath warmed her skin, but his lips never quite touched her. "You're cold."

"I don't feel cold," she said, her voice shaky. She pulled her hand back. "That's enough of your flirting. You can't distract me from what is about to happen."

He stopped. But only because her father and the lady were exiting the theater. Her stomach twisted, and her shivering continued.

"It's him," he said. "Let's follow." He knocked his walking cane on the ceiling of the hack.

They took off, but it was not her idea of a carriage chase. They drove at a snail's pace, three carriages behind, caught in the traffic of society coming and going from soirees and balls. In fact, urchins walked alongside the hack.

Eventually the glut of carriages and horses thinned a little, and they took Holborn Road for miles and miles.

"Where are we?" she said.

"Cheapside," he said. "An area for merchants and vendors."

The road was wide, and five-story buildings with shops at the ground-level went for what seemed like miles.

Her father's carriage took a side street where the shops turned into housing. They stopped in front of a large townhouse. He alighted and handed his partner down.

"Do you think he lives here?" she said, the words catching in her throat. "I've never heard of this address, not in any of his correspondence."

She felt lost, and desperately wanted it not to be him. But it was. You could mistake a face in the dark, but not the way his shoulders slouched when he walked, or the familiarity of the flourish of his hand when he helped his lady down from the carriage. He'd done that a thousand times for Mother. That hurt.

The house, one of many new terraces built around the square, had long elegant windows, with candlelight peeping through the drapes. It was not a hotel and it was not a brothel, as she had first feared. It looked like an ordinary house, for an ordinary family.

While they stood on the step, Father fumbling with his latchkey, Daphne had the chance to look at his companion. She had an ample, jolly figure, and even from across the street, Daphne could hear her booming laugh as he fumbled yet again. She had an arm looped through his, which was why he was finding it so hard to open the door.

"I've seen enough," Daphne said, unable to spy on their intimacy any longer. None of the questions she'd had when she'd first spotted him in the audience would be answered by continuing the surveillance.

Hugh knocked his cane on the roof of the box. "I'll send word to Wolfe tonight so he can make enquiries tomorrow. He is discreet, despite appearances."

Daphne listened to Hugh's murmured voice as he instructed the driver to take them back to Curzon Street. They traveled in silence, but when he switched position to ride forward with her, Daphne didn't quibble. And then, when he picked up her hand and held it in his with the warmth of an old friend, she accepted the comfort.

"I'm sorry," he said, as if it were his fault Davenport disappointed her.

"I just don't understand." Her voice broke, despite her efforts to control it. "Why is he here? What is he doing?" *Why would he lie to us?*

"Hush," he said, reaching forward to brush away a tear she wasn't even aware had fallen. His touch was gentle as snowfall and made her feel all the more like crying. "These are questions for tomorrow, after a cup of chocolate and a night's sleep."

It was all too much. His kindness and Father's betrayal in the space of a few moments. The tears became a flood she couldn't stop, and the next moment found a large soft handkerchief thrust toward her.

"It will all be fine. You'll see." It sounded less like a comfort and more like a vow that he wanted to help her out of her mess.

That only made her cry harder. He reached behind and pulled her close, and if she ruined his beautiful jacket with her tears, he never complained.

CHAPTER 14

IN WHICH DAPHNE MAKES A DUBIOUS CONNECTION

Daphne woke early, not from the first rays of light that crept between the curtains but from a heavy dread that clung to her like a wet blanket. It took a few moments to remember why she felt so sad.

Father. Hugh. *Damnation.*

She needed to speak to him *before* Hugh and Mr. Wolfe made their move. She'd have to be quick. The thought made her empty stomach squirm with nerves as she slipped out of bed and pulled on one of her old dresses---the kind that didn't need half an hour and a maid to put on.

The house was quiet and cold as a tomb as she crept down the hall toward the back stairs. She reached the landing when a door behind her opened. Daphne whirled around.

"And where are *you* going?" Celeste stepped out into the hall, dressed in her dusty brown velvet cloak.

Daphne let go of the breath she was holding. "Just for my walk in the garden," she lied.

Celeste joined her on the landing. "I shall come with you. I'm awake in any case."

"I'd rather you didn't," Daphne said, keeping her voice low. "Go back to our room."

"Ha!" Celeste said. "I've been waiting since daybreak for you to sneak out. Why should you have all the fun?"

She should have known there was no way she could do this without Celeste. Although there was no way in Hades it was going to be fun.

"You saw him last night?" Daphne asked but knew the answer by the glint in Celeste's eyes.

"Oh, yes. I know that hacking cough just as well as you." She folded her arms across her chest with a militant air. "And if you think I'm not coming, you're very much mistaken."

Daphne took a deep breath. "In that case, I suppose we should stop wasting time and hope we can get out of here without being spotted."

"I took the liberty of telling my maid last night that we might take an early morning walk."

Clever girl. She should have thought of that herself. "Won't she expect us to take a groom?"

"By the time she realizes we didn't, we'll be back again and no one the wiser." Celeste took her hand. "Let's be off."

They crept down the stairs and to the front door, the heels of their boots echoing on the marble floor, and the chill chasing away the last remnants of the sleepy warmth of bed. But finally, they were out on the street.

London was swathed in morning fog, horses and carriages emerging from the gloom at a slow pace. She linked arms with Celeste, and they walked in silence to the corner where they waited for a hackney carriage. It took two laden wagons, countless horses, and ten minutes before a hack lumbered into view. They hailed it and Daphne gave the driver their direction before they climbed into its ancient box.

Celeste wrinkled her nose. "It smells."

"Worse than Mr. Ferguson's farm cart, and I never thought I'd say that," Daphne replied, taking her handkerchief and wiping a small circle in the grimy glass so she could see out the window.

The fog enveloped them, blurring the buildings and providing just the right atmosphere for a secret journey.

Once in Cheapside, Daphne directed the hack to Father's house and nudged Celeste to leave the carriage. "Come, dearest," Daphne said. "It can't be any worse than we imagine."

Celeste looked up sharply. "What do we imagine?"

Daphne rolled her eyes, trying to make light. "Oh, you know, that he's a thief and will land himself in a noose." She tried to smile but failed miserably. "That you and I will have to start fresh over on the continent where we have no infamous relatives."

And no Hugh to comfort her when it all went wrong.

Her joking tone made Celeste smile in return, but it was just as miserable. Celeste stared at the shiny black door of Father's new house with foreboding. "I vow, if he makes me miss the ball tonight, forget our dash to the continent; I shall never forgive him."

A rude knocking on the carriage roof brought them both back to attention. "Do I wait then, ladies?" the driver said in his brash Cockney.

"Should we have him wait?" Celeste wrung her hands in her lap. "Perhaps we should. He may be very angry with us."

"Father angry with us? It's more likely we'll need the hack because I've just throttled him and we need to escape." A laugh erupted from her mouth, and she wished for a moment she was still back in that luxurious feather bed with only the ball tonight and dancing with Hugh to think about.

As she daydreamed, a carriage pulled up across the road from them, outside the house. It spilled four Bow Street Runners onto the street, led by Mr. Wolfe.

"Too late," she whispered, her voice weak with nerves.

Daphne drew in a breath so fast she almost choked as Mr.

Wolfe looked around and spotted them inside the carriage. He lifted a hand and smiled.

"What do we do?" Celeste breathed.

"What *can* we do?" Daphne replied.

She watched in horror as the maid at the door was replaced by Father dressed in a red velvet dressing gown. He pulled his shoulders back and lifted his chin in defiance, but his eyes darted up the street as if searching for an escape route. Mr. Wolfe showed Father a letter that made him step back and allow them entry. Half the soldiers guarded him; the others followed Wolfe inside.

"Miss?" Another insistent knock on the carriage roof. "I'm sure you're not paying me to sit here all day. What's your orders?"

Daphne snapped to attention. "Back to Curzon Street," she said, sitting as far back in the seat as she could. "Drat him."

"Drat Father or Mr. Wolfe?" Celeste asked.

"All of them," Daphne replied. "We'd be better off without *all* of them."

Hugh, for all his lovely words and kindness, had Father arrested. And it was only a short step from there to discovering Lady Spellwater. Then he wouldn't want to help her; rather, he'd want to throw her into gaol too.

Because poor though they might be, she had apparently been using stolen goods to turn a profit, and there was no way that was the right thing to do. Somehow, she had to fix this and pay Hugh back the money she owed him.

"They wouldn't arrest him without reasonable cause," Daphne said. "We have been using stolen goods. That's the only conclusion."

"What do we do?" All the anguish Daphne felt was in Celeste's voice. She took her hand and rubbed it against hers to get some warmth into her sister.

"We come clean. We do what we can to make it better."

~

HUGH WAITED for Wolfe's carriage to arrive, watching the Bow Street Magistrate's court through the hazy glass window of the Brown Bear tavern. He pushed the tankard of warm ale away, still trying to find a solution to his dilemma.

It was bad either way.

If Wolfe came back with enough evidence to arrest Daphne's father, he'd have to watch the light in Daphne's eyes die along with her trust in him. And equally bad—if there was no evidence, this charade continued on until he was either bankrupt, crazy, or both.

Finally, Wolfe's coach arrived, red-coated officers alighting from the box followed by a very rumpled looking Edward Davenport. Hugh shook his head in a mix of disappointment and disgust. They must have found enough evidence to have him questioned. What would that evidence be? He expected to feel jubilant, but his heart fell. How was he going to tell Daphne? What was he going to tell Daphne? Wolfe had been adamant that he not accompany him to Cheapside this morning, and so not only did he have bad news, he also had no new information to tell her about the lady they'd seen or what her father had been doing during his time in London.

He paid his shot and left the tavern, crossing the road in time to follow the party through the front door of the magistrate's court. From there, they went down a hall and into a plain room with a desk in the corner and two sturdy wooden chairs placed in front of it. The fireplace burned low, crackling as the officer in front of him placed a box he was carrying on one of the chairs.

Hugh entered the room, and Wolfe gave him a broad smile in greeting, a smile that was all teeth and bad intent. Davenport was forcibly seated on one of the chairs, his hands tied in front of him and an officer on either side.

Davenport spotted him. "Ah, now it all begins to make sense," he said, his dark gaze so like Daphne's that Hugh was momentarily taken aback.

"Funny, that's just what I was thinking," Hugh replied.

Davenport eyed him belligerently. "Couldn't you find anyone else who hated your father enough for revenge?" he said lightly. "I could think of fifty men who would throw a spoke in the wheel of the Mandeville Empire."

"My father is dead," Hugh said. Perhaps if he'd lived through his illness, he would have made up for the wrongs he did. *It was unlikely.*

Davenport leaned back into his chair. "But his cherished son is alive. The one he did all that extorting for. He told me once. 'Edward,' he said, 'I can't afford scruples. I have a family to keep in style and a son to elevate to the peerage.' How does that make you feel, knowing he stole from so many people who could ill afford it, just so you could have that lovely blue barouche and call yourself Mandeville?"

Hugh remembered the barouche. Father had given it to him for his twenty-first birthday along with two shiny gray mares to pull it. It had been one of the happiest days of his life. They had driven to Brighton on a whim, taking turns with the reins. He pushed down the swell of guilt and met Edward's gaze.

"He was a good father as you well know. A son has no influence on the way his father runs his business affairs. If I thought anything, it was that he did whatever was necessary to protect his family and ensure future generations were prosperous. If he did things I would not, it is not for me to judge. Especially not after I watched him die a slow and lingering death. Any anger has long since dissipated. However, when it comes to people who are currently stealing from us, I assure you, my anger is quite fresh and real."

Damned if he would tell Davenport the lengths he'd traveled to right his father's wrongs. Damned if he'd let him know how his words cut. How every good memory he had of his father had been tainted since the first discovery, less than a month after inheriting, that money landed in the Mandeville coffers from a variety of questionable sources that looked suspiciously like blackmail.

"It has bearing if you want to find your thief," Edward said. "I am by no means the only one with money to recoup from Alistair Mandeville. You ruined my family, but you ruined many others. Even my lovely Minerva has a tale to tell."

Hugh might want to right the wrongs, but he refused to take the blame. "I never ruined anything, Davenport. You, however, have done a fine job of ruining your family all by yourself."

His bushy eyebrows drew together. "What do you know of my family?" His teasing note was gone.

"Well now, you should know that, shouldn't you? If you were a good father and at home taking care of your daughters instead of your lovely 'Minerva.'"

Edward made a leap at Hugh and was held back by the officers. "You dare touch my girls—"

"Touch them? Edward, I've been feeding them for a week. They are skin and bone. What have *you* been doing?" He smiled, ready to make his last strike. "Oh, that's right, you've been going to the opera." Suddenly, all the worry he had over Daphne was no match for the fury he felt at how Davenport had treated his own daughters. "You know, I hope you rot in Newgate. The hangman's noose is too good for you."

"You'll need some evidence before that happens, boy," Davenport said with a smug smile on his face.

"You wouldn't be here if there wasn't evidence."

Edward scoffed. "Evidence of what exactly? That I've been in India? That I've purchased oils?" He lifted his finger in mock thought. "Wait, yes, that's right—I'm an oil and spice merchant, too! Is that all you've got, Mandeville?" He scoffed. "Alistair had more than that when he framed me for fraud and stole my customers."

"You think I'm framing you? Why would I bother? My only aim is to stop the thefts. Mr. Wolfe, could I see the evidence you found?"

Wolfe grabbed the box by the door and placed it in front of Hugh. Hugh lifted the lid, revealing rows of glass bottles with amber-colored liquid inside. The air immediately smelled of Persian Essence. Heart hammering, Hugh pulled out a bottle of golden oil and turned it over in his hands. "Well, well. What have we here?"

Wolfe looked at Hugh eagerly. "They're yours?"

Hugh inspected it. It was identical to the bottles they used, and although they weren't entirely uncommon, the scent was.

"They are identical to the ones we import." He raised his nose to the bottle. "And we do have the sole import of Persian Essence."

"Poppycock," Davenport burst out. "Those bottles are like hundreds of others sold in India. And you can have all the sole import agreements in the world. That doesn't stop me buying the product in India itself, and you know it. I didn't import those bottles, sir. I bought them in India late last year."

"Who did you buy them from?"

Davenport waved his hand. "Who remembers?"

But he should remember. Harsha Agashe was one of India's foremost scientists. "Was it Mr. Agashe?"

Davenport nodded. "That's the one. Lives in Benares in a big pink house." He gave the old palms-up gesture of innocence. "I truly didn't steal these from you, my lord, no matter how convenient it would be for you if I did."

Hugh wanted to believe him. The look on Davenport's face when Wolfe had recited his supposed crimes would be hard to feign.

Hugh's conscience nagged. It looked like his product and it smelled like his product, but without the Mandeville stamp on the boxes, he couldn't be certain. His head told him Davenport was lying, but his heart was thumping happily away at not having to press charges that would grieve Daphne.

He looked at Wolfe, who must have read his expression because he cursed and beckoned Hugh to follow him to the corner of the room. "If you identify them as your goods, then placing them in Davenport's house is enough to warrant an arrest." He lowered his voice. "Mr. Wallington is the Magistrate today. He can get a confession out of anyone. We've shown our hand, now we have to follow through. We can only keep him for six days on suspicion."

"He seems quite at ease," Hugh said. "Not at all nervous."

Wolfe shook his head. "I've seen this a thousand times. Bravado a plenty until they get in front of the Magistrate. Then it all falls apart."

Hugh wasn't so sure, and he had to be one-hundred percent certain before he acted. "Let him go. Maybe he'll give us more evidence when he runs."

Wolfe laughed. "I'm not letting him go. Not after what it took to get him here. Don't go all soft on me now."

"Thoroughness is not softness, Mr. Wolfe," Hugh said quietly, both eyebrows raised in derision.

Wolfe nodded and bowed his head.

Hugh turned to Davenport. "As luck would have it, Mr. Agashe is in London at the moment on his way to Paris. Mr. Wolfe agrees that if he can verify what you say, all will be well."

Edward gave a start of surprise and then slumped in the chair with an expression of sadness and resignation on his face. Then he straightened and seemed to brace himself. "No need to call him in. Let the case be tried with the evidence you have. Very well, gentlemen. Do your worst. Where do we go from here?"

"Are you saying you did not buy them from Agashe, after all?" Hugh frowned at Davenport, trying to guess where the sudden change of heart came from.

"They're yours, Mandeville. Took them all by myself." He crossed his arms over his chest.

He was protecting someone, and not very well. But who? Lady Spellwater?

He had to get close to Lady Spellwater again and ask. Where had she said he would find her? Glittering balls in London? He would try tonight. All of London society came to Devlin's ball. Surely she would be there too.

Wolfe motioned his officers to escort Davenport. "The public office, the bench, the magistrate, and if you're very lucky, someone to post bail for you."

"Very good. Let's get on with it then. The sooner you do that, the sooner I can be on my way."

Wolfe dusted his hands. "Well that wraps it up for now." He motioned to the men guarding Davenport. "Take him to the lockup and the boxes to the evidence room."

"Take good care of my girls," Davenport said over his shoulder, and his antagonism was gone, replaced with what looked like genuine fear.

Hugh clenched and unfurled his fist and flexed his fingers.

Wolfe crossed his arms over his chest and raised his eyebrows at Hugh's fists. "Imagining how good it will feel to draw Davenport's cork?"

Hugh ignored the jibe. "You think you can get everything out of him?"

Wolfe escorted him to the front door. "No doubt. My hunch is that he's covering for others. Lady Spellwater for one. She has received stolen goods at the very least. I have a hunch on her identity."

Hugh took Wolfe's hand in a firm grip. "She is definitely a lady, so tred gently. In fact, there is a grand ball this evening at Lord Devlin's. I may be in a better situation to find her. With luck she will know the accomplices."

"Have at it," Wolfe replied. "But if you don't succeed, I'm sure I will. I should have chased that blasted balloon instead of letting you do it."

More than ever, he had to know who Lady Spellwater was. He'd find a way to lure her out, before Daphne's father was sentenced to a death that he hadn't earned by himself.

Wolfe called him back. "Have you got Mr. Agashe's details? I'll contact him tomorrow."

"I made it up, Mr. Wolfe. He'll be in his big pink house overlooking the Ganges in Benares."

The sound of Wolfe's laughter followed him down the hall.

DAPHNE ALIGHTED FROM the hack she'd hired with her last shillings to take her back to Cheapside. She couldn't pretend to embroider her petit point a moment longer. Hugh could be all day, and in the meantime, she could meet her father's lady. Celeste had stayed behind, moaning that her first ball that evening might well be her last. Daphne had left her with promises of a walk to Hyde Park if she could cover for her for an hour.

Lombard Street now teemed with wagons and horses, carriages and people, like a circus in full swing. The perfume was horse dung with undertones of straw and baking bread. Strange and a little disturbing. Daphne quickened her pace, trying not to inhale too deeply.

A quick glance around the street answered her first question —Wolfe's carriage was gone, meaning Father was at Bow Street undergoing questioning. His lady friend was likely alone inside and beside herself. Suddenly, it barely mattered they'd never met. This was a time of crisis and they needed to pull together. Maybe they could help each other through this difficult time. After all, she must love Father, too.

She knocked on the front door and stepped back, heart

hammering. Scuffles and heavy footfall filtered through the heavy wood. A maid opened the door a crack, staring out onto the street with wide, scared eyes.

"Nobody's home for visitors," she said, and made to close the door again.

Daphne put her foot in it. "Your mistress will be home to me. My name is Miss Davenport."

The eyes widened further, if that was possible, and she opened the door to allow Daphne entry. It was a commotion inside with a crew of people carrying furniture and crates toward the back of the house. She stopped short. What was this? Were they fleeing?

She was led to a bare room with lurid green paper on the walls.

"Sorry, Miss. The furniture's gone. She won't be long."

Good Lord, should she and Celeste run too? The thought never crossed her mind.

With nowhere to sit, Daphne walked to the mantle where a letter was set up against the wall, addressed to William and Bartholomew. Looking for answers, she put it in her reticule. Now she was a thief in earnest, but she'd do it if it brought some answers.

Just as she was closing her bag, Father's new lady swept into the room. Today she wore a mauve and black silk dress with a scalloped hem and a red ribbon caught underneath her matronly bust. The effect was dazzling and bold.

"Get us some chairs," she said to the maid. When the maid had gone, she turned to Daphne. "You'd think she'd never done a midnight flit the way she's carrying on." She looked around her. "I only have a few minutes." She held out her hand, like a man, for Daphne to shake. "I'm Minerva. You must be Edward's Daphne. I've been waiting for this moment."

Daphne placed her hand in Minerva's, feeling as though she should curtsy along with it. "Then why have we never met?"

Minerva smiled indulgently. "Edward went to such lengths to keep you secret, I didn't want to burst his bubble. He was so diverting with his 'I have to visit my old aunt in the country' fabrications."

The maid brought two kitchen chairs into the room and dumped them with a clatter.

"You knew?" Daphne lowered herself slowly onto the seat, crossing her ankles underneath in a neat efficient movement, as though by controlling her body, she could control this situation.

"You don't think I'd marry a man without a thorough check of his family, do you? But I've got sons enough without adding two beautiful but penniless stepdaughters to the mix. So, I let him have his secret."

"Married?" she said in a shocked whisper.

"I gather you didn't know."

Daphne hid her shock by taking a deep breath. "And sons? How long have you been married?" Did she have half-brothers? Daphne pushed down the tug of longing for the family she had missed out on. Minerva might be brash, but maybe it would have been better than the heavy weight of responsibility she'd worn since Mother died.

Minerva correctly interpreted her shocked expression and let out a jolly laugh. "Not with your father; I'm long past that age. From my previous marriage. William and Bartholomew, both young hotheads."

Keeping calm, Daphne stared at Minerva. "If you'll forgive my impertinence, how did you and Father meet?"

"On the boat from India. By the time the ship was a league from Calcutta, we were tight as a drum. So much in common, you understand."

She didn't. What could they have in common? "That you were both English and both on a ship?"

Minerva laughed. "No, both having been sent up the river tick by our good friend Alistair Mandeville. Suffering united us, you might say."

Daphne's heart fell. It just got worse and worse. They were *all* in it up to their ears.

And being there, listening to Minerva was the stupidest idea she'd ever had. The lady had a dangerous edge to her. Nobody but Celeste knew where she was, and if Minerva discovered they were staying with Hugh, who knew what she might do?

"We've all suffered. Celeste and I don't seem to have stopped suffering."

"My boys said I was selfish keeping you in the country. And perhaps I was. But if you're honest, you'll admit this would have been an awful place to live. Raucous lot."

Daphne stood and paced the room, tired of pretending this was a social visit. "What a convenient argument. Taking our father, offering nothing in return, then telling yourself we're better off."

Her anger at him mounted by the minute. And why was she tiptoeing around this woman who knew of their existence and plight and yet ignored them? It was unconscionable.

Any thought that they could deal well together vanished. Minerva was no better than Father. Not an ounce of integrity between them.

At once, she thought of her own integrity, and lack of it, when dealing with Hugh. She'd fix that, too. Or she was no better than Minerva, seeing what was convenient.

"Sit." Minerva pointed to the chair. "I had the boys keep an eye on you when they were in the area."

Daphne tried to hide her surprise. The thought of two men she'd never met checking on her welfare brought her skin out in gooseflesh. What had they done? Perhaps hidden some stolen oils in the barn while they slept? The temptation was great to blame anyone but Father.

She pointedly did not sit. "Then you should've known our

situation." Had her sons caught any hint of the perfume-making? Hopefully, basing their operations at Ayah's had saved her once again. "Did Father know?"

Minerva looked at Daphne as though she were a half-wit. "I thought we established that Edward thinks me ignorant of your existence. No. I kept an eye on you because dear Edward can be forgetful. I just wanted to make sure you were fed. I'm not heartless."

"We were fed because I worked." Daphne felt her anger rising. "Risking our reputations every day."

Minerva leaned forward, needling Daphne with a curious stare. "Worked, did you? And what exactly did you do?"

Too late, Daphne realized Minerva was much more intelligent than she'd given her credit for. She thought quickly.

"Darning and mending for the village ladies." It wasn't a falsehood; it just wasn't the entire truth.

Minerva relaxed back into her chair. "Oh, well, that's harmless enough."

"Indeed," Daphne said frostily. She was eager to leave, so she needed to discuss the reason she came. "However, Father being taken into custody isn't quite so harmless. I gather that's why you're jumping ship?"

"Jumping country, more like. You should do the same. Don't get caught up in his misery."

"But who will bail him?"

Minerva cocked her head to one side as if Daphne were an interesting puzzle. "No one. Edward should know I can't wait around to see what happens to him. Not that we thought Mandeville was smart enough to catch up with us."

Yet another sign she was either complicit in his activities or the actual instigator of them. "He stole from Mandeville, didn't he?" She tried to say it with relish, as though she was proud, but she found herself sitting down again, her knees unable to take the weight of what she knew Minerva was about to say.

"That's for a jury to decide, young lady. Not the likes of you or I."

As far as denials went, it wasn't very convincing.

Minerva stood. "It's a shame Mandeville couldn't be bankrupted. I understand he still owns all his land and the contents of the houses. He'll be rich as Croesus again in no time. I thought those investors would sue when entire shipments went missing."

Minerva was very well informed for someone who had nothing to do with it. Daphne knew what that meant. "Do you also consider his arrest a failure?"

Minerva stood and went to the door, opening it for Daphne to leave. "Anything less than the obliteration of Mandeville's fortune is a failure. He hurt so many, he deserves ill fortune."

Daphne stood, wondering if Minerva was queer in the attic. "The old Lord Mandeville is dead, you know."

"Father, son, what difference does it make? If he was to compensate all who lost their fortunes at his father's hand, it would be a mighty long list. I only wish I could've done more." The bitterness in Minerva's voice was frightening.

Previously, Daphne would have thought it inconceivable that a woman should orchestrate such a large-scale criminal activity, but Minerva led her to believe otherwise. She had obviously suffered at Mandeville hands, and her nature was not a forgiving one.

The visit was a monumental mistake. Daphne stared at Minerva's five sausage fingers bedecked in emerald and sapphire rings, one of which looked terribly familiar. She forgot her manners and the fact she desperately wanted to escape. "That's Mama's engagement ring!"

Minerva smiled as though Daphne had somehow amused her and looked down at her fingers in surprise. "Is it? Which one?"

"The square-cut sapphire with diamonds." It was a beautiful ring. She'd been so angry with Father when he'd said he'd sold it.

Now she wasn't sure what was worse; his lying, or seeing the ring on another woman's hand.

Minerva pulled the ring off and tossed it to Daphne. "Keep it," she said, unconcerned. "I have many more. Although, I still regret the necessity of selling the rubies in that necklace."

So *that* was where the rubies went. Daphne caught the ring and resisted the urge to throw it right back, instead slipping it onto her finger where it fit like it had been made for her.

The saddest part was that she could confess all to Hugh, and it wouldn't make a whit of difference—he would know everything by now. It was too little, too late. But still, she had to go to Bow Street and face the consequences.

CHAPTER 15

C hurch bells rang in the distance, announcing the time to be eleven o'clock when Daphne arrived at the Bow Street Magistrates Court. The Runners' office was a jumble of people waiting to be attended to with little semblance of order. She took her place in the throng and hoped she would somehow make her way to the front so she could ask for Mr. Wolfe.

Finally, an officer took her request and within moments, Mr. Wolfe stood in front of her. His red coat was beautifully cut and obviously an expensive version of the classic Runner's coat. It made him even more threatening, as though he had the might of both the law and wealth on his side. And to her shame, it worked. She clasped her hands in front of her to stop them shaking.

"Miss Davenport. I must admit surprise. I thought you were more the run-and-hide type." He turned and motioned for her to follow. "If you could follow me to a more private room?"

Since she would rather not admit her Father's guilt with an audience, she happily followed him down the hall into a small office that had a simple wooden desk, three chairs, and a cheerful fire. A portrait of King George looked down on them.

He waited for her to sit and then sat himself. "If you've come to beg for leniency, you're wasting your time. He is to see the magistrate tomorrow." His voice was dark and dangerous and caused the hair to rise on her arms.

"No. I have just come from his house and thought to inform you that his wife is leaving. I believe she and her sons to be involved also, and thought you should know."

His gaze narrowed. "What makes you say she is involved? Knowing about something and being an accomplice are two different things."

Daphne took a deep breath. "She said the Mandevilles had ruined her, and that her sons had been dropping the goods at our house in Reading and also checking on us at the same time."

He steepled his hands. "Of course."

Daphne opened her reticule and got the letter out. "I have no idea what this says, but she left it on the mantle for them."

Wolfe took the letter, unsealed it, and scanned the contents. His face broke out into a wide smile. He looked younger, although still predatory. "I see I have misjudged you, Lady Spellwater. Thank you for this, you have made my job much easier."

Lady Spellwater? "Yes, well, I am not surprised you worked it out, but if I could rely on your discretion? I am not quite ready to leave London yet. There is a ball tonight my sister has her heart set upon."

"You should confide in Lord Mandeville before the ball," he said, eyeing her steadily.

She nodded. "Yes, yes of course. But if it doesn't interfere with your investigation, can I ask that you do not?" It was the last thing she wanted to do. To look him in the eye and tell him the person he'd been looking for was right in front of his nose. That he'd been a fool to trust her because she was untrustworthy. To see the light of friendship die in his eyes would be too much to bear. She looked down at her hands. "I also got my mother's engagement ring back. I am hoping to give it to Lord Mandeville to pay for the oils I used."

He looked down to the ring and then up to her face, his expression softening. "I will not tell him today." He rose from his chair. "Shall I take you to visit your father?"

Daphne blinked at the unexpected offer. It may well be the last time she saw him before his trial and as such was a generous gesture. "Thank you."

They took the short trip to Newgate prison. They entered the main building where Mr. Wolfe signed himself in with the turnkey. The man, who was thin and pale with pockmarks all over his cheeks turned to her.

"Sign yourself in, then," he said.

She looked down at the book, at the lines and lines of signatures and addresses.

The turnkey waited patiently with his hand held out and she realized it was for payment. Wolfe grunted and threw a few coins on the counter. Then he led them upstairs, but still in the main building. He opened the door to a clean but sparse room that was a long way from what Daphne thought a prison would be like.

He led them down the hallway, the keys attached to his belt jangling with each slow step.

He opened the door of a private cell, and when she entered, she was relieved to see whitewashed walls, a swept floor, table and chair with a plate with bread and cheese on it. A single candle sat on the dresser with a bowl of water and soap. There was an orange cat on the windowsill, basking in weak sunlight.

Mr. Wolfe stayed in the hall.

Last night, in Hugh's carriage, she'd imagined what she'd say to Father. None of them had her feet feeling glued to the floor, wretched and numb simply by seeing him.

"Daphne! My dear girl, you came. In my hour of need, my own flesh and blood stands by me." He opened his arms to pull her into an embrace.

It didn't precisely look like his hour of need. His mandarin-colored waistcoat looked laundered, and he'd clearly had his beard trimmed. But more than that, he had an air of joviality about him that belied where he was.

It wasn't cheap to live well in Newgate.

"Indeed," she replied, pulling off her bonnet and veil, then her cloak, and placing them on the bedstead. "You seem to have the best of Newgate here. Who's paying for it?" she said, giving him a "barely there" curtsey. No kiss or embrace.

"Some benefactor," he said easily. "I started out in the main ward, but was quickly moved here. Hopefully I have not already caught the typhus. It carries them all away. I'm surprised anyone makes it to the gallows."

She stepped around him and went to the window. It looked out onto the jail yard, where a handful of prisoners took their exercise. They looked as numb and miserable as she felt.

"You don't seem concerned about your trial on Monday."

He sat with an audible sigh. "Trumped-up charges. It won't stand up in court."

Daphne shook her head, unable to believe what she was hearing. "No need to bamboozle me. I would prefer it if you didn't lie."

He leaped from his chair in a clatter of wood. "Lie to you? I cannot believe you would level something so dishonorable at me."

Drat men and their stupid sense of honor. "You have done nothing *but* lie to us. We didn't even know you were married."

He brushed the idea away with a wave of his hand. "Minerva said she was glad I didn't have any children. Her boys are handful enough, so I just kept mum. I could never have done it if I didn't know that Ayah and Mrs. Pike were taking good care of you. I regretted it soon enough, but what could I say then? We were married, and the deed was done."

He was a coward, Daphne thought with calm clarity. "And

then you just went along with her criminal ideas, or were you part of them?"

His eyes snapped up, and she knew she'd scored a point. Unfortunately, it wasn't the point she'd hoped to score.

"Mandeville's gotten to you, too," he said. "My own daughter."

She must have blushed, because he groaned and put his head in his hands. "Ah, so that's the way it is, is it? Ah, Daphne, my duck, he's not the man for you."

The use of the old endearment angered her. "And why not? You lost the right to dictate our lives when you started a new one without us." Father didn't need to know he was already spoken for. That would only make her look more foolish.

"He's still an arrogant little princeling. If you could have seen him coming in here, lording it about…"

"He visited you?"

"Bah, he's trying to get more information out of me. I'm not telling him anything."

"I think you will find," came a deep voice in the doorway. It was Mr. Wolfe. "That Lord Mandeville paid for your current accommodations."

He rolled his yes. "I don't believe you. Why would he do that?"

But Daphne knew. It was for her. He wouldn't care if Edward Davenport rotted in jail, but Daphne's father was another thing entirely. "Perhaps he hopes you will tell him of Minerva's role in all this."

Father scowled. "Minerva knows nothing. No point you asking her."

Daphne turned to Father, incredulous. "Not quite the impression I got when I met her."

Confusion flitted across his indignant expression. "You met?"

"Oh yes, didn't she tell you? Or, let me guess, she hasn't been to visit you. You know why, of course? Because she's fleeing the country."

"Are you sure?" Father asked, searching her face, perhaps hoping to see a lie there.

"You may lie to me, but I won't lie to you," she said simply. "The house was almost entirely packed when I visited."

He just sat there, looking as dejected as a man who'd just been betrayed by his wife could be. Daphne wished she could muster some sympathy for him, but she was just glad his eyes were opening to whom he'd abandoned his daughters for.

"Where would she go, Papa?"

He looked up at the endearment, his eyes filling with tears. "What would your mama say of the mess I've made of things?"

"She'd say 'make it better, Edward.' So tell us where she might go. Tell us where the stolen goods are."

"She might have said she was leaving the country, but she's more likely in Yorkshire," he replied simply. "Her family home is in Yeadon, just south of Guiseley. The oils and spices are in a variety of places, small lots everywhere. Some in our barn at Reading, some in a warehouse by the docks, some at her son's house. I'll make a list."

It was hard to believe she knew him at all. "Help Bow Street so you don't end up in a noose."

"I could make a case for transportation if that list leads to recovery of the goods," Wolfe said, rubbing his hands together.

"Ah well," Father said. "In time it could be the start of a new business venture. I hear the sheep down there are something to be believed."

"Father, it's not adventure, it's a penal colony. You will be lucky if you survive the trip."

But he might avoid the noose. The relief made her light-headed. Was he the instigator of the thefts, or did he go along with Minerva and her sons? She may never find an absolute truth, only these confusing shades of gray that took forever to unravel. Was the truth always thus?

"I'll survive and thrive. That's what we Davenports do." He raised a dramatic fist in the air.

"I see." Daphne said. "So, you will look forward to being a prisoner in the colonies without the least regret. We suffered. We missed meals, ate things that should have been thrown away, had to beg for charity from our neighbors. You have now ruined us both. Have you nothing to say?"

He scowled. "It's not your place to judge your own father."

"Oh, does my criticism annoy you?" The years-long anger at their situation bubbled to the surface. "New South Wales will not be far enough away as far as I am concerned. I had hoped we might reconcile, but I see you are too selfish even for that. When word gets out that you are a convicted felon, Celeste may never marry. Never have children. I worked myself ragged to create opportunities for her, and you have leveled them in one fell swoop. I am so glad Mother is not here to see this."

Her hands shook. Saying these things was as hurtful as feeling them.

"I'll take my leave of you," she said, glaring at her father. "Enjoy your time in the colonies."

As she turned to leave, he yelled out to her. "Daphne!" Tears pooled in his eyes, and his cheeks were red. "I am sorry, you know. I kept thinking I could make it all better. Instead, I made everything worse."

She nodded. "Yes, you did, but my thanks for the apology."

It struck her that he would not see Celeste marry and that her children would never know their grandfather. The sadness kept spreading like ripples on a pond.

There was no more to say, so she embraced her father, inhaling his smell perhaps for the last time. "Godspeed. I'm so very sorry it has ended this way."

She left the neat cell and was escorted back downstairs and into the sunny afternoon. She turned to Mr. Wolfe. "Is there a chance he will survive it?"

The Bow Street Runner nodded. "He is older, that is of concern, but if anyone can survive transportation it's a well-connected man who has skills to offer to the colonies."

He may have been saying it so she could sleep at night, but Daphne appreciated it all the same.

"Thank you, Mr. Wolfe. I am very sorry to have been proven wrong about my father. His life turned in a direction I had no control over."

"I would not have expected you to, Miss Davenport. I am only relieved to find you had no part in the criminal activity. I say again, you should trust Lord Mandeville with your identity."

"Of course. Excellent plan." He was right, but that didn't mean she was looking forward to it. And she certainly wasn't doing it before Celeste's first ball.

CHAPTER 16

IN WHICH MANDEVILLE THROWS OUT A LURE

L ater that evening, Hugh tried to empty his mind of the day's events as he climbed the front steps of Lord Devlin's town house for the ball.

He needed to speak to Daphne alone and explain about her father. But he also needed to discover if Lady Spellwater was at the ball and if she was, let her know that Davenport's wife may be dangerous, if what Wolfe had just told him was true. Which to do first?

But if he could divine more information from Lady Spellwater, then he could tell Daphne more. He nodded to himself. Lady Spellwater first. He put his hand around the cool five-carat sapphire that sat in his coat pocket. If Lady Spellwater was desperate for money, the jewel should bring her out of the woodwork. Or alternately, someone in this huge throng might think a sapphire enough of a bounty for her identity. Either way, Hugh would get what he wanted.

A footman took his coat, issued him with a numbered card for its retrieval, and left him to walk through the throng toward the ballroom. The dancing had begun in earnest, the orchestra playing a lively jig. The floor bounced with the efforts of fifty or more dancers. He scanned them for Daphne's dark hair.

No luck, which was strange, because Daphne was an unlikely wallflower, with her lively eyes, ink-dark hair, and ruby lips. Any man in his right mind would whisk her onto the dance floor.

In fact, the thought of dancing with her was so alluring, he almost walked directly past one of his childhood friends, James Cosgrove.

Cosgrove waved a hand in front of his face. "Evening, Mandeville," he said, the brass buttons on his dark blue uniform catching the candlelight. "Don't bother going to the supper room; there's nothing more filling than a cucumber sandwich."

Hugh laughed. "I'll have my hands full keeping my young charges in check. Have you seen them?"

"Saw your mother in the card room with some young ladies."

"Must be them," he said flatly. He should have known. Where else would his mother be? And without any other connections, Daphne and Celeste were obliged to stay with her, spending the entire ball watching hand after hand of whist.

As he made to leave, Cosgrove blocked his way. "I'd be obliged for an introduction. She's dashed pretty," he said.

"Certainly," Hugh replied, with absolutely no intention of introducing his handsome and charming friend to Daphne. The thought gave him pause. When had he decided Daphne was his alone? "Perhaps you mean the sister with the fair hair?"

"Who else?" Cosgrove shrugged.

"She's a lovely girl," Hugh said. "I wonder, while you're waiting, if you'd put it about that I have a large sapphire for information on Lady Spellwater's identity?"

"One of the gems from your stash?" Cosgrove asked.

When Hugh nodded, he smiled broadly. "Perhaps *I* can find her myself if that's the prize."

"Didn't you win enough prizes at sea?" Hugh laughed and left his friend to go to the card room. A quick scan revealed his mother presiding over whist, as only she could. He moved around the group milling in the doorway and walked toward them.

Celeste stood behind his mother, and Daphne on the side, closest to him. While Celeste looked lovely in a modest white gown, it was Daphne that made his breath hitch. She wore the same dress he'd seen on her at the modiste's, the mauve gown caught under her bosom with gold ribbon, then flowing in regal lines to the floor. Tendrils of her wild hair were shaped into a large curl and lay against the creamy expanse of her neck.

While he was busy yearning like a pup, she stared at the mirror on the opposite wall, watching the festivities with a wistful gaze, one foot tapping in time with the music.

Poor girl. His mother should be ashamed. Then Daphne spotted him. The color fled from her face, and her entire body stilled. She lurched forward as though about to run to him, before checking herself and staying in place.

The hand of cards finished just as he arrived at the table.

"Good evening, Lady Mandeville, Miss Davenport, Miss Celeste." He didn't recognize any of the other players, and his mother didn't make introductions. Instead, she turned and lifted her chin in defiance.

"As you can see, Mandeville, I have been successful tonight," she said, sweeping up a small pile of golden guineas.

"Successfully shirking your duties to our guests, madam." He beckoned Daphne and Celeste toward him and held out an arm each for them to accompany him. He eyed his mother's small pile of coins. "We'll leave you to your ruin."

Daphne and Celeste curtsied to his mother, and they moved out of the card room and into the ballroom.

"Thank goodness you came!" Celeste said artlessly. "I thought I would faint if I had to stand still for a moment longer." Then her face fell. "But Daphne should dance first, being eldest."

It was a long time since he'd seen a young lady look at a dance floor with such longing. No false air of ennui for Celeste.

"No need." Cosgrove stepped in front of them with a broad smile that Hugh was delighted to see was directed toward Celeste, not Daphne. "Perhaps I may be of service?"

"Miss Davenport, Miss Celeste, may I introduce Captain James Cosgrove, my neighbor, recently of the Royal Navy and genuine English hero."

"That's me, bona fide hero." Cosgrove smiled modestly, but he was obviously happy with the compliment. "I don't know what the next dance is, Miss Celeste, but will you join me?"

"I should be delighted!" Celeste replied, putting her hand in his outstretched one.

Ah, perfect. Two lovely people dancing together, allowing him time with Daphne alone.

Daphne put her hand on his arm, allowing him to escort her to the dance floor.

"We have much to discuss, but not here." He smiled as though she'd made a jest as he led her toward a small group of dancers forming for the reel near the balcony doors. "Some people spend the entire evening pretending not to listen to other people's conversations. They gather their eggs and sell them on the morrow in the best drawing rooms."

"Oh." She let go of his arm, leaving the spot where her hand had been cold despite the heat of a hundred bodies in the room. He rubbed it, wishing she were still touching him. "Yes. We do not want this news served with tea."

She nodded. "I should tell you that I have been most active today and am probably abreast of all the news you have. So, there is nothing to discuss. Let us just enjoy this night, for when word gets out, I'm sure we will be on the first coach back to Reading."

Daphne kept her eyes firmly ahead, not betraying any emotion but for small patches of red on her cheeks. He heard the underlying desperation and was powerless against it.

"All will be well, I promise."

"No, all will not be well. But it is not your fault. She looked around. "I need some fresh air."

They had thrown the doors open for propriety's sake, but the balcony was empty at present. "A stroll on the balcony instead of a reel, perhaps?"

She nodded and almost ran out the doors, stopping at the marble balustrade and bracing herself on it. She looked distressed and yet beautiful. Both made him ache.

The balcony was lit with hanging lanterns, so it was as bright as the ballroom, although the night sky lent it intimacy.

Daphne took a deep breath and clutched both hands onto the balustrade, looking out over the garden. "I suppose you could tell me what happened at the first interview? I was not there."

He felt an urge to soften the blow for her but had to quash it. It wouldn't help in the long run. "Mr. Wolfe found products exactly like mine at your father's house in Cheapside and took him to Bow Street for questioning." He glanced sideways at her, but she said nothing, so he forged ahead. "After questioning, he admitted his guilt and is now in remand. He will stand before the magistrate on Monday morning. It looks bad."

"It is bad," she said bitterly. "I met his wife and then took a letter I found there to Mr. Wolfe. He may have more leads, he certainly seemed happy."

"He mentioned he had new information on Mrs. Davenport. Thank you." He searched her face. She looked as though the bottom of her world had fallen out.

She turned to him, her eyes awash with tears but her expression angry. She strode across the balcony. "All these years, we have lived so poorly...and all this time—"

"He built a family without you. I know." It made his chest tight to think Davenport had done that to two such lovely ladies.

"He never sent for us," she said more to herself than to him. Then she straightened and lifted her chin. With her shoulders pulled back and her chin up, she was a picture of defiance. If he didn't know better, he'd think she didn't care a jot for her father.

Lady Johanna stepped out onto the balcony, her eyes trained on him.

He bowed. "Good evening."

"Oh, excuse me," Lady Johanna said as if interrupting wasn't what she had intended. "Good evening, Lord Mandeville, Miss Davenport." She curtsied, although not very deeply, as she *was* a duke's daughter. The light from the ballroom illuminated the white muslin gown she wore. At first glance it was a simple dress with capped sleeves and a demure neckline. But further inspection revealed the sheer fabric was embroidered all over in white flowers and motifs that took the dress from simple to exceptional. And expensive. Her fair hair was elaborately dressed and punctuated with pink rose buds.

He hadn't seen her since the balloon ascension. The way Lady Johanna glared at Daphne told him she blamed Daphne for his absence.

"Lord Mandeville, I heard you offered a large sapphire as a reward for the identity of Lady Spellwater?"

He heard Daphne's sharp intake of breath. "Indeed. It has become urgent I speak to her."

Lady Johanna smiled, but her smile was at odds with the gleam in her eye. "You spend quite some time chasing after her! But I will find her for you and hopefully keep that sapphire in the family. I know her voice from the balloon ascension, I believe I can identify her."

He ushered her back toward the balcony door, trying to give Daphne some time to regain her equilibrium. "It would delight me to give it to you. Bring me Lady Spellwater's name and you can gladly have it."

She curtsied with a winning smile. "I will see you for our supper dance." She turned to Daphne with a kind smile. "Rest well, Miss Davenport. Perhaps an early night?" And with a pointed glance, intimating he should make it happen, she left the patio in a swish of skirts.

When Hugh turned back to Daphne, it was to find she'd taken a seat on the stone bench, clutching her hands in her lap.

"Miss Davenport?" In the warm light of the lanterns, her pallor was alarming. He kneeled in front of her.

"I need a moment to collect myself," she said, sending him a weak smile. "Go inside, I'll follow directly."

"I would rather escort you," he said as the reel finished. Three couples, puffed and laughing, spilled onto the balcony. They marveled at the lanterns, then hushed when they saw Hugh and Daphne.

Frowning, Daphne rose to her feet and allowed him to take her arm. "Could you take me to the ladies' retiring room?"

"Of course."

Why had she gone from defiant to pale and frightened in the space of a heartbeat? Strange, but he could swear it only happened after he mentioned the sapphire and finding Lady Spellwater. Surely not a coincidence.

CHAPTER 17

The retiring room was not empty, although Daphne wished it were. Then she could collapse without an audience.

Two ladies were having a quiet coze in the corner, and one elderly lady sat with her head tipped back and turban askew, snoring like an old cat. Daphne took the seat by the window and closed her eyes. Being Lady Spellwater at this particular moment in time was the most wretched thing imaginable.

The elderly lady jerked awake, looking around as though she'd forgotten where exactly she was. "I wasn't asleep."

"No, of course not," Daphne replied with a small smile.

The lady straightened her turban. "You look like you could use a kip, young lady." She frowned. "Or do you need my smelling salts, m'dear? You look awfully pale."

The kindness in her eyes made Daphne's heart squeeze. "I just need to close my eyes for a moment." *And think how to extricate myself from this mess of an evening.* Not least of which that everyone in the ton who had the least liking for enormous sapphires would be hunting for her.

Daphne shuddered. She had to surrender and face the consequences. It was past time.

But even thinking about it gave her a headache. Celeste might hate her, but her path was clear.

Her thoughts were interrupted by a familiar voice. "You *are* in here," Celeste said. "I barely believed Lord Mandeville when he told me." She crouched in front of Daphne, not caring for crumpling her dress or that other ladies were in the room. "Are you unwell?"

Daphne nodded. "Sadly out of form. But I'll be right as a trivet in no time. Just give me a few more minutes of quiet, and I'll come and sit with Lady Mandeville."

"No, let's stay here," Celeste said, resting her head on Daphne's lap.

"Your dance partners will never forgive me if I keep the most beautiful lady at the ball in the retiring room." Daphne reached out and touched the pale green velvet ribbon threaded through Celeste's hair.

Celeste smiled. "It's hard not to feel beautiful in this dress! I've danced three dances in a row." She smiled and sat on the edge of the seat, tapping her foot. "What a glorious night." She turned to her sister. "Do you think it's possible to fall in love in the time it takes to dance a reel? Because I think I have."

"Captain Cosgrove?" It felt good to put her woes aside for a moment and revel in Celeste's happiness, even if she was about to quash it.

Celeste nodded. "He's very dashing. I do love a naval uniform."

Daphne smiled. "He is." She envied Celeste's ability to enjoy the evening.

"Perhaps he will call on us tomorrow." There was a light in Celeste's eyes, a true elation Daphne hadn't seen there in years, if ever, that made her feel sick for what she had to say.

The two ladies in the corner returned to the ball and the

elderly lady rose to her feet too. "I will let you have your conversation in peace, my dears."

She took Celeste's hand. "Dearest, Lord Mandeville is looking for Lady Spellwater here at the ball. I must confess."

Celeste's face fell. "Oh must you? Couldn't it wait until tomorrow when it's over and I've had one perfect evening?" She tapped her foot, thinking, and then her face brightened. "I know!" Celeste leaned forward to whisper in Daphne's ear. "Let him find Lady Spellwater, but don't tell him it's you. Then you can tell him the truth, and I'll still be able to go to supper with Captain Cosgrove." She leaned back. "Please say you will!"

"Dearest, it's such a risk. If he finds out, it will be worse again. I've lied so much already. I just want to be truthful."

"He won't find you out! Meet him in a dark room. Wait here, I'll get your cloak, then if you just make your voice low like you did in Reading, he'll never know."

No. No. This was a terrible idea that would just be icing on a day of terribleness.

Celeste ran to the cloak room, leaving Daphne with a sense of foreboding no amount of lively music could lift.

Celeste returned. "I've left the cloak in the library. Then I snuffed all the candles, leaving one lit so you can find your way, and drew the curtains. It will be more than dark enough." She hugged her sister. "Thank you. I know I'm asking a great deal."

"Do you?" Daphne couldn't help asking but also found it impossible to refuse, which she had an inkling her beautiful sister knew. "I'll do this for you, but only because I believe this is the end. There will be no balls and no Captain Cosgrove after this."

"Then I'd best go wear a hole in my slippers dancing," Celeste replied and almost ran from the room.

She still didn't seem to understand the risk of the situation. Or perhaps she did and was determined to ignore it.

Daphne wandered down the hall until she found the library.

There was one candelabra on the desk, making it easy for Daphne to locate the parchment and quills.

Daphne picked it up and penned a brief note to Hugh. Then she entered the ballroom and dropped the note on a footman's tray, praying he'd be clever enough to deliver it for her.

She watched Hugh read the note and squirrel it into his pocket with a triumphant smile.

It was time for Lady Spellwater to make an appearance. What would Hugh say? How would he react? Would he be angrier than he was in Reading, or would he just be grateful for the information?

With the weight of such serious issues, her whole body shouldn't be alive with anticipation of meeting with Hugh in a darkened room.

HUGH WAS BALANCING a glass of champagne and a plate of very ordinary cucumber sandwiches, watching the door for Daphne's return, when the footman delivered the note. He read it and smiled.

She took the bait!

It sent a thrill through him that was well worth the price of the sapphire and whatever else it took to have her meet with him. Despite his previous doubts, she truly must move in the upper echelons of society.

"What is it, my lord?" Lady Johanna tried to read the note over his shoulder. He crumpled it and pushed it into his pocket.

"Just my coachman needing my assistance." The lie came easily, and she nodded, accepting it. Daphne wouldn't; she would know immediately something was afoot.

The note said to meet her in the library, which discreet questioning revealed was also on the ground floor. He made his way to the back of the house and quietly opened each door until the unmistakable smell of leather-bound volumes en masse became apparent. He was greeted by pitch black. The light from the wall sconces behind him were no help, but he stepped into the room anyway, taking a deep breath.

"Madam?" Perhaps he was in the wrong room.

Silk skirts rustled to his right, over by the window. "Move to the fireplace, Mandeville, so I can close the door. We can't have the entire ballroom knowing we're in here together."

The use of his name and the deep huskiness of her voice had his blood pounding. Just as Daphne brought out his protective instincts, Lady Spellwater seemed to bring out his more sensual ones. Following her voice around the darkened room was like the most delicious chase. He moved quietly to the fireplace, the glowing embers of the hearth doing nothing to help him identify her.

She closed the door and locked it, the rustle of her skirts telling him she'd positioned herself somewhere between him and the door for an easy escape. Clever. He moved with stealth until he was only a foot from her, seeing her outline perched on the edge of an armchair. Her fragrance spun around him again with a sweetness that took his breath away.

"This is intimate," he said, unable to hide the delight in his voice.

Her silhouette straightened. She was prim for someone who made fragrances that captured desire in a bottle. "It has nothing to do with intimacy and everything to do with secrecy."

"Still," he said, reaching down and touching her hand lightly. "I'm not sure it was a wise move. Locked in a dark room together."

He could feel the heat radiating from her. It matched his own.

"You wouldn't touch me." Her breathing was short and sharp.

"No, of course not," he said. "Unless you wanted it."

He took her hand in his and was surprised when she didn't pull it away.

Instead, she changed the subject, her voice a little shaky, her hand still in his. "I hear you've taken to offering precious gems for my identity."

"You can have the sapphire for yourself if you'll just help me." He strained to make out the shape of her dress.

"I would feel uncomfortable taking anything from you with what I am about to say," she said.

He dropped her hand and sat on the sofa, hoping to make her feel more at ease. "Ah. It is bad news then."

She was so close he could smell her when he inhaled. Not her sensuous and arresting perfume, but something uniquely her, warm and earthy. It was somehow familiar and much more alluring.

"Yes. I am certain my ingredients are yours. I am mortified. Nothing is as I thought, and thus we find ourselves here in the library. Not for the sapphire, but to help you and hopefully stop you from exposing me."

"You did not lie to me on purpose," he said, not quite understanding his need to comfort her. "I'm sure of it."

"And yet I did lie to you. My stock came from a man called..." She paused, as though giving him the name was the hardest thing she'd ever done. "Davenport." She took a deep breath.

He sighed. What he would've given for this information weeks ago, even days ago. "Thank you. I interviewed him today. He admitted to the crimes and said he worked alone."

"He most certainly did not work alone. His wife is at this very moment running away. He is in it up to his ears, and so is she. *She's* the one he's covering for. I have given Bow Street all the information I have." Her voice trembled.

It was just as Wolfe had told him. That he'd met Lady Spellwater and she had confirmed Mrs. Davenport was involved. He was relieved she was helping Bow Street, but it was just so hard to think of a woman thieving on that scale. But Davenport said she'd hated his father, too. It was the common denominator.

He closed his eyes against the sense of failure. Never had he blundered so badly at such an important juncture. They could have easily had Minerva in custody, too. "Do you have any other information?"

He realized he'd switched from gentleman to inquisitor in the space of a heartbeat, but there was nothing to be done about it. She seemed to understand, just as pleased to answer as he was to question.

"I have given Bow Street all I have. They will be able to recover much more now, I think."

He took a deep breath. All was not lost. "Then I must thank you."

"That is not necessary." Her voice broke, and he realized how deeply affected she was by the events. She sounded like a scared young lady, not confident like Lady Spellwater usually was. "I will repay you every shilling of what I used. I have kept accounts, and it will be entirely accurate. I have a ring I could give you in good faith."

He shook his head, not that she could see it in the dark. "No need for the ring, although I appreciate the offer. I would like something else, instead. If I am to supply your oils in the future, I need to know who you are." Never had he wanted her to trust him more. Especially if it were Daphne, as his intuition was screaming at him. In the dark, Lady Spellwater and Daphne had merged as one and there was no reason for her not to confide in him.

She stood from her perch on the side of the armchair and slid her hands up until she had cupped his face. "This is who I am," she replied huskily. Then she stretched to kiss him, not softly like a gently reared lady, but with a headlong rush of passion. Not that she seemed to know quite what she was doing.

He fell into the sofa and pulled her onto his lap. He slowed the kiss, turning it into something lazy and delicious. She responded deliciously, too, melting into him, the sweetness of her lips setting a trail of sensation.

She groaned, a husky sweet sound that called to him. Everything about her called to him, asked him to take a risk and damn the consequences.

Lord, what was he doing? This was crazy. He pulled away, but she took him by the lapels of his jacket and pulled him back to her, to kiss her again.

He had no resistance.

All semblance of thought fled as her hands curled around his collar and ran through his hair.

She tasted like champagne and strawberries and smelled like Daphne. All lingering questions were answered. "Interesting."

She pulled away in shock. "Drat, I should not have done that," she said and with a swish of silk, she ran to the door.

"Come back!"

"No, time for me to disappear. I just had to stop you from revealing me."

First, he heard the key in the lock, then there was a crack of light as she opened the door and slipped out. He lurched toward the door, punch-drunk, as it slammed shut.

"Daphne! Come back this instant!" How dare she kiss and bolt like that? She had some explaining to do.

He shook his head to try to clear it, but when he opened his eyes, everything was just as murky.

He wasn't worried until he heard the key turned in the lock again.

The wretch had locked him in the library.

CHAPTER 18

Daphne forced herself to walk steadily down the corridor to the cloakroom, where she left her cloak on a chair. Her heart was torn between dancing for joy over the kiss or running from Hugh before he confronted her.

Dancers pounding the floorboards rumbled in concert with her thumping heart. Her cheeks were hot and her lips swollen and tingling. She must look a fright.

Why did she have to kiss him? Why did she ask him to meet her in that small dark room where anything could happen?

Because she'd *wanted* him to kiss her, and her heart kept hammering on about how it was worth it, how she'd never felt this way, how Hugh Mandeville was the only man worth kissing.

And now she was undone. He knew who she was and how much she'd lied to him. But at least Celeste could enjoy her ball.

The rooms were overfilled and stuffy, the odor of so many people and badly aired dresses made her queasy. Somebody should *definitely* open a window.

Celeste was dancing a country dance with Captain Cosgrove. The rapport between the couple was obvious. There were some very speaking glances that told of instant adoration on both sides.

In the distance, she could faintly hear Hugh thumping on the library door. Surely, someone would let him out soon?

It was time for her to take her leave as Lady Spellwater, to show Hugh she meant what she said about being horrified by her part in it all. Her alter ego had run out of time.

After a quick visit back to the ladies' retiring room with the note and pen from her reticule, Daphne dropped her note on the ballroom floor and retreated to a sofa by an open window to wait for someone to pick it up. It might take a while, but in the meantime, she could easily content herself with observing the theatrics of the Ton.

The air coming from the garden smelled like a full-blown rose, ripe and decadent with all the primness of the bud long since gone. A last hurrah before the petals fell to the ground.

As her gaze moved on, a footman handed Lord Devlin the note. Daphne felt a stab of triumph as he waved the note above his head and motioned for the music to stop.

The dancers stilled, looking around for the reason.

"She's here!" he said. "Lady Spellwater is in this room!"

The room murmured. "What does it say? Out with it!"

"Dear Guests," he read out. "Sometimes you amuse me, sometimes you disgust me, but forever you entertain me. If I made a perfume from tonight's ball, it would be ambrette seed, which is musky and floral like your exuberant dancing—"

Tittering filled the room.

"Ylang ylang for the heat and joy of a room full of dancers and lovers. Then perhaps some lemon for that tart I ate at supper, and finally a drop of rose absolute for the lingering kiss on my hand by Lord Gibson." Devlin stopped and looked around the room for Lord Gibson, who raised his champagne glass to the applause. Devlin continued on, giving her note the right amount of drama.

"A mess of a fragrance, you say?" Lord Devlin continued. "No.

My fragrance, like London, is much more than the sum of its elements. But alas, I must leave you for I have a large debt to repay. Perhaps one day I will play with you again, but for now, adieu."

He looked up. "Lady Spellwater, if you're listening, we would be happy to help you with your debts. There is no need to hide your identity. We can be trusted with it."

The crowd applauded, and Lord Devlin motioned for the music to begin for the next dance.

Daphne smiled. She had said goodbye, now it was time to leave.

She was still shaking when she made her way to Celeste, intercepting her as Captain Cosgrove escorted her back to Lady Mandeville. "I have quite the headache, would you mind if I return home?"

Celeste curtsied to Captain Cosgrove. "Please excuse me for a moment, Captain."

Arm in arm, she walked Daphne to the refreshment table, handed her a glass of lemonade, then pulled her onto an empty settee. She looked around to make sure nobody was listening. "I gather from your letter, that did not go well."

"He knows it's me. I may have locked him in the library." Daphne frowned. "This is all about to ignite like a keg of gunpowder."

"Drat! Can we not even have one ball to enjoy ourselves? You have barely danced and you look so beautiful." Celeste stamped her foot in frustration. Because her foot was shod in a dancing slipper, the effect was somewhat disappointing. Still, it was such a typical thing for her sister to do that Daphne smiled.

Daphne lowered her voice. "I was a fool to think I could get away with this and naive to think nobody will find out about Father. Everyone will. I'm afraid those gentlemen that danced with you tonight will disappear when the news spreads."

Celeste stared at her toes. "Yes, of course," she said quietly. "I would like to think Captain Cosgrove would be made of sterner stuff, but I have only just met him. I can expect nothing."

At Celeste's long face, Daphne held her hand, wishing she didn't have to bear such bad news on such a magical night.

"It may still work itself out," Daphne said, knowing she was telling a fib if not an outright lie.

Celeste rolled her eyes. "Yes, and we'll find evidence that Father is innocent of all wrongdoing," she said sarcastically. "And the magistrate will drop all charges and give us an apology and a big dowry as compensation."

"Sweetheart, we've tried our hardest. Some things are beyond our control."

Celeste shook her head. "I'm tired of that. Tired of always having our needs scuttled by our irresponsible father." Her anger evaporated, and she deflated before Daphne's eyes.

Daphne took her sister's hand and looked her in the eye. They had shared every tragedy and triumph of the past decade, and she was so very dear and precious. "I will see you safe," she said.

"You always do," Celeste replied, a hitch in her voice. "Thank you for all you've done, but I think this is even beyond your capabilities. We should leave London after tomorrow. Captain Cosgrove said his mother is having a house party and he'd like her to invite us. Perhaps we should accept?"

Celeste squeezed once and pulled her hand away. "We should definitely accept."

Captain Cosgrove and another gentleman came to stand in front of them. "May I introduce you to Mr. Wetherly, Miss Celeste?"

Introductions were made and Celeste took her partner's arm.

"I would like you to stay here and continue dancing. Tell Lady Mandeville I have gone home with a headache if she asks." She would be in trouble for leaving, but what did it matter now?

"I shall enjoy myself enough for both of us."

Daphne collected her cloak and made her way outside. There

was a steady stream of people both arriving and leaving the Devlin's ball, meaning the road was clogged with carriages and horses.

She needed a hack but could find no footman to help her; they were all too busy fetching the carriages of people more important than her. She shrank into herself, keenly aware that she had no chaperone and eyes would be on her.

A lady stood next to her and she turned to see Lady Johanna. Her carriage pulled up almost immediately, as if to illustrate the difference between them. "Come, Miss Davenport."

"You would drive me home?" The door was opened by a footman and Daphne got in.

"Eventually," Lady Johanna replied cryptically. "I need to talk to you for longer than a two-minute journey."

AFTER PUMMELLING the door until a passing footman let him out, Hugh found the ballroom in an uproar about Lady Spellwater. He searched the crowd for Daphne but did not find her. Celeste, however, was sipping a drink by a large pillar, his good friend Cosgrove by her side.

He made his way to them. "Where is Miss Davenport? I should like a word with her."

Celeste's eyes narrowed. "I thought she would have told you. She went home. She has a pounding headache."

A spike of frustration lit through him. She'd run and it was his fault.

He knew her well enough to know she'd feel guilty for using stolen oils. He'd heard the horror in her voice as she admitted what she knew about Minerva. He'd kissed her, but he hadn't told her he understood, or that he didn't blame her. And most importantly, that he had no intention of disclosing her identity to anyone.

Surely she wouldn't think that of him?

He couldn't care less if she never gave that money back. All that was important was that the thefts should stop. The rest he could make up over time.

Daphne. Victim of her father's crimes.

Daphne. Lady Spellwater.

Hugh felt a spurt of anger that she hadn't trusted him with the truth from the beginning. But that was when she'd thought her father innocent.

He walked as swiftly as propriety would allow to the front of the house. He was at the top of the steps when he saw Daphne and Lady Johanna step into a well-heeled carriage. He took an involuntary step forward, although there was nothing he could do to stop the carriage taking off into the traffic.

He called for a hack so he could follow them.

Where was she taking Daphne? And why? It would be disastrous for Daphne if Joanna identified her, but he couldn't put a stop to it five carriages behind. A smart man would have borrowed a horse so he could catch up and not be caught in traffic.

Too bad that when it came to Daphne, he acted first and thought later.

CHAPTER 19

IN WHICH LADY JOHANNA BARGAINS FOR HER MAN

Daphne leaned into the squabs of Lady Johanna's carriage, clasping her still trembling hands, willing herself to be calm.

Lady Johanna didn't need to know she was nervous. Or was she trembling with anger? She was too exhausted to tell. All she wanted to do was curl up in a corner and sleep. Then wake up in a world where she hadn't come to London and fallen in love with Hugh. Again.

Johanna sat across from Daphne, her chin raised, looking out the window at the passing buildings as though Daphne wasn't even in the carriage with her.

They trotted along in an uneasy silence, for what seemed like forever, and Daphne certainly wasn't going to be the first to speak. The carriage was filled with the strong scent of lavender, bay, and rosemary, along with hair powder, a sickly combination that made Daphne put her arm over her stomach.

The moment drew out, punctuated by the horse's footfall.

Lady Johanna broke it first. "I suppose you're wondering why I rescued you," she said crisply.

Did Johanna know she was Lady Spellwater? Her stomach

roiled with nerves. "I did not need rescue. A hack would have come along shortly."

Lady Johanna laughed, a trill that flapped around the hackney cab like a caged bird. "Indeed? I saw you drop that note Lord Devlin read out."

"Oh dear, did you?" Daphne said slowly, feigning ennui, determined not to be intimidated. Typical of this day that it would end with her being unveiled. It was unavoidable. She regarded Lady Johanna with what she hoped was a sardonic eye. She probably just looked annoyed. "Satisfied?"

Johanna rubbed her hands together. "I can't tell you how happy it makes me to see it is indeed you."

"I cannot think why." The carriage was feeling like a prison. If only she could just open the door and jump out. But she had to see this through.

"Because you're not a daring temptress; you're just a little mouse from the country." Her eyes bored into Daphne's, challenging her to disagree.

It was how Daphne often thought of herself in any case, so it did not feel insulting. She shrugged. "And therefore?"

She reached forward and patted Daphne on the knee. "Therefore, you are not a threat to me. I have been worried about Lady Spellwater for weeks, watching Mandeville slip away like a ghost as he chased her. Now I have found you and I have a draft on my father's bank in my reticular to offer you a handsome sum of money to leave London. After all, you said you had debts."

In other words, Daphne was to be bought off. Again. As Lady Mandeville had bought her off, as Father had found it so easy to leave her behind. Because Daphne was not worthy of better treatment. It was obvious, in retrospect.

"Then Lord Mandeville will finally set a date?" Daphne couldn't keep the sarcasm out of her voice. "Although he could have done that any time over the past three years. Makes one wonder..."

She pursed her mouth. "That is none of your concern. I'm sure we will set a date."

Perhaps it was true. The mystery of the thefts was solved, and he could turn his attention back to Lady Johanna and that transactional marriage they had planned.

Daphne closed her eyes against the wave of heartache. Despite everything, she'd held onto the hope that he saw her for who she truly was, a spirited and ingenious woman who wanted to leave her mark on the world. And she saw him for who he was too. A principled man who protected those who were vulnerable, who believed in justice, even when he had to look in the mirror and see where his family had hurt others.

Foolish girl. None of that mattered.

Lady Johanna lunged for her final strike. "What I have with him is real. What you have is some silly scent and an illusion."

Daphne was long past playing nicely. "I wish I'd known *that* before I kissed him a few minutes ago."

There was a sharp intake of breath. "How *dare* you?"

"What? Be so thoroughly kissable? I don't know. Has he kissed you?"

The silence was telling. "He knows better than to show me such disrespect. I don't believe you." And she was right, in a way. Daphne had instigated the kiss, not Hugh.

"Of course," Daphne said with as much false pity as she could jam into two words.

Johanna looked at Daphne with exasperation. "Even if he were free, he would never marry you." She regarded Daphne in the moonlight. "But I will not tolerate a mistress."

Daphne's eyes widened. "What makes you think I would tolerate *being* a mistress?"

It was all very well that a single kiss between them was explosive enough to fuel the Vauxhall fireworks, but if he chose the woman opposite her for his wife, then he could have her. Just like Father had to pay for the choices he made, so would Hugh.

She suddenly felt powerful and wise beyond her years.

Lady Johanna shrugged. "I am glad to hear it." She reached inside her reticule and pulled out a bank draft. "As you can see, I prepared for this eventuality. I had thought to give it to you at the balloon ascension." She handed the draft to Daphne and dusted her hands like a dirty job was done.

Daphne's eyes widened at the figure that she knew would be enough to keep them clothed and fed for almost five years if they were careful. Or less time if she gave Celeste a dowry. Or she could go home to India. "How much is a passage to India, I wonder?"

Lady Johanna's eyes widened. "India? Well, I'm sure I could have my father add that to the bargain if you truly mean it."

But the question was not about what she could do with the money. No, this time the decision was about giving up Hugh. Was there no hope for them? Would she accept this offer and discover that he loved her and she'd given up a lifetime's happiness?

"Why do you want him so badly? You could have anyone."

"I'm sure you will agree that men with breeding and wealth that look like Adonis come to life are not so thick on the ground. Why should I not have the best? I was in love with him by the time we finished our first quadrille."

Daphne nodded. They had something in common, after all. "Yes, that I can understand. Having fallen in love with him at an early age and discovering myself just as susceptible years later, it is not surprising."

Their eyes met and a moment of understanding passed between them.

Well.

In the end, there was actually only one truth. That Hugh had courted Lady Johanna so long that his honor would never permit him to cry off.

Never.

And *her* honor would never permit her *not* to pay him back what she owed him for using his goods in her perfumes.

Sometimes honor demanded a high price.

Daphne closed her eyes and took a deep breath. This felt like the kind of decision that changed the course of one's life and one that would come with no small component of regret. Because in these past weeks, life felt like it had color again. The spark she used to have had been kindled back to life. Even discovering the truth about Father had been liberating in a way. She could stop making excuses for him, trying to please him or make him proud of her. Her life was hers to live.

Perhaps she could keep the spark alive by leaving Lady Spellwater behind and bringing her perfume-making out into the open. These funds could pay back Hugh and help them expand. They could do it all out in the open, as Madam Le Favre suggested. If only she could still work with Hugh, because his abilities and connections would make it a reality. Madam Le Favre had given her a taste for what good connections could do.

She took the proffered draft, her hand trembling. "I will accept, if you will allow me to keep my trade connections with Lord Mandeville. By letter only, you understand."

"Oh, that will all stop," Johanna said blithely. "Lord Mandeville will no longer be so directly involved in his business matters."

Daphne felt her eyebrows draw together in confusion. "Are you sure? He has told me how much he enjoys it."

Johanna looked confused. "Not that it is your concern, but my father sees great potential for him in politics."

"I see," said Daphne, foreseeing an interesting conversation ahead for the couple. "Very well, then would you agree to me still being able to trade with his company Oriental Spice and Fragrance? If you agree, I will take the draft you have so kindly offered."

"I agree. If you are to continue in trade, then deal with the company as you will with my blessing." She handed Daphne the draft. The paper was as crisp and new as the tidy sum it represented. She wasn't sure whether to be happy or appalled at being bought off for a second time, but needs must when the devil drives.

Daphne smiled, amused at the way the blessing was condescendingly bestowed. "I wish you both happy." Hugh had *chosen* to marry Lady Johanna. If that meant social standing was more important than love, such bad judgment wasn't worthy of her.

Lady Johanna patted her on the knee, a patronizing touch that made Daphne recoil. "And now, I feel our business is at a close. Where can I drop you? Here?"

Here? Daphne looked out the window with no idea where they were. It was dark, the lamps only illuminating a small circle around them. Not that much in London looked familiar after such a short time. But at least there were plenty of people about.

"Here is perfectly fine." She had a few coins in her reticule to get her home.

Lady Johanna nodded. "Good. You won't come to any harm in Covent Garden." She certainly didn't sound sure.

"Thank you. I wish you well." Surely, someone, somewhere would give her points for keeping her poise. Daphne stepped out of the carriage and closed her eyes, glad for her voluminous cape and hood.

Everything had gone to plan. She had the money to pay Hugh back and hopefully enough left over to start again. So why did her heart ache?

The street was teeming with activity, and in the distance, a clock chimed the hour, half past midnight. A new day was beginning, her life had to begin again too.

Perhaps she could just tell herself that over and over until it stuck.

She looked down the street, hoping beyond hope to find a clean hack with a friendly driver.

But every hack had a passenger, and even those seemed few

and far between. At least it was a warm night, a light breeze keeping it from being outright muggy.

She would have to find somebody to ask directions. Perhaps a night watchman? Everything would be fine. People walked home alone every night. But this was not the way she thought the night was going to end.

CHAPTER 20

THE COUNTRY MOUSE DECIDES ENOUGH IS ENOUGH

"Faster, my good man." Hugh knocked his hand on the roof of the carriage to get the hack to hurry up as he chased Lady Johanna's carriage.

Daphne was Lady Spellwater, which meant Lady Spellwater was no beguiling temptress—she was a young lady from Reading who had no money, lived on tallow candles, and had a threadbare rug. A young lady who still had dreams about India and maharajas and jasmine. Lady Spellwater was the alter ego with the color Daphne felt she had lost in England.

She had kissed Hugh and kissed him properly. His blood was still heated from it. But trying to sort the truth from the lies was challenging. One thing he knew, she had never lied about her circumstances. They were every bit as dire as he thought they were. And her father's were the opposite. And he had abandoned them for a new wife without so much as a backward glance. Hugh knew in his heart she wasn't an adventuress, but she wasn't afraid to be expedient, taking the dresses from his mother, accepting their entrée into the polite world. Although, it was all for the sake of Celeste, if he was truthful. She partook little of it for herself.

Was it any wonder she didn't trust anyone but Celeste?

But.

She had lied to him, over and over, and about things he was desperate to discover.

She hadn't trusted him, and he hadn't trusted himself when his intuition told him she was withholding something.

The question was, why was she in a carriage with Lady Johanna?

He wanted to believe the best of Johanna, that she wouldn't be capable of ruining another young lady's life. On the other hand, he'd seen the jealous glint in her eyes at the ball and did not discount it.

The carriage trundled along until finally pulling over in bustling Covent Garden in front of a tavern. It was a strange place to stop, and soon, the throng of theatergoers of all classes and ages would spill out onto the street from the nearby theater. Drury Lane was busy even without that.

To his surprise, Daphne alighted from the carriage alone, the door closed, and the carriage resumed its journey. He frowned, confused.

How could Johanna leave Daphne to the whims of the street? Or had Daphne given her no choice, demanding to be released?

Whatever the reason, Daphne would be hard-pressed to find her way home. Even though Covent Garden was only a mile and a half from Mayfair, it was still a very long way after midnight. Thank goodness he had been able to pursue them.

He knocked on the roof of the hack to pull over so he could get out and walk with her.

Daphne's head snapped around as they pulled alongside her, her hood fell back, and Hugh saw her distressed glance turn to one of relief when she recognized him.

He closed the door behind him like he had all night and flipped a coin to the driver. "My thanks."

He turned to Daphne. "Can I offer you escort, Mischief?" He

hoped his voice was light-hearted. The only question was whether she was going to beg forgiveness or brazen her way out of this. Daphne would beg forgiveness but Lady Spellwater would take the brazen path. Who was he walking with?

She raised an eyebrow. "Only if you do not spend the *entire* time chewing me out," she said crisply.

Lady Spellwater, it seemed, was in residence.

He shrugged and slowed his pace to keep in step with her. "I find it prudent not to admonish ladies who kiss me. It could dissuade them from doing it again."

She huffed. "It might be best if you forgot that. It was not well thought-out considering your understanding with Lady Johanna."

"That understanding…" He searched for the right words. *Was a mistake.* He couldn't say that. It wouldn't be fair to her. "Yes, of course." Better for her to think he had no feelings for her at all.

He sighed and turned to her. "Can we start again and be the friends we should be?"

"I'm not sure that is possible when my father has been stealing from you." Her voice was flat, like she had suffered a great disappointment.

"I'm too scared to ask if you knew he was stealing from me, because I don't want to find out you did. Fool that I am."

It all came out in a rush. "You must believe I didn't know the oils were stolen. I only found them in the barn, under the hay, and thought 'what a waste' when I could make them into something beautiful. And then the local ladies loved them, and gave them to their friends, and before I knew it, I had my own small enterprise. And we could eat and pay the rent too."

He couldn't help but be impressed, even though she had risked a great deal, both for herself and Celeste. "Why didn't you tell me straight away?"

"You took me past the *gallows*, Mandeville. To show me what was coming. I had to find Father before you did."

"To warn him?"

She closed her eyes. "If I thought he was innocent, then yes, I likely would have."

They walked in silence. He offered his arm for Daphne to take, looking ahead and not down at her as she looped her arm in his. But the warmth of her and the awareness that sparked within him was almost his undoing. "You can't save them all. You tried."

She nodded, then seemed to come to a decision. "You're right," she said, closing her eyes. "I can't save Father, I can't save Celeste. I can't save you."

He laughed. "How would you save me? I feel like you've been actively working *against* me."

Her gaze was serious. "You need saving too, you just don't know it. Your passion calls you to pursue your trade interests. But society doesn't want you to do that. It wants you to laze around all day, visit your clubs, and pretend there's no such thing as business. But you should be able to follow what makes you happy. And it won't happen. If I thought you could, I would offer you a business partnership to make up for what I have inadvertently stolen from you. I told you about the gentlemen's cologne. I could have that finished within a month, I'm sure. The notes are all in my journal."

"I…" He didn't know what to say to such an offer. An offer he would take up in a heartbeat if the yoke of the earldom didn't weigh so heavily on him.

"No, do not answer. Lady Johanna won't marry you if she thinks you will increase your involvement in trade, and I have promised her I will only deal with your company by letter in the future. I understand all the reasons the idea is silly. I just wish it weren't."

"I wish the same." She was not wrong. Society's judgement would be swift and brutal, with none of the curiosity they reserved for Lady Spellwater. Now seeing Daphne, worried for his happiness rather than his social standing, his future felt bleak.

Wealthy, but bleak.

Something like despair bloomed in his heart at the thought. His hand rose absently to his mouth, as he remembering the kiss they had shared not long ago.

She dropped his arm and continued walking.

He caught up with her. "Did Johanna discovered your identity?"

"Yes, although I'm sure with the right encouragement she would keep the secret. For the second time this month, I was offered a great deal of money to leave you alone."

"Truly? How much?"

She pulled a piece of parchment from her reticule and handed it to him. He read it and whistled. "It seems you have been in the wrong business."

Her expression broke into a smile. "They all overestimate how attractive I am to you."

Sadness echoed inside him. "No. No they do not."

Their gazes connected for a long moment before Daphne looked down at her toes. "Unfortunately, attraction does not a marriage make."

Just a few weeks ago, he would have agreed with her. Now, along with a budding friendship, it felt quite appropriate indeed.

He tried to hand the draft back to her, but she pushed his hands away. "No, no. You keep it. I will send you my accounts and you can refund the difference if there is any."

He shook his head. "Very well. Get me your figures and I will work it out and then set up an account at the bank for you." *Where upon with interest coming in and your spending going out, you may never figure out that I kept none of it.*

She hooked her arm back through his. "Look at us haggling."

"Our natural state, I think." They walked in companionable silence for a while.

"What will you do?"

She shrugged."Go back to Reading after Father's trial next

week, if you can spare your carriage. Make perfume without trying to hide that I am in trade. Poor Celeste's chances were scuttled before she even began. She will have to find her own way."

"And she will. I do not underestimate your charming sister. I will go to Reading tomorrow, to claim any goods that are mine from your barn. I have sent a letter to the local magistrate asking him to meet me there at nine. I hope this is acceptable?"

"Oh, Hugh, how could it not be? I'm sure they were only targeting you. All of the stock there will be yours. But I have not yet told Ayah about Father, so please be gentle."

Her inadvertent use of his first name felt right. "Your Ayah is there?"

"But of course! You don't think I could make all those perfumes on my own do you? Her husband works at the Auction House Coffee Room but hopes to save enough money to start his own curry house. This was supposed to fund it."

"I'm truly sorry. If it helps I think you have a very good basis for your future business and I will ensure you are successful."

DAPHNE FROWNED. "Ensure we are successful from afar, I suppose."

They turned the corner into Curzon Street. "Yes, from afar. I can avoid my obligations no longer." He slowed his pace, seeming to be deep in thought. "Miss Davenport," he began, and his tone was regretful.

She held up her hand. "No, I don't need to hear it."

He looked taken aback.

"We've said all we can say. Done all we're going to do. Best leave it now. I beg you."

"I only want to tell you how deeply I admire—"

Gracious, it was even worse. *Now*, when there was no hope,

he was going to declare his undying admiration for her. Well, she wouldn't hear it.

"Thank you. I'm very grateful for your admiration. Grateful it will all be finished soon and I will get to leave this horrible time behind. Thank you for everything, but surely you understand that saying such things causes me anguish."

She ended the sentence slowly and deliberately, letting him see how truly she meant it. And in that moment, she supposed she did. Her life was a great mess and the temptation to run away as far and as fast as she could was great.

Hugh became suddenly stiff, the tiny muscle in the corner of his strong jaw twitching. "I don't want to make you uncomfortable, however, if you could just—"

He wasn't listening to her. He had something to say and he was going to run roughshod over her until he said it. Well, he could say it to thin air if he wanted to say it that badly.

"I'm tired. Please, we must let each other go." The weight of the entire day suddenly made her weak. All she wanted to do was curl up in bed and pretend none of it happened. Perhaps that made her cowardly, but now that it was over and she didn't have to be brave, it seemed awfully appealing.

"Of course," he said, picking up his pace again. "Please forget I mentioned it. I hope you know I always tried to do my best by you and for you."

They reached the house, which had lamps lit and a footman at the door, awaiting their return. "Of course. I appreciate all you have done, especially considering the circumstances."

Parting ways forever in such a polite fashion came near to breaking her heart.

CHAPTER 21

IN WHICH THE SON OF A BUFFALO VISITS THE PERFUMERY

The sun was rising by the time Hugh reached Reading, sending streams of marmalade light through the eastern sky. It was beautiful, although he was going to get no happiness from what the day would hold.

The Davenport house was quiet, with smoke coming from the chimney that suggested Daphne's tiny staff was still in residence. He would pay their wages before he left.

They drove through the crumbling front gates, and Sir Barkley, whose canine ears heard the carriage long before anyone else, came bounding out, running alongside them, barking. The horses had been slowed to a walk, so Hugh opened the door, and the dog leaped into the box.

He jumped all over his coat with dusty paws. Hugh scratched under his chin and received a lick in his ear for his efforts.

"She'll be home soon," he said.

Sir Barkley whimpered and nuzzled closer, both paws on his lap.

The carriage drew to a halt, and Hugh opened the door and stepped down, happy to stretch his legs after the long ride.

O'Keefe grunted and hitched up his pants. "Told you it were Davenport. We'll find all your stuff is in his barn."

Hugh stopped in his tracks. "But you said you checked the barn thoroughly last time we were here." He turned slowly and regarded O'Keefe's ruddy complexion. The man couldn't even meet his eye. "Something about finding only a litter of kittens, I seem to recall."

"Kittens and a jug of ale with old Mr. Pike," O'Keefe said sheepishly, bowing his head.

"Ah." Hugh took a deep breath and let it out with a frustrated groan.

"The old blighter distracted me, he did."

"Of course. It's impossible to see past a jug of ale."

"The ale is damn good here in Reading. Especially after the drive we had that day. You may not remember the rain and mud, but it was a toad of a drive."

It had not rained that day, but Hugh couldn't find it in his heart to be angry at O'Keefe. The series of events had led to bringing Daphne to town and discovering her all over again. That same part of him was wretched about the distance between them now.

It was too cruel, but it was necessary. Only distance would stop him doing something impulsive like asking her to run away with him.

"Just unbridle the horses, will you?" He turned away from the house and back to his manservant. "Then, find me some men and a wagon. We'll have cargo to transport. The magistrate should be here soon, but I want to get started."

O'Keefe mumbled something under his breath about even the horses getting a break before he did.

"I can hear you, old man," Hugh yelled after him.

"Good!" came the sharp reply. "You owe me a pint."

"I probably owe you three." Hugh laughed when O'Keefe's step visibly brightened.

Hugh made his way through the garden to the large wooden barn. The neighborhood birds continued their cacophony, and the round edge of the rising sun was just visible on the horizon. Berkshire was beautiful in spring. So, if everything was so rosy and he was about to find some of his stolen stock, why did he feel like something important was missing?

Daphne. It felt wrong to be here without her.

He took a deep breath of clean country air and opened the creaky barn door. The smell of hay and cow dung wafted over him, but underlying it was the smell of nutmeg and vanilla. Inhaling again, there was a faint whiff of rose, like a long-forgotten bloom left in a dry vase.

He strode across the barn and up the ladder to the loft. A quick glance told him everything he needed to know. Crates lined the loft and he searched until he found the faint shadow of his crest on one of them. The nutmeg smell was stronger, but the rose had disappeared. He didn't bother bringing them down but climbed up and investigated each crate to ascertain its shipping date. Most originated from the large theft of the warehouse last Christmas Eve. They hadn't even discovered that theft until the New Year, but here much of it was safely stowed in Edward Davenport's barn.

He sat by the top of the ladder with his head in his hands. He was about to haul the crates down one by one when a portly, silver-haired man entered the barn, his gaze lighting on Hugh.

"There you are, Lord Mandeville. I received your letter." He walked to the bottom of the step and waited for Hugh to descend. O'Keefe stood behind him.

Hugh leapt down the ladder. "Lord Wills, I presume?"

They shook hands. "Lord Wills. Local magistrate. I've brought ten men and some wagons with me at the direction of Bow Street. I understand you believe this property houses goods belonging to you?" There was a twinge of disbelief in his voice.

He'd probably prefer to be at a leisurely breakfast with his steak and eggs.

"Unfortunately, my lord. I've uncovered one lot in the loft already, and I know there are more, although not exactly where."

"Oh! They're definitely yours? My understanding is that Mr. Davenport was once involved in the import of oils and spices himself. How do you know they belong to you?"

"My crest on the crates was the first clue. It has been scrubbed, but I can still see the remnants."

"Oh." He stared at Hugh, seemingly lost for words. "Well, that's a shame. Two lovely girls. I suppose I'll have to start the process of searching for their father."

Lord Wills looked chagrined at having to go to so much effort.

"No need. Bow Street are questioning him." He did not mention the arrest and could only hope for Daphne's sake that Lord Wills didn't have a loose tongue.

Lord Wills stroked his chin. "You know, you should visit their old nurse while you're in the area. I understand her husband was Mr. Davenport's valet. They may know where more of your goods are."

"Yes, Miss Davenport mentioned as much. Where is she?"

"A small cottage to the north. Can't miss it. Just walk across the field. She's a respectable woman, though; I won't have you intimidating her." The older man regarded him sternly. "In fact, I think I might come with you."

"As you wish, although I have known Daphne's Ayah for many years and hold her in great esteem. I just want my products back."

Lord Wills considered him for a long moment. "Very well. If I have your word as a gentleman."

"You do." He shook Lord Wills hand again. "Thanks for all your help."

The older man scratched his head. "Yes, well, I can't say it's been a pleasure."

~

It was still early, but smoke came from the chimney of the small cottage, and there was a woman, dressed in a pink sari in the garden, picking leaves off a small bush. Her black and silver hair fell in a plait over her shoulder, and if he strained he could hear the soft lilt of her voice singing a Hindi lullaby. One that had been sung many times to him as a child.

"Ayah?"

She turned to the title, as he knew she would. Then her mouth dropped open and her hand fell to her side, long thin leaves falling to the ground. "Bhains ki aulad."

She just called him the son of a buffalo. He smiled despite himself. "True enough. But I'm here to pick up the rest of my oils."

She blanched. "No! You stay out of here!"

He stood behind the closed gate, not wanting to alarm her. "I know everything."

She moaned and looked as though she was about to faint.

"But all is well. You are safe, and Daphne and Celeste are safe. I only want my products back."

She looked at him sharply, obviously not trusting him. "Really? You give your word no harm will come to me, my daughters, or Daphne and Celeste?"

"I do."

She sagged with relief. "Come to the stillroom."

He followed her, bemused. They had a stillroom? That sounded very organised. She grumbled all the way, a mixture of Hindi and bad English, until opening the door to an old dairy.

There, laid out in a very orderly fashion, were enormous pots and rows of amber glass bottles with tags in Daphne's handwriting. "Frankincense, ginger, rose."

"This is surprisingly open considering you were using stolen goods."

"Nothing to hide!" she said, outraged. "How could we know what Mr. Davenport was doing? We just saw the oils and used them. Otherwise..." She waved her hands around wildly. "We starve!"

"Daphne was close to starving, anyway."

"Daphne is good at making perfume, but selling it is harder, and we are only just now selling in London."

Which made him wonder how her perfumes had found their way there. "Then how have you been selling?"

She shrugged. "To the tinkers. They come and buy or swap our boxes and sell them on their travels."

Ingenious. They would not have been charging enough, but at least it got the product out without the cost of transporting it.

Rows of glass bottles lined on a table on the far wall drew his eye. There had to be at least a hundred bottles, and at least triple that of the snuff tins. Then, as he looked further, the underneath of the table was stacked with boxes filled with bottles and snuff tins.

A blast of perfume hit him like a cudgel to the head. Her name rose to his lips like an anguished prayer. "Daphne." Look what she and Ayah had created. A swell of pride overtook him.

He had his eyes closed but opened them when he felt a light touch on his forearm. Ayah was looking up at him in wonder.

"You like it then?"

"Yes, all of London loves it. You are all very talented."

"I would be happy to move this equipment and my family to London to be with my husband. I would be happy to run this production in the city." She twisted her mouth. "And I would be even happier if someone was in charge who had a knowledge of how business works and where to sell things too. It's hard for a woman."

Hugh couldn't help the bubbling of joy that thinking upon this venture gave him. Working closely with Daphne, with Ayah, creating something together. When Daphne suggested it, he'd rejected the idea, because if being in her company for a few days led to him being this captivated, imagine how excruciating it would be to see her over an extended period.

But if he could just deal with Ayah, could it be possible?

He shook his head. No. Going into the perfume business on that scale would also be the opposite of the life his father had planned for him and what society expected. If he wanted to marry and raise a family in that society, he had to follow its rules and not break them before he even began.

That must be why it felt so good. Despite what his head was telling him, his heart had other ideas. Despite what his father had drummed into him from birth, he was still his grandfather's grandson. Still the boy who loved to hear of trading in faraway lands, of bolts of the finest muslin running through one's hands. Spices that filled his senses and called to his heart.

He smiled slowly. "I have a feeling you will bargain your contract quite hard."

She shook her head. "It's not hard. Profit split three ways, and everybody that works gets paid."

"Daphne has had enough of me, I think."

She blinked slowly, a hard look in her eye. "Not if you treat her as a business partner. Don't play with Daphne because it makes *you* happy."

"I'm not sure what you mean by that."

She smiled a knowing smile. "I watched you as a young man; I have eyes in my head. You loved India *and* your grandfather's enterprise. I saw you with him. Now you can't do that. You're stuck being a nob." Ayah looked him up and down as though this did not impress her. "But Daphne is a link to those years and those times, and *she* is not afraid to do what you would love to do."

Was that it? It was true, talking about flowers with Daphne, chasing her down in a balloon, being in a darkened room and holding her hand, it did make him feel more alive than he had since he left India. Like the dull gray of London was being washed away to reveal a bright, clean under layer.

Ayah nodded. "You know it's true. And she is beautiful, my girl is. She thinks herself inferior to her sister, but we both know that's not true."

"It's not true." The more Ayah spoke, the more he realized that being captured by Daphne was not a passing fancy. Not something he could neatly put away in a box and pretend didn't exist.

"I will convince her to go into the venture with you."

"Things between us are not good," Hugh said. "And Edward will be convicted."

"That is as it should be. And if things are not good between you, then fix it. She has loved you since she was a girl; just don't let her down. *Do* you love her?" Her sharp eyes assessed him.

He found he did not want to dissemble. "I do. But I am promised to another. Betrothed." He already felt guilty enough about kissing Daphne while courting Johanna; he could never do Joanna the disrespect of jilting her. He'd spend his lifetime regretting he couldn't, though.

"Then simple." Ayah shrugged one shoulder, her brown eyes sparkling. "Unbetroth yourself."

Easier said than done.

CHAPTER 22

IN WHICH MANDEVILLE TAKES HIS CHANCE

Hugh arrived home from Reading to find Daphne and Celeste gone. Their rooms were empty.

"Departed where exactly?" He'd thought they were waiting until their father's trial was over.

His butler was apologetic. "Her ladyship stood at the top of the stairs and waved them off, my lord. I assumed you were aware."

"I was not," he said darkly. What on earth had his mother done? "Where is Mother?"

"Taking tea with Lady Johanna on the terrace."

"I see." He could not see them in his dusty travel clothes. This would require his valet, who, knowing Jenkins would already be waiting for him in his dressing room.

He sighed inwardly and prepared himself to try to get the answers out of his mother and Lady Johanna in the most polite way possible. Sometimes putting on the mantle of the Earl of Mandeville was tedious. Especially when he just wanted answers.

A quarter hour later, much more polished and gentlemanly, Hugh made his way downstairs.

In any case, he was feeling particularly charitable toward

Lady Johanna, since he had not heard a word of Daphne's identity breathed after the ball. That kind of trustworthy behavior would help their friendship grow after they were...married. Perhaps one day the thought would not feel as wrong as it did now.

It was a beautiful day, and they were taking tea on the terrace overlooking the garden. There was a tiered tray with a myriad of small cakes and sandwiches, and Hugh noticed his mother had ordered her very best tea set for it to be served with.

His mother was smiling as one would to a young lady soon to be your daughter-in-law, and Lady Johanna was talking animatedly. "And then, up she went in the balloon. The crowd was deafening."

Bless her. Once again she had every opportunity to hint at Lady Spellwater's identity and chose not to.

"I do hope it was worth it," his mother said. "One cannot help but be shocked by such behavior. Did you sample the new perfume?"

Lady Johanna sat up a little straighter. "I did, but would not wear it."

"Oh?" His mother bent her head politely. "Not to your taste?"

"Why would I wish to smell like everyone else?" Lady Johanna said simply. "I will continue to go to Ross's where they hold the recipe for my own personal blend."

He stopped in his tracks. What a wonderful idea—Lady Spellwater could charge a fortune for bespoke scents. "A missed opportunity, I would think. You could have had her create you your own signature scent. I'm sure she would have done it."

Mother whipped around and saw him leaning on the door jamb. "Do come in, Mandeville. Lady Johanna will pour you a cup of tea, I'm sure." She bestowed Johanna with another beaming smile and motioned for the footman to get another cup and saucer.

He entered the room, taking one of the spare seats next to

them. "That would be lovely." *And I can find out how much more you know.*

"I was telling Lady Mandeville all the juicy on-dits about Lady Spellwater."

Hugh shrugged one shoulder. "It seems she has left London, if her note at last night's ball is real."

"As I was telling Lady Mandeville, I had the honor of driving her home after the ball."

"Now *that* is interesting. Did you discover her identity? London is waiting with bated breath."

Joanna smiled brightly. "They won't hear it from me. I am no prattle." The expression on her face suggested she knew she was doing him a great favor.

He breathed a sigh of relief and reached for a sandwich and ate it in one bite. *Egg.* "So, Mother, I see the Misses Davenport have left us. Where have they gone?"

"Lady Cosgrove's for a house party. The good lady invited us at the ball last night after you left. I think her son put her up to it. He seemed quite enamoured of Miss Celeste. I was invited, too, of course, but I don't need to go to a house party five miles from my own house." She rolled her eyes at the thought. "Miss Davenport said they would go home to Reading from there." She huffed. "All that effort for one ball! I can't complain, though. It was all quite fatiguing."

He picked up his teacup, willing it not to shake. "I do wish you had convinced them to stay."

"What, beg them? I think not."

Lady Johanna sighed and put her cup of tea on the table. "At least now, my lady, you can order your day around your own preferences." She looked out to the garden. "How lovely the garden looks. Do you care for a walk, Mandeville?"

Hugh frowned and turned to Lady Johanna. "Of course." He stood.

"Lovely. There's no rush. Please enjoy your tea."

They continued chatting while he drank, Lady Johanna darting glances at him every minute or so to gauge his progress.

He drank the last of his tea and placed the cup and saucer on the table. "Very well, shall we go? I will enjoy sharing the rare plants my father brought home from the Orient. I like to think they have made England their home."

Her face brightened. "Sounds enchanting!" She then threw a meaningful look at Mother that he did not miss.

He felt his stomach tighten in reply to it.

"There is a parasol by the wrought iron, my dear," Mother said kindly. "Although the sun does not have much heat left in it."

"Thank you, I would prefer to feel it on my face today."

Hugh suspected she didn't want anything to block his view of her or poke him in the eye as he attempted to woo her. *I should do that.*

She took the arm he offered her, and together they walked slowly down the steps to the terrace and into the garden.

It was a beautiful afternoon. He could hear bees buzzing in the distance, probably swarming over the hedge of lavender that he remembered Daphne running her hand over. She always lifted her hand under her nose after she touched a plant, as though it was the way plants communicated with her.

It had always been a disorganized garden, being the place Grandfather had loved to plant the things he'd carefully transported home for his mother's pleasure. Those plants, the ones that survived, were now mature, and the gardeners had made a good effort of propagating them, but the result was an unplanned riot of color and greenery.

"Oh my," Lady Johanna said when they passed through the large wrought-iron gate that marked the entry to the walled garden. "What a...mess."

Her mouth was a sad moue, and her brows were drawn together. It was the complete opposite of the wonder and awe he'd seen on Daphne's face what seemed like an eternity ago.

"What kind of garden do you prefer?"

"I like box hedges and topiary," she said, scanning the garden for her favorite. "I can see none here. Although that one might have been a box hedge some time ago..."

"It is not that kind of garden. Many of the specimens here are unique; many of them are the herbs which Father would import already dried. He liked to see how the dried version compared to the plant actually growing."

She blinked, slowly and noticeably. "He continued his involvement in the business? I knew you had merchants in the family through your mother's side, but I was led to believe you relied on your lands for income. My apologies for speaking frankly."

He nodded. "Yes. Our lands in Surrey are well over ten thousand acres. But we did not sell the Oriental Herb and Spice Company."

"But you will divest yourself once we marry, will you not? Our honor demands it."

Hugh politely sidestepped her question. "I let go just a little in the past year and have lost a sizable amount of money for my trouble. Wouldn't you want to know about the businesses that fund your life?"

"Oh no. I would just need to take care of my children and my household and trust my husband to take care of us all."

He nodded. "Of course." Not all ladies, or in fact, any lady, would find business dealings as enthralling as Daphne did.

Lady Johanna stopped and bent to smell a small purple flower, creating a lovely picture, glancing back to check he was watching her.

But all he could think about was Daphne right here in this very garden with the golden sun making a halo around her.

He looked down to find he had grabbed a fistful of mint that he had freshly crushed with his hand.

She smiled brightly. "Now, let us not talk of such mundane

topics. Did Miss Davenport tell you I have given her a small sum to get her started?"

"She did." His stomach sank at the bargain she had made. "Does anyone else know her identity?"

She smiled at him, like someone expecting thanks. "No one else knows. My gift to you, since we are to be betrothed. I thought to do you a good turn."

"A good turn? How so?" Hugh said quietly.

Lady Johanna shrugged, unconcerned, and continued through the garden. "She has been dogging your every step. Now she can return to her beloved India and do whatever it is she does. She was interested, I assure you!"

"She would! She thinks she can only be happy there and nothing here will make her so."

"You *are* in love with her!" Her eyes flashed dangerously.

He massaged his forehead. "No, of course not." *Yes, most definitely, and for some time now.*

"Then why do you care?"

"Her family is here; her life is here. She has this crazy thought that everything will be grand if she can just get back to India. I don't want her to be four thousand miles away and alone when she realizes it isn't."

He'd never thought about it before he'd said it, but it was true and broke him out in a cold sweat.

"She won't be alone. Surely she would take her sister with her."

Celeste. But after watching the young lady at supper with Captain Cosgrove, it seemed unlikely she'd want to live thousands of miles away with such a lovely courtship in the offing. Or that a loving sister would ask it of her. Captain Cosgrove lived in the adjoining property to the Mandeville in Surrey. He would go there and find out.

He was still thinking of Daphne, alone in India and trying to feed and clothe herself when he realized that Lady Johanna was still talking.

"I will forgive this outburst, but really, Hugh, you must bring yourself into line. Your association with her is quite unbecoming. I would think you would be relieved I have solved the problem for you. It will be no mean feat to get a passage in next week's voyage, I assure you!"

"Unless, of course, I have misread you." She looked at him, searching for something in his expression. "I think perhaps I have."

"No, you have not." He looked up at her. Late afternoon light softened everyone's features, but it did particularly lovely things to Lady Johanna. He remembered how she often dropped by just to entertain his mother without thinking he might be there, too.

She had done the wrong thing buying Daphne off, but often she *did* do the right thing, and just because his feelings had altered and his life turned on its head in the space of a few months, none of that was her doing.

"You may think I did not notice, but I did," she said softly. "You did not answer my previous question. It was a neat side step, but a side step nonetheless. Will you lessen your involvement in your business dealings after we marry? I ask not only for myself. I don't have to remind you of my father's standing or the family you are marrying into. I will not have society saying I smell of the shop." She dusted her hands on her dress, although she was perfectly clean. "I apologize for my directness."

He liked her directness, even when it surprised him. He never thought it mattered to her what he did as long as he was her husband and looked good on her arm.

He shrugged. "I hadn't thought about it. Do I need to?"

She blinked rapidly, as though calculating something. "Only if you want to marry me. And I know you want to marry me or you would not have been courting me all these years."

She said it lightly, but he knew she meant every word. She put a single finger on his lips, as though to stop him answering.

He lifted the finger off, gently. "Unfortunately, it has been hugely satisfying to put things right with the company. I think if I gave it up, I'd miss it. All I can think of are the adventures I have waiting for me with it."

"Adventures?" she said sharply. "Whatever would you want adventures for if you are to settle down and start a family?"

"Why can't I do both? I could use the raw ingredients we've always had to make something so much more special with the perfumes. I don't have to actually see Miss Davenport to pursue it."

That was the biggest adventure of all and something he wanted to share with Daphne, even if only as a business partner. "And if I can't do both, perhaps a family can wait a little while…" He let his voice trail off and looked up to find her regarding him in horror.

"Oh no, that will never do. I am so glad we had this conversation. I have lived as a duke's daughter a little too long to reduce myself to that." She smiled ruefully. "I was so looking forward to having a ring from the maharaja's chest."

He took her hand in his, feeling like a window had opened, letting in a fresh spring breeze. "And so you shall. I have a lovely emerald one inside. I will have it delivered to you. It is quite beyond compare."

She stared into the distance for a few long moments, looking as though she thought of an idea only to discard it two or three times. He waited patiently.

"Would you, when asked, say I discovered your sad penchant for trade and broke off our courtship? You will, of course, be in your clubs looking absolutely heart-broken—extra credit if you cry about all you have lost in the hearing of Lord Eldridge."

The elation in his heart was at odds with the gravity of the conversation. "You have my word that I will do that. Do I have your word that you will keep Miss Davenport's secret?"

She held out her hand to put into his. "Yes, you have my word."

They shook hands and she smiled, but he saw sadness in her eyes. "I do believe I'm glad I spoke to Lady Spellwater. I may have made a grave error in judgment if she had not been so forthcoming about your endeavors."

He still had her father's bank draft in his pocket. "About that…" He gave it to her. "Miss Davenport has repaid me, and you have kept your part of the bargain, but I assure you, I do not want this money."

She took the draft, folded it, and held it tightly in her hand. "Thank you. That is quite honorable of you."

He clasped her hand. "I'm sorry my other endeavors are not so gentlemanly."

"You will be an embarrassment to your entire family, I am sure of it." She rolled her eyes and pulled her hands free, walking back toward the house.

"But not to my grandfather," Hugh said quietly. "I believe he would be quite proud."

CHAPTER 23

SOMETIMES THINGS DO NOT COME ABOUT

L ater that week, Daphne took a deep breath of Surrey country air. The grass was green as a bowl of peas, the birds were singing, and she could almost have believed the entire London trip was a bad dream.

Or she might be able to, if Captain Cosgrove's family would stop asking sticky questions. *And* if only Celeste and her beau had chosen to tell the entire truth rather than a rosy version of it. Then there wouldn't be so many awkward moments.

For example, now. It was just past ten o'clock, and she and Lady Cosgrove were taking a morning walk. One she insisted on and that Daphne had unsuccessfully tried to avoid.

Lady Cosgrove was solid and athletic, with the look of a woman who would stride through the fields rather than take the sedate and deliberate pace they took at the moment. She had raised five children, Captain Cosgrove being the third in line, and was nobody's fool.

"I hear your father," Lady Cosgrove said, walking slowly in a way that suggested deep thought, her parasol angled to catch the morning sun, "is migrating to New South Wales. Is he a pastoral man?"

Daphne took a deep breath. "To be truthful, he is not a pastoral man. It will shock you to learn that he has been involved in a criminal enterprise that has stolen vast amounts from the Mandeville family. He was lucky not to be hanged and Celeste and I are mortified."

During the week, Father had helped the authorities recover the remainder of Hugh's goods from Minerva's property in York-shire but had not escaped penalty, and Daphne wasn't sure that he should have, in any case.

Even the love she had for him could not blind her to the fact he was a thief.

In any case, he was to be transported to Botany Bay, where, from all accounts, he was looking forward to angling his way out of his sentence with exemplary behavior so he could start on his pastoral enterprise. Minerva had yet to stand trial.

Lady Cosgrove stopped walking and regarded Daphne with a mixture of relief and sadness. "I am very glad to hear you admit as much. We knew about it, in any case," Lady Cosgrove said mildly. "The thefts from Mandeville, the conviction, and all of his inferior connections."

Daphne stopped walking. "Oh thank goodness!" If Lady Cosgrove knew and allowed them to stay, surely it meant Father's crimes were to be overlooked? Or had she only just found out and they were to be summarily dismissed?

"I hate to say it, but you are well rid of him. I'm not one to blame the daughters for the sins of the father. I just wondered if your sister could be encouraged to share the truth, but she would not, even though I could see that it pained you. Your loyalty to your sister is commendable, my dear...Lady Spellwater, I believe?"

Daphne's heart wrung itself into a knot. Now it was not only Father's secrets coming back to haunt Celeste, but her own.

"At your service," Daphne said.

Lady Cosgrove took a deep breath. "Your sister is naïve to

think that we would not investigate the family of anyone James courts. We have contacts at Bow Street."

"Mr. Wolfe, I presume?"

Lady Cosgrove nodded. "He was quick to tell me how helpful you had been to the investigation."

Daphne shook her head. "He does *so* like to put a spoke in one's wheel. Would it help if I left the country too? You see, dear Celeste has had nothing to do with any of our foibles—not Father's criminal ones, nor my socially disastrous ones."

"Oh, I hardly think you are disastrous, my dear. Although, having Lady Spellwater wandering around society when I have a daughter to debut next year could be."

Daphne nodded. "I see, I truly do. If Celeste and Captain Cosgrove continue their courtship, I will take a passage to India." Her heart constricted at the thought of never seeing her future nieces and nephews. Her heart ached at the loss of her beloved sister. They could write to each other, but it was not the same.

"Goodness, no need to go that far!" Lady Cosgrove said with alarm.

"It is probably for the best. I like India, after all. And if I understand correctly that you will not stand in the way of Captain Cosgrove and Celeste, I will, in all honesty, do anything you ask of me."

Lady Cosgrove laid a hand on Daphne's. "You will not need to do that because I'm afraid I will not give them my blessing. This is not a good alliance for our family."

Daphne felt a vice squeeze around her heart. "Oh."

"I am sorry to speak so bluntly. I will, of course, tell your sister and James myself when we return. If you want to leave, you may have our carriage for the trip home. I know this is hard to hear, but you must know I have enjoyed meeting both you and Celeste. You deserved better, but we must deal with what is rather than what we would like things to be."

Daphne turned to her. "Thank you for your hospitality. I

know it would have presented challenges, but I can honestly tell you that my sister is beyond compare and any man married to her will be the luckiest man alive. I think your son knows that, and I hope you don't live to regret this decision."

Lady Cosgrove nodded. "I'm sure that is true. But we all must do what we can to protect our families. Now, let's head back? We have almost talked ourselves onto Mandeville land."

They stood atop a hill where they could see across the valley where a large country house stood atop the neighboring hill. It must be Mandeville Hall. How perfect it would have been, if Celeste had married Captain Cosgrove and she had married Hugh. They could have been neighbours. If she looked hard enough, she could almost see their children chasing each other down this very hill.

Daphne's heart leaped at the Mandeville name being spoken, then crashed when she remembered that it was supposed to mean nothing to her. They turned and walked back to the house, amicably talking about everything from gardens to needlepoint and even how Daphne created perfumes. It may have been idle chatter, but by the time they arrived back at the house, Daphne was exhausted, her mind racing a thousand miles an hour at how Celeste would react to the news.

She found out a half hour later. The answer was...badly.

Celeste flew into the bedroom they shared and closed the door behind her. There were red splotches high on her cheeks and she rounded on Daphne.

"You *told* her."

Daphne wrung her hands on her lap. "She already knew, dearest. Mr. Wolfe's family lives on the other side of this estate. She had a letter yesterday and was hoping we would be honest."

"And we were not. Another strike against me, I suppose." She buried her face in her hands. "I really liked him, Daph. He would be the best in any room of gentlemen, anywhere."

She burst into tears, but of course, being Celeste, she even did that beautifully. Tears that spilled artfully down her cheeks and broke one's heart.

"I know, love." Daphne got off the bed and pulled Celeste into her arms.

"I hate Father," Celeste said into Daphne's hair.

"I know, love." She didn't want to mention that her perfume-making had definitely been a factor.

"What did Captain Cosgrove say?"

Celeste sobbed. "That was the worst part. He said that perhaps it was for the best if we slowed our courtship down."

Daphne considered it. "That may mean he is just biding his time?"

"He does not have courage is what it means."

Daphne pulled back so she could look into her sister's tear-streaked face. "Dearest, you only met him last week, I think his response is entirely prudent." She did not add that Celeste was used to getting her own way and this was one of those rare times she was not.

Celeste shook her head. "No." Her mouth was a stubborn straight line, her eyes narrowed. "Can we leave now?"

"We can leave as soon as we have packed our bags." It wasn't like spending more time would change Lady Cosgrove's mind.

Celeste nodded. "Good. She pulled their trunk from under the window and proceeded to empty the contents of the wardrobe into it. "You go and tell that dragon that we need their carriage."

Daphne did, and it was amazing how quickly they were ejected from the Cosgrove property, seen off by nothing more than the housekeeper who wished them safe travels.

The road to Reading took them past the front gates of the Mandeville estate. The drive was lined with leafy oak trees although it was impossible to see the house. "That is where Hugh lives," she said to Celeste.

"Do you want to see it? All those great houses allow tours if nobody is in residence."

Daphne shook her head. "Surely you jest. I would rather drown myself in its ornamental pond than tour it. The Cosgroves, the Mandevilles, they can all go to Jericho."

Celeste dabbed her handkerchief on her face. "A sentiment I thoroughly endorse."

～

Hugh returned home to Surrey as soon he was assured his plans were almost complete. He'd spent the last few days organizing the new perfume venture with Ayah, letting her choose where they would run the enterprise and how she wanted it set up. They had agreed on processes and distribution ideas but there was one very important thing missing..

Everything will be for nought if there is no Daphne.

Driving his curricle to Surrey had been a good decision because the task of driving took the edge off his nerves, and the journey through the countryside made him feel more alive than he had in years. Or was it just the thought that finally his life was his own to live?

Now he was a few miles from the Cosgrove Estate and about to pass his own gates in less than a mile. Sir Barkley was on the floor of the curricle curled up on a blanket. He just hoped Daphne hadn't left already for India or he'd be chasing her halfway around the world. That would not be quite so exhilarating.

The road ahead went down a gentle hill leading to a bridge that crossed a creek. He could see another carriage coming toward him that would likely meet him as he crossed it. He felt gooseflesh raise on the skin of his arms without any reason. Was this them? The driver lifted his whip and pulled over to allow Hugh to cross first.

Hugh crossed the old stone bridge slowly and came to a complete stop as he drew alongside the carriage. It was the

Cosgrove carriage and a tear-stained Celeste was sitting closest to the window. She lifted her hand and waved, but it seemed a sad "farewell" wave.

Poor child. The revelation of their father's imprisonment must not have gone over well. He wasn't surprised by Lady Cosgrove but thought his childhood friend would have more stamina than that.

He turned to the driver. "Where are you headed?"

"Reading, my lord. Hoping to make it to Bath by sunset."

Hugh frowned. "I hope that will not be necessary. Can I have a word with the ladies? If they agree, I will bring them to Mandeville Hall." He always had what felt like hordes of distant family members in residence to lend the girls chaperone.

"If it is acceptable to the ladies. Otherwise, I have my orders," the driver said.

"Benny!" Hugh called for his tiger, perched on the seat in the back. "Hold the horses."

Sir Barkley must have thought the call was for him because he raised his head, jumped on the seat next to Hugh, and when he saw Celeste started to alternate between barking and whimpering.

Celeste opened the window and broke into a smile. "Sir Barkley! What an excellent surprise!"

Daphne joined Celeste at the door. She glanced at the dog. "Hello, good boy." Then up at him. "Lord Mandeville. Is something amiss? Why do you have Sir Barkley?"

"Nothing is amiss. I have a proposition for you both, but I cannot do it standing on the road with our horses waiting. In addition, Sir Barkley desperately needs a run. Shall we adjourn to Mandeville Hall?"

The both looked apprehensive, which was not the desired effect.

"I assure you that my carriage will be available for you both tomorrow to take you onward to Reading if you choose not to accept. And that I have an abundance of elderly relatives to act as chaperone. I have spoken to Ayah and have some ideas for your perfume enterprise."

He watched as Daphne's eyes widened slightly and her mouth dropped open. "Very well. If you have spoken to her, then I will hear you out." She reached across the small distance between the carriages and patted Sir Barkley on the head. "You, dear thing. I am so glad to see you."

The dog definitely got a warmer welcome than he did.

"Yes, I must apologize, he stowed away." It wasn't quite true, for Hugh had discovered him in the curricle long before he left, but dashed if he didn't hope the dog might win them over somehow.

They were on their way in a few moments, Hugh leading the carriage the few miles to Mandeville Hall. The house would soon come into view. It was modern by estate standards, only completed fifteen years ago in a glorious Palladian style.

When they arrived at the front of the house, footmen came out to take their luggage and Sir Barkley bounded off around the side of the house toward the gardens.

Daphne watched his retreating form with a frown. "Will he come to any harm?"

Hugh shook his head. "No, although we will go and fetch him as soon as you are rested."

Celeste walked with her head bowed, but Daphne looked up brightly. "We need no rest. We only just left the Cosgroves."

A sob escaped from Celeste. "I would prefer to go inside and rest."

Daphne took her sister's hand and clasped it. "Of course, my dear. I will chase Sir Barkley and listen to Lord Mandeville. You will get a tea tray and put your feet up." She turned to Hugh. "Shall I meet you in the garden in an hour? I would like to see Celeste settled."

All he wanted to do was pull her into his arms and tell her all would be well. That he was free to marry whomever he chose and all he wanted was her. Instead, he bowed. "I will see you there and make sure Mrs. Herbert sends up some of her famous scones for Celeste."

Daphne curtsied. "If anything can mend a broken heart, it's baked goods."

~

AN HOUR LATER, Hugh realized he should have narrowed down his meeting point with Daphne.

She could be in the fields, or inside the temple of winds, or the walled garden, or any one of the indulgences his father had spent vast sums on when he became the first Earl of Mandeville.

He tried the walled garden first, and as soon as the gate had creaked shut behind him, he could hear feminine humming and a definite creaking coming from the vicinity of the swing hanging from the ancient oak.

She'd left the heavy iron door open, so he walked quietly through and closed it behind him, nerves fluttering in his stomach as it clicked shut.

He took another step toward her and stopped, because she looked so beautiful swinging with such gusto, her toes touching the branches of the old oak above her.

She saw him coming and scowled, but then the scowl was replaced a moment later with a broad grin. "I should be embarrassed you'd find me doing this, but I am having such a lovely time that I can't."

She seemed entirely carefree, her brown boots sitting on the grass next to the swing, her toes peeking out from under her dress on each upswing, while her cotton dress billowed around her legs.

Her hair had fallen down and was windblown and out of control, a dark mass of curls. It suited her.

"Someone should use it."

She laughed. "I feel years younger. Why, I haven't swung since before my mother died."

She swung forward and avoiding the possible sight of her legs, he fixed his eyes on the grass. "I remember that swing you had in India."

"Yes, on the blackwood tree. Why do you stare at the grass?"

"Oh, no reason." He would not ruin her fun. He looked up, carefully fixing his gaze on her face.

She glared at him, doing a fair imitation of a stern governess. "How do your wedding plans go?"

"I must marry someone," he said with a grin. "And I'm sure *you* wouldn't want to marry me now."

"No." Her voice was resolute. "I can't abide a man who makes bad decisions."

"How about a man who makes bad decisions for the right reasons and then tries his hardest to fix them?"

She swung through again, a trim ankle sweeping past his face. "That depends."

"On what? I feel I must tell you that if I look the wrong way, there is a good chance I will see your ankles."

"Ah!" she said in triumph. "That is why you were looking at the grass! How noble of you."

"Indeed. However, perhaps you should swing a little lower if we are going to continue this mad conversation."

"No," she said simply.

He gave up trying to concentrate on her face and threw himself into taking peeks of her ankles as they streaked past him. "What does forgiving me depend on, again?"

"On *how* you fixed it."

A flash of ankle this time, a glimpse of petticoat the next, it was all up to the wind. He could sit there all afternoon and perhaps even miss dinner.

Which, as anyone knew, was saying something.

"Hugh Mandeville, *are* you looking at my ankles?"

He looked up to see her smirking with a mischievous look in her eye. Who was this woman? But he knew who. Mischievous Daphne from his childhood was awake.

"Yes," he said. "I do believe I am."

She demurely hid her ankles, only to lift them into the air the moment she was just past his view.

"Minx," he said.

"I cannot believe you would look at my ankles, with me talking about something as serious as your betrothal."

"I believe I would prefer your ankles over my betrothal at any time." *Unless it's my betrothal to you.* He smiled and sat back. "Please, keep swinging if it pleases you."

"No, of course not. I am a *lady,* not your light-o'-love."

"Now that's where you're wrong, dearest. You are my light and my love." He tried valiantly to keep his voice carefree, knowing he failed miserably.

She stopped the swing, looking stricken.

"I am leaving," she said flatly and jumped off.

"Leaving?" It wasn't precisely the answer he was expecting after a declaration of love.

She turned to look over her shoulder. "You insult me."

"How so?" He was trying to get this right, but only succeeding getting it very wrong.

She stopped and turned. "I will *not* be your mistress, you wretched man." There was no heat in her insult, like she had moved on and he had no ability to hurt her.

Understanding dawned. "My apologies, that was a bad choice of words. I do not want you as my mistress either." He took her hands. "You light my life and my world. Daphne. What I'm saying is that I cannot live without you. And I would have you as my wife."

Her eyes opened wide. "Wife? What of Lady Johanna? Your

honor won't let you leave her after all this time and I would hate it if you did." Her voice was quiet and sad.

"Apparently, she only became aware of how much I enjoyed owning Oriental Spice and Fragrance from you. When I confirmed my inclination to continue my involvement, she decided such a fall in her standing could not be brooked." He turned her to him by placing his hands on her shoulders. "She has released me."

She closed her eyes. What was she thinking? Her expression was one of pain, as though he was inflicting an injury.

"Daphne. I want to marry you. Please say you'll have me, bad bargain that I am."

Never in his wildest dreams did he imagine that his marriage proposal would include a healthy dose of begging. But if he had to get onto his knees to make Daphne believe him, he would.

"Come, I have something to show you that might convince you. It's the proposition I was talking about earlier."

DAPHNE HESITATED, wondering how hard she should make this on him.

Hard. Yes, definitely, hard.

"I can't think of a single thing that would be big enough."

He simply took her hand and smiled.

"I mean," she continued, "if you're thinking that redecorating a bedroom in my favorite color will work, I can tell you it isn't going to change my mind." Because her heart was singing and her mind fully made up.

They trod the lush green lawn that a bevy of children could play cricket on. Her children, perhaps? And forget the manor, in all its Palladian glory. More importantly, there were trees, ones to climb when one was little and in search of adventure.

"No, of course not," he replied affably.

Those old buckskin breeches he wore showed his muscled

legs to perfection. She could let herself indulge in watching him, if she thought it might be forever.

He led her around the house, to a large courtyard with outhouses. "This is more like it," she said. "I'm to be shown the servant's area?"

He didn't stop holding her hand, even though there were people everywhere. "Thank goodness you didn't make it to India."

"I thought you'd want to send me there yourself!"

He stopped in his tracks and looked at her. "Only if I purchased myself a passage, too. Couldn't have you going all that way on your own."

They were interrupted by barking that seemed to be coming closer. A very familiar barking.

Daphne whipped around. "Sir Barkley! Come here, you big beautiful boy."

The big beautiful boy in question took that suggestion as a command and leaped at her, knocking her sideways. Hugh braced her as the happy dog put his paws anywhere and everywhere.

"I'm going to be filthy." Daphne looked up at Hugh and could feel the happiness she was radiating. "I'm so glad you brought him from Reading." She stood but continued to rub behind his ears.

Hugh looked taken aback. "Goodness, if I'd known how easy it was to impress you I wouldn't have gone to half as much effort. Come look through the window."

She followed him and peered into the window.

It was a large rectangular room with windows every five feet.

Large work tables had been set up in two rows, and on them was an assortment of equipment that Daphne used to make her perfumes.

It smelled familiar.

She looked more closely at the vials that stood in little wooden stands, and the shelves filled with dark amber bottles.

"A perfumery," she said in wonder.

"Your perfumery," he said in reply, and picked up her hand and pressed his lips into her palm. "Please say you'll forgive me for being a fool. Please say you'll marry me. Nothing else is important if I don't have you by my side. Not this place." He swept his arms wide. "Not my life. Say you will share it with me."

Daphne's thought faculties seemed to have fled with any semblance of control over her emotions. She felt tears spring to her eyes, unbidden and unwanted.

He pulled into his arms, held her close, and whispered in her ear, "Let's make a life together. Let's have dogs and children and a house that smells beautiful. Let's make a lifetime of memories to cancel out the bad ones. Say you will."

Daphne kissed his neck, then his cheek, and then his lips. "I will."

He leaned down to kiss her. She closed her eyes and felt his lips brush against hers and his hands cup the sides of her face. A rush of heat came over her, and she stood very still, not wanting to make a mull of it like she had at the ball. She pulled back a little.

But he was so attuned to her that he pulled back too. "Daphne?"

"I...don't know quite how."

"And I'm sure you do." He kissed the side of her mouth, which tickled, and when she smiled, he took full advantage of it to deepen the kiss, gently and slowly. So slowly she thought she might die or at the very least keel over. She felt lazy, like she was lying in a garden surrounded by brightly blooming rhododendrons and orchids. There was a blanket beneath them, a leafy canopy above. And Hugh, returning her love as she'd always dreamed he would. And who knew, all she actually had to do was be truly herself, be Lady Spellwater without her disguise.

Something bloomed between them that was the sweetest thing she'd ever smelled, grass and wind, love and Hugh.

His kiss was a promise that he would always love her. His hands in her hair were a vow that he would hold her forever, gently, just like this.

She would hold him, too. She was brave enough, even though his mother would probably never love her and society would turn its back, too. It didn't matter. Not if they had each other.

It seemed like an eternity when he drew away, tipping his head down so they were forehead to forehead. As though the kiss had made him weak, just as it had her. "We'd best go inside before they all come out here."

"All?"

"Your team, of course. Come inside and say hello. We've had to move heaven and earth to make this happen within a week."

Hugh pushed the heavy wooden door open.

There was a group of people employed at the tables, their heads bent. The complex scent of Scandal was in the air.

Daphne took a few steps toward them. "How did you do this?" she said.

"Perhaps I had some help."

Daphne looked closer at the people working at the table. They were Indian, each one. And what's more, she recognized at least five of them. Then one of them turned around.

"Ayah," she almost yelled, running to her childhood nurse and throwing her arms around her.

The hug she received in return brought tears to her eyes. The strong and steadfast love for her nurse, the same love that had encouraged her every step of the way, was now comforting her. "There, there," she whispered in Daphne's ear. "All will be well now."

"But how?"

"Lord Mandeville offered everyone lodgings and a good

paying job to make our products. And now Mr. Khatri is with us too. The girls are happy we are all together."

Hugh smiled with obvious pleasure at her surprise. He knew her well enough to know that taking care of her Ayah was the same as taking care of her, if not better.

Daphne smiled. "No wonder you found it so easy to set this up; Ayah and her family know how to make perfume better than I. Indeed, they taught me."

Hugh nodded. "It made perfect sense. Ayah and I would like to be equal partners with you. You create, Ayah makes, and I will distribute. I have already established relationships with Penhalligon and also Ross's in Bishopgate Street. So if we do go ahead, we have willing customers."

He pulled some cards from his pocket, large cards of thick stock that were emblazoned with the crests of the establishments she had only dreamed about. In all honesty, it made her feel a little annoyed that those doors that had always stuck for her, opened for him so easily.

Daphne gasped. "Ross's? I have only dreamed of selling there. I sent samples perhaps three or four times earlier this year, always returned with a short note explaining that an account would not be opened. If I had more money, I would have employed a man of business, but alas, I never could." She shook her head. "All I ever wanted was financial stability for both Ayah's family and our own. It's where the whole idea of selling perfume came from. Their talents and their ability to make beautiful things and my palate for scent. And now in the space of one week, you have succeeded where I failed."

Ayah shook her head. "Don't think like that. This will be your success too. None of it would be happening without your talent."

Hugh picked up a nearby stool. "Now you just have something you didn't have before, that's all. I also plan to send letters to the largest stores in Paris and New York."

"Oh my," Daphne said. "That's exciting and a much better way of looking at it. What of Lady Spellwater? How can she disappear if you continue to launch new products?"

"From afar," he said. "In essence, Daphne, you will be able to make what you want to make, without the risk of being discovered. And yes, I would like that to be as my wife. A separate issue, but more important to me than anything."

Daphne was dazed. Her mind couldn't process that not only was Hugh free to marry her, but that he had gone to all this trouble to make every wish she had real. She must be dreaming.

He turned to Ayah and Daphne heard him say quietly, "Did we make a mistake? I thought she would love it."

She could feel Ayah watching her as she inspected the work area. Ayah had set it up much the same as their benches in Reading, with each different element done in a different area by a different person. The bottles were all well labeled, and at the end of the benches, the storage area where the product would mature for a month before being ready for sale was well organized and safe.

"You've done a wonderful job," Daphne said. "I can't think of anything I'd change. Except perhaps that you might need to replicate this area a few times."

"Why?" Ayah asked. "We have plenty of room to grow."

"But I have two new creations," Daphne said. "One will be especially for gentlemen and one will be for the ladies. I have started on both."

His eyebrows raised, but there was a glint of excitement in them. "You mentioned the men's fragrance before. It's a wonderful idea. What will you call it?"

She looked at him with only a small amount of the mischief she was feeling. "Barkley's Blend."

Hugh smiled. "Well, it's a step up from being dressed in a bonnet."

Daphne gurgled. "I was jesting. I thought maybe, Corinthian."

"After me?"

She rolled her eyes. "Are you a Corinthian?" She shrugged, as though she hadn't thought about it. "No, I did not create this fragrance for you."

"Fibber. I'll check that journal of yours. Come here."

In a moment, she was in his arms, nestled into him as though she belonged there. "You're right. I've been working on this in my head since you kissed me in the library."

He should be outraged, but he loved the memory, too. "And here I thought you met me there to tell me about your father."

"Maybe I just wanted to be kissed by you." She tilted her face up, feeling the warmth of the sun on her face.

"And you shall be." He bent his mouth to hers.

EPILOGUE

IN WHICH SIR BARKLEY FINDS HIS HAPPILY
EVER AFTER

The tiny chapel in the grounds of Mandeville Hall was full to overflowing with well-wishers. Soft organ music filled the golden-lit space, candles burned, and the air was heavy with the smell of roses and lily-of-the-valley. Daphne stood at the open double doors, her sister holding her hand and tears of joy already filling her eyes.

"I am so happy for you," Celeste said. She somewhat ruined the sentiment by scanning the chapel for someone in particular. She had been so careful never to be in his company and had thus far managed not to even have a conversation with Captain Cosgrove. Letters were sent back unopened, invitations refused. It had been difficult considering they were living so close. Lady Mandeville had graciously agreed to return to Mandeville Hall to chaperone Daphne and Celeste since Hugh refused to have them return to Reading to live alone.

"You will have to speak to him one day, my dear. Surrey is too small. Or do you want him to go off to sea again with so much between you unspoken and unfulfilled?" It was what Daphne had not dared to say all these months, but she felt protected by the

237

fact this was her wedding day and Celeste would never do anything to ruin it.

"Humbug," Celeste replied. "Not even a married lady and already lecturing me."

"As though I need to be married to do that. It's my job as your elder sister." They were all waiting for her, and all she could do was close her eyes and breathe in the smells of her wedding day.

It was a peculiar mix, like all the most stunning fragrances. Sunlight and lilies, soap and freshly washed dog. Then a highlight of old frankincense reminding her that this was the most reverent of occasions, a rebirth into a new life. A happy and full life, if the past months had been any indication.

At her feet, a yellow-haired retriever in a bonnet topped with flowers sat calmly waiting for his cue. She reached down and gave Sir Barkley a pat on his hind end. "Off you go, boy."

Amazingly, the dog made the front of the chapel without incident and then let out a huge bark for Hugh to give him his biscuit, just as they'd practiced.

Her husband-to-be looked up, and their eyes locked for a moment that seemed to stretch out to eternity. The look calmed her in the sea of excitement she was being tossed about in.

She took a step toward him, and another and another, and with each step he smiled a little wider until she reached him and he took her hands in his.

Celeste gave her to Hugh, who lifted the veil from her face. "No more veils."

"Agreed," she whispered, her insides fluttering.

Then Hugh lifted her hands and kissed the tops of her fingers. "You look beautiful." He looked down at the dog. "Not as beautiful as Sir Barkley," he added. "But beautiful."

She wanted to say something witty but was tongue-tied. She inhaled deeply, knowing his scent would steady her. He was wearing the new cologne she had made for him, a strong thread of artemisia mingling with the bergamot and nutmeg. And after a few hours, when the wedding breakfast was over, all that would be left was warm cedarwood and Hugh.

She looked up and beamed at him. "Would you like to marry the dog? He's available."

Hugh tilted his head back and laughed, despite the solemnity of the chapel and the vicar waiting for them to begin.

It felt like all the lines in her journals had led her to this one true perfume.

And it smelled like hope.

THE END

THANK you for reading A Whiff of Scandal.

I hope you enjoyed it and I would love to hear what you thought. It would make my day if you could leave a review where you purchased this book or any review site you enjoy.

Your opinion goes a long way to helping others decide if a book is for them.

BUT WHAT HAPPENED TO CELESTE?

Find out by joining my newsletter!

I'm currently writing a short story about Celeste finding love that I will send to my newsletter subscribers. Join me here!

https://www.robynchalmers.com/newsletter

A Song of Secrets

In opera circles...

 ...she was without equal.

But was her career more important than love?

From the tender age of 16, Sarah has used her beauty and voice to become a diva on stage. The crowds loved her and her family depended on the money she sent home.

Was it too late now to have a family of her own?

And would any man love her if he knew her secret?

Evander Ambrose, the second son of the Earl of Wrotham, is a vicar and a widower. He longs to remarry but everyone knows vicars can't fall for opera singers. And he has a secret.

Has the loss of his wife...

 ...cost him his faith?

When mother nature and a terrible accident conspire, they

are forced into a situation that neither is prepared for, but they both just might need.

You'll adore this wholesome regency romance, because everyone has regrets but if they try, they can change, and their forever love will be waiting.

Get it now from your favorite bookstore.

https://books2read.com/u/mggP5v

A Song of Secrets is a sweet regency romance.

ABOUT THE AUTHOR

Robyn Chalmers is an emerging author of sweet regency romance.

She lives in a country town in southern Australia with her family and a white fluffy dog. She reads a lot, walks a lot and gets caught on Pinterest too much.

When not reading, you can find her writing her favorite kind of novel – Regency romance.

She loves hearing from readers and you can find her on Facebook and Twitter.

Made in the USA
Las Vegas, NV
12 September 2021

30080521R00146